THE DOWNTRODDEN BREED

JAMES S. KELLY

The Downtrodden Breed

A NOVEL

James S. Kelly

ISBN: 978-1-963565-06-5 (Paperback)

Printed in the United States of America

Published by

info@thequippyquill.com
(302) 295-2278

OTHER BOOKS

By

JAMES S. KELLY

Westerns

A Man of Breeding
A Breed Apart
The Wounded Breed

Mysteries

I Didn't Forget
Not In My Backyard
Interned

Civil War

Magnolia

Viet Nam War

The Long Walk Home

ACKNOWLEDGEMENT

Spouse

Patricia

Children

James Jr.

Mark

Nancy

Michelle

Editor

Mike Peterson

Contents

THE INCLUSIVE BREED

PROLOGUE

Raindrops began to collect on the main sail and drop down on the deck as the sun slipped below the horizon. With lightning visible in the east, a storm was on the way. In the back of the crew's mind, they were in an area where pirates were prevalent, and the cargo they were about to accept was precious. The scavengers of the ocean had boarded many unsuspecting merchant vessels, their cargo confiscated, and the crew sent to a watery grave.

However, the advantage was only sometimes with the pirates. The time it took to track a target, board it and subdue the crew had to be precise and well-planned. However, many of the pirates were former sailors from a country's navy or were ex-merchant seamen, which didn't give them a leg up. Even if they were successful, many didn't have the expertise to steal cargo and sell it for a profit.

The first mate, Charles Bookers, guided the Gaff Rigged Schooner, christened Serpent, close to shore, yet cautious of any shoals between the ship and the coast. Under the Captain's direction, who was his father, he turned the boat into the wind and dropped anchor. Both father and son were experienced seamen.

As per the plan, six armed sailors headed by Bosun Mate Jerry Jones crawled over the side and went down the rope ladder to the rowboat waiting below. Their charge was to accept the cargo, escort it to shore and supervise bringing it onto the ship. As many as twelve boats would be used in the operation. Proximate to their departure, half of the crew went below to prepare the two holds for the cargo. Some of the remaining team set charges for their two 24-pound cannons; others prepared the boat for a potential attack.

Thirty minutes later, Bosun Jerry Jones and his men reached land. He jumped out of the boat, pulled it ashore, and secured it on the sand. The rain was coming down harder now, and they could hear thunder overhead. His party was armed as he led them to the village. The crew members were alert and maintained quiet, with only the chirping of the Horn bill breaking the silence as they made their way in land to their destination. The often-used path was wide enough for the sailors to walk two a breast. This was a prime area for an ambush, and the men were nervous. The sailors on the right kept their eyes to the right, while those on the left were alert to anything on the left side of the trail.

Fifteen minutes later, they walked up to the entrance, and a feeling of foreboding took hold. This was a village of five hundred natives. Usually, the children and some villagers would run out to greet them; no one came. Jones halted his group and assessed the situation. One of his men said, "let's pass on this, Bosun. I have a feeling."

Jones ignored the man. "Let's spread out and find the chief but be careful. Any sign of trouble, we'll stay together and head back to the beach. Shoot as a last resort."

The chief, with some of the villagers, was huddled on the ground around a fire in the center of the two-hundred-plus huts. He told Jones he became nervous when a villager reported that another ship had anchored on the south side of the peninsula, so he moved the cargo north about two miles up the beach. Though his English was limited, he wanted his goods now. Jones held fast, and the chief finally agreed to accompany him and show them where the cargo was hidden. The chief also clarified that he expected to be paid at that point. Six of his warriors would accompany him.

The rain was steady and reduced the visibility on the Serpent somewhat, so the Captain, Silas Bookers, ordered the lookouts doubled and those on deck to be vigilant for borders. The two 24-pounders were loaded, and the firing crews stood ready to carry out the captain's command.

Just as Jones and his crew, along with the village chief, reached the boats, lightning illuminated the sky.

They were startled as they saw that another large ship had appeared and was within a mile of the Serpent. In addition, two boats loaded with fifteen to twenty men were approaching their craft and were already one hundred yards out.

It was one of the lookouts that spied the other large ship coming around the south side of the island and alerted all below. Although there was some light from the occasional lightning, the other vessel was dark and steering directly at them. The Captain ordered all below to come up on deck and be ready to repel any attempt to board them each of the 50 member was armed with muskets; the Captain and his officers had pistols. Shortly after that, he ordered Charles to fire on the two boats carrying the potential boarding party. The threatening ship was out of range for the small guns on board, though the Serpent gunners were skilled at their craft.

However, the two small boats were within range of the 24-pounders with an effective range of twelve hundred yards. Each gun hit its mark with its first shot, and the boats sank, with those on board drowning or swimming back to the black ship about three thousand yards away. One more crack of lightning confirmed that the two small boats were sinking and the aggressor ship was turning about; no one was making any effort to save those in the vessel. Crew members from the Serpent were firing on the men as they were swimming back to their boat. The Captain felt they had repelled the attack and ordered his men to cease firing.

Soon, Jones and his group arrived back at the Serpent, and he briefed the Captain on the change of plans. One hour later, the Serpent anchored two miles north of Porto Novo and unloaded their cargo of metals, decorative items, guns, and textile items that would be paid to the chief who brokered the sale. The actual sellers had been waiting two days at the rendezvous point near the cargo the Serpent would carry. Their payment would be mostly in linen goods plus some coin.

The heavy rain and the constant lightning and thunder made the crew hurry to load their cargo. As the first enslaved people were put in the boats, the sailors on the beach were fired on from the heavy foliage about twenty yards away; two of their men were wounded.

There were about thirty armed men from the Serpent firing back at where they thought the attack was coming from, but they couldn't tell how many were in the attacking party. When Charles Bookers saw the action on the beach, he ordered his gun crews to fire the 24-pounders on the aggressors. However, as soon as the guns opened up, the assailants left their secluded place and charged the Serpent's sailors who were attempting to load the enslaved people.

Bosun Jones rallied his men, pulled the wounded to safety behind one of the boats, jumped behind other boats on shore, and fired back, killing three attackers. The enslaved people, already in the boats, hunched down to

avoid being shot. The outcome was in doubt until Charles Bookers had his gunners fire on the raiders on the beach and disperse them. Jones tried to capture   one of the aggressors, but the five who lay on the sand in front of him were dead. There were no telltale signs that would help identify them or their ship.

It took four separate firings of the canons to disperse whoever was involved in the attack. Safety for his men and the cargo was his prime concern, so Charles sent twenty more men from the schooner to patrol the beach while Jones and his men worked the rest of the day and into the night to complete the loading of two hundred and fifty enslaved people and put them in the holds of the ship.

The women were placed in one hold, unshackled; each man was jammed into the other hold and shackled to another male. The gunners reloaded the 24- pounders, but the black ship remained out of range as the Serpent made its way out to sea. Even with the holds filled, they were faster in open water and soon extended the distance between the two ships until they could no longer see it.

Charles wondered if they heard the last of the black boat as it made another about and came after the Serpent. Charles Bookers had a good idea who the master of the phantom ship was, even if his Captain ignored the threat.

CHAPTER 1

The Bookers Legacy was born when Silas Bookers parlayed a small inheritance into two merchant ships. But it was the decision to enter into the triangular trade that made his fortune.

He'd seen yesterday's scenario play out before. In that case, his ship was boarded by pirates, but he and the crew fought them off and killed most of the marauders. They had enough canons on board to keep the pirate ship at bay and could sail away from further danger. Today, his success was based on careful planning; he was alert that they might be in trouble, and he and his crew were ready.

As soon as the cargo was loaded, the Serpent was on its way to Kingston, Jamaica. While the black ship was slowly disappearing in the distance, Silas went to his cabin to enjoy the rum he brought from New England on the first leg of this voyage, which he held out from the English buyers.

This was his fourth trip to Africa, and he planned at least two more before he turned the company over to his son, Charles. He had at least two glasses of rum before the second mate knocked on the door and brought in two sixteen- year-old females for him to look at. He liked their looks but chose the shorter of the two and offered his second mate the other, plus a bottle of rum for his work. The mate didn't decline. Typically, the first mate would perform this ritual, but his son, Charles, was strait-laced and didn't condone his father's lifestyle.

For Silas, this was one of the perks of these trips. He'd enjoy the woman's nubile body until they reached Kingston, Jamaica, where he'd sell Maria, or along with those who survived the trip.

On his initial trip carrying enslaved people, he lost twenty percent of his cargo, mainly due to the brutality of his officers. From then on, he was careful about who he hired and how they ran his ship. The changes paid off because, on his last two voyages, he kept his losses under twelve percent.

On only one of the trips, he had any semblance of a revolt, and that occurred on his third voyage. Ten enslaved men in the hold chained close to each other were from the same tribe and spoke the same language. They were able to overpower one of the crew and make their way on deck but were quickly neutralized and thrown overboard. The sharks that followed the ship made quick work of them.

Besides an occasional storm, they had smooth sailing and made good time across the Atlantic Ocean. Bookers knew a new law would be implemented in 1842, abolishing enslaved people coming into Jamaica. Luckily, they arrived around Christmas in 1841 and were within the legal time frame.

Charles found a buyer while the crew cleaned up the enslaved people, making them presentable for auction. The sale took place on the pier where they docked. Since this would be one of the last slave ships allowed into Jamaica, prices for the enslaved people were at an all-time high. The Bookers were very happy, and so were the crew. More profit meant a more significant bonus. The officers and the staff would stay a month while Charles bought sugar, molasses, fruit, coffee, and rice. Most of the crew were from the east coast of America and enjoyed the warm environment and the friendliness of the natives. Silas would pay them half their share in Kingston and the balance when they docked at home. Human nature was what it was; some would be out of money quickly and must stay on the boat until it was time to leave. Those who were more prudent in their spending would enjoy the month.

Silas was a New Englander by birth from Bristol, Rhode Island, with a wife and two sons, Charles and William. His wife was originally from Indiana and had come east to live with her brother, who introduced her to Silas. Their courtship lasted two weeks, with a one-week honeymoon in Boston. The Bookers had a prominent home in downtown Bristol and considerable holdings in land and small businesses in the surrounding area.

Marriage for a man like Silas was more a convenience than anything else. He was home for only one month out of the year and rarely spent time with his wife after she bore him two sons. William and Charles were spirited young men who made two trips with their father to Africa between their studies at Brown University.

Charles, the oldest, would inherit the shipping business and, therefore, follow in his father's footsteps. William had a rich endowment, with little interest in business, and was studying to become a physician. Yet, William was closer to his father and enjoyed his lifestyle. And it was William who would go into town with his father, enjoying several glasses of rum and the natural beauty of the native women. Charles, on the other hand, would stay on board while in port, supervising the buying and loading of the cargo to be brought home or to the different destinations in the triangular trade.

The stay in Kingston had other benefits for Silas. He owned a home in the central part of town, and his housekeeper, aged twenty- five, was a brown beauty trained to satisfy his every need. He wished he could stay two months at a time with her instead of the one month he allocated to her. When he retired, he could live here instead of in Rhode Island, which was cold and dreary, and so was his wife.

Three weeks after they arrived in Kingston, the Black Ship lay anchor in the harbor. Soon many of their crew took boats into town and returned around midnight. Charles observed this pattern for the next week, and a plan took hold in his mind. He went into town and met with Silas, and told him what he had in mind. Silas agreed.

The day before leaving for Bristol, Silas decided to sell his home in Kingston, then returned to the Ship while Charles rounded up all his crew. There were six crew members Charles trusted above the others, and he briefed them on what he wanted to accomplish.

That evening just after the crew from the Black Ship went ashore, Charles and the six sailors made their way by boat to the other Ship. They approached the schooner quietly, and when they were below the rope ladder, the six followed Charles up onto the deck above.

They made their way to the bridge, looked in the window of that room, and saw three sailors enjoying a drink. Charles and his men burst through the door and quickly overpowered the three members of the black Ship. One of the three- spoke English, but he refused to tell Charles where the captain was.

One swing of the musket was all it took for the chap, who was now bleeding from his nose, to point to where the captain and the other crew members were. Again, those from the Serpent burst into the stateroom where the captain was and quickly overpowered the four. All seven were marched out onto the deck, and Charles asked if any more sailors were on board.

No one responded, so Charles struck the captain in the face, and he fell to the deck. He yelled out, "everyone's in town."

Three of the Serpent Sailors set charges in the hold, and when they came back on deck, they threw the seven captives into the water and told them to swim ashore. Charles and his group returned to the Serpent and prepared to sail. With the new abolition law, most thought this would be the last time they'd come to the island, so they didn't care if their identity was known.

Before he left Kingston, Silas told his lady friend he wasn't coming back next year. She cried, and he was sad, but he was over it by the time he was on board. Just as they got underway, three explosions from the Black Ship rocketed the harbor. Charles smiled, and Silas had a glass of rum.

With a fat cargo, they landed in Bristol and were greeted by their families, and Silas turned the offloading and sale of the goods over to Charles. Silas and his wife

Priscilla took a carriage to their home. When they retired for the evening, Silas had difficulty getting aroused but finally performed his husbandly duties, and his wife was satisfied, at least he thought she was. Charles would wait until he was finished selling all goods and then go home to his wife and son. He was a family man and spent time at his home port with his wife and son.

It was Silas' choice that he spent only a month at home before taking a cargo to England. Again, Charles supervised the purchasing and loading of the shipment.

On this voyage, they carried their most popular items, cod, maple syrup, rum, and whiskey. On previous trips, they took livestock and lumber. Their Destination would be Liverpool, England. William returned to Brown University to pursue his studies; Charles accompanied his father to England.

Other than a storm as they passed south of Iceland and some of their foodstuffs had spoiled, the voyage was nondescript. Silas leased a flat in Liverpool annually, and each time he arrived in England, he extended it for another year. On this trip, he was met at the pier by his cockney girlfriend, Gladys, and the male child he had fathered fourteen years earlier. This was the first time Charles met his father's bastard son. As he watched the three walk off, he wondered how many other children his father had sired.

Gladys named the boy Frederick Smith. It didn't cost Silas much to keep them, and he enjoyed playing with the boy and, of course, the mother. This time he spent two months with Gladys before carrying guns, ammunition, and cloth from the mills in Manchester to Porto Novo in

Africa. The three legs of the Triangular Trade made New England Shipping Companies like his very, very rich.

The slave trade was pretty new to America. It began when a Dutch ship unloaded twenty enslaved people in Jamestown, Virginia. The problem the colonists were trying to cope with was labor. Initially, they used indentured servants and soon found that the enslaved Black people were cheaper to feed and worked long hours; therefore, more were targeted for the colony. Soon after, the colonial economy boomed; consequently, more enslaved people were brought to America in significant numbers.

Initially, the Portuguese and Spanish captured African Villagers and sold them to Europe. They were amazed at how little regard the African power groups had for their fellow citizens. One reason was that tribal feuds had permeated the African Continent, and the captured members of one tribe would most likely be killed. Now they had another more lucrative option. The African sellers accepted guns, ammunition, and staples from the buyers, which increased their power and allowed them to continue the process.

Even though the slave trade in America only lasted two hundred and fifty years, it was the catalyst that made the southern economy boom and created the plantation way of life. It probably was the impetus for the American Civil War.

Before Silas departed from Liverpool, Charles constantly called on him at his home to set a sailing date. He was worried about keeping the crew occupied and the food from spoiling. Silas reluctantly agreed to go after exhausting all the excuses he and Gladys could dream up. Along with his mistress and their child, Silas took a carriage to the pier, was piped aboard the ship, and said goodbye to one of his families.

His father was without female companionship on the leg to Africa, but once on the Dark Continent, that situation changed. One of the comely native women had become his companion in Africa starting four years ago. When they arrived this time, Charles was surprised to see a little boy with her as she waited to greet Silas at the dock. He didn't recognize the woman, but he knew she'd stay with his father in the house he had built.

It took nearly a year to build a home on the shore for Silas. A contractor started to work on it after his first voyage and had it ready when Silas arrived on his second trip. The scion of the Booker Family would spend at least a month each year with this native woman; Silas was a natural family man; he couldn't confine himself to just one.

It was but a short walk to the beach for Silas from his three-bedroom home outside Lagos. Most afternoons, he could be found walking on the sand or fishing with some English retirees enjoying some of the rum he brought from Rhode Island. He sometimes couldn't decide which of the destinations he liked the best.

Unlike their layovers in England and Africa, Silas didn't have a woman waiting at the dock when they arrived in Rio De Janeiro. However, Silas was resourceful, and within a few days, he found companionship with a very young native woman. Charles didn't see him until it was time to leave. As usual, Charles spent his time selling the cargo and lining up another one to take to Bristol.

It'd been his job to handle the business side of their company for as long as he could remember. There never was a problem finding products that his countryman would buy. After unloading the enslaved people, he spent the next month picking up tobacco, rum, fruit, and lumber to be sold in New England.

Despite professing to be a god-fearing disciple of Christ, Silas had no conscience and looked upon his slave trading as nothing more than business. As far as his wife was concerned, he gave her an above-average standard of living and enough help so she didn't feel neglected entirely, which she was. Yet, she seemed happy with the month he was home. Silas always wondered if she preferred this way of life rather than having him around all the time.

When the civil war between the states erupted, Silas turned the company over to Charles and retired to England, where he lived out his remaining years with his girlfriend and their son. He never visited the other three women he left behind. He had Charles deliver a letter to his mother in which he wished her a good life; he provided her a generous pension, letting her live the remainder of her life as she wanted. The women and children in Africa and Kingston were just abandoned.

Charles was more of a businessman than his father; in fact, he'd been running the company for the past twenty years. When Silas turned the company over to Charles, he retained a minority position. The ownership transition was smooth because all the decisions had been made by Charles for some time. When the civil war erupted, Charles saw an opportunity to make more money by running the Union Blockade and delivering munitions to the south. Instead of a company that bartered for a living, he turned it into a company that accepted gold upfront as payment. Silas was content to let Charles run the business and accept annual payments to keep him living the lifestyle he desired in England.

Since the company had been using Liverpool in the triangular trade, it gave Charles a base of operations when he switched to bringing arms and munitions to the south. Liverpool was the hub of shipbuilding, and it was here where he learned about the sleek blockade runners he could purchase.

He transported cotton from the southern states to England and munitions to America. It was still the same company; they just dropped a leg from the triangle. Charles, like his father, had no conscience. He saw the trade with the south as business, and it didn't bother him that other considered him a traitor.

Bookers' Maritime Company had six merchant ships when Silas retired. They were perfect for delivering a lot of cargo but useless when delivery had to be made down shallow draft rivers at night in southern ports. Charles expanded their office in Cuba, bought four sleek blockade runners in Liverpool, and used some of the lesser-known Cuban ports to offload his goods from his larger ships onto the smaller quick craft. From England to Cuba, he avoided the north's blockade of the eastern and southern coast and therefore didn't lose one of his merchant ships during the war. Occasionally, they lose one of the runners, but profits were so enormous; that the risk-to-reward ratio was in his favor. Besides, anyone with gold could have a runner built very quickly.

Unlike his father, he wasn't promiscuous. He'd spend time off with his wife Patricia and his only child, Hiram, named after a maternal uncle. When the end to the civil war was in sight, Charles went back to the Triangular Trade, but instead of selling the enslaved people in the Caribbean, he did business with Brazil and Argentina.

Young Hiram spent his teenage years training to take over the company. He'd graduated from Yale, majoring in business and finance. He'd tried out for the varsity football team in his sophomore year with limited success. In his junior year, he could see that he wasn't going to make the football team, so he switched to boxing. Over his last two years at Yale, he amassed a record of nineteen wins and two losses by decision. He fought a couple of exhibitions with professional fighters but never considered joining them. It was at this time that he met Jane Thornhill, a lovely brunette from Haverhill, Massachusetts. Her father was a doctor at Massachusetts General in Boston.

He'd grown into a sturdy young man standing five feet ten inches tall and weighing one hundred eighty pounds. He had an engaging smile and a firm handshake. Like his father, he had a receding hairline and probably would be bald by his forties.

The couple met through mutual friends. Within a year, their relationship had reached the stage where he was invited to her home for Sunday dinner. Soon her parents gave their blessing, and the father announced their engagement over the Christmas holidays of Hiram's senior year. They planned to marry over Christmas the following year.

Although it was assumed by everyone that Hiram would take over the family business, he wasn't sure he was ready, but he decided to give it a try. He finished his studies in January of his senior year and sailed as first mate with an experienced Captain. The company had re-started the Triangular Trade Route years earlier and added two more merchant ships. This was his first voyage involving enslaved people. As first mate, he was responsible for purchasing the cargos they'd take to Liverpool, then to Africa, and finally to Rio De Janeiro before returning to the states.

He'd never experienced the slave trade in person, and what he saw, he didn't like. When they landed in Porto Novo, he knew he couldn't refuse to purchase enslaved people, but he procrastinated somewhat. The hardest part of the operation was when he looked into the eyes of these poor people. The human degradation was more than he could bear. The captain became impatient with him and interceded with the sellers. Once on board the ship, he couldn't accept the stench of the human cargo; the discipline gave out to make the enslaved people obey and the substandard living conditions they had to endure across the ocean.

He spoke several times to the captain, who had to walk a fine line because Hiram was the son of the owner and the future master of the company. As diplomatically as he could, he made sure Hiram understood the captain's role and authority.

One day, after a discussion with Hiram about the treatment of the enslaved people, he lost his temper. "Young man, you may be the owner's son, but I'm your captain; you either follow my orders, or I'll have you replaced as first mate and placed in the hold until we reach home. I have orders from the owner of this company to have a successful voyage. My livelihood is dependent upon how much we make on this trip.

You'll not jeopardize that. Do we understand each other?" Hiram saluted and left the cabin. For the remainder of the voyage, he kept his mouth shut.

After the enslaved people were offloaded and sold at auction in Brazil, Hiram was different; the albatross had been removed from around his neck. He handled his duties with precision and effectiveness and made several lucrative purchases for the trip home to Rhode Island. Just before departing Brazil, he received a telegram that his father had passed away. Charles had been diagnosed with an irregular heartbeat that he hadn't divulged to his wife and son. Hiram was shocked and took it very hard. He loved his father and would miss him.

Hiram relinquished his duties as first mate and took over the Captain's Cabin and ownership of the ship and cargo. He didn't speak to the captain for the remainder of the trip. All dialogs went through the new first mate. However, when they arrived in Bristol, Rhode Island, he thanked the captain and told him there would be no repercussions for his disagreement with Hiram. He was surprised that there was no one to greet him upon arrival. Soon he learned that his beloved mother had passed away within a month of his father's demise.

Two funerals the first week he was home caused a great deal of stress, especially with his fiancé. Hiram was an introvert, and the pain he experienced when learning of the death of his parents was difficult to share with anyone. His mother had been his rock and confidant. He didn't know what he'd do without her guidance and counsel. He needed some space and perhaps be free of the company. The cruise from England to Africa and, finally, Rhode Island after stopping in Brazil would never be repeated by him. He hired a firm to assess his company's value and, after six months, sold the company, including its ships, real property he inherited, and all his holdings. His grandfather, Silas, had passed away five years earlier, and William, now a prominent physician, readily accepted a buy-out from Hiram for his family holdings. Hiram was a wealthy man. If he'd been more patient, he probably would've been able to obtain substantially more for his share, but he just wanted out.

Jane was devastated when he postponed their wedding, especially since she and her family had spent considerable time and expense to plan and prepare for the event.

The cake had been ordered, a deposit was placed on the hall, and her wedding dress was ordered from the foremost designer in Boston. "I need time." Was all he could say to his fiancé.

The pressure got to her. During a luncheon date with Hiram, she lost her patience after he stated he didn't know when they'd be married. "Well, you can have all the time you need." She threw her engagement ring at him and walked out of the restaurant. This wasn't the outcome he desired. But all he could think about was that he had to get away to think all of this through.

On the spur of the moment, he took a cruise to England, a ferry to France, and a train to Paris. Initially, he wrote to Jane every week, but as the year went on, he was lucky if he wrote once a month. After a year in Paris, he returned home to find out that his fiancé had married another man; he never saw Jane again.

CHAPTER 2

*T*he letter that came by mail was barely legible. It was written in Lakota language and traveled from The Pine Ridge Reservation in South Dakota by stagecoach to Cheyenne and then by train to Santa Ynez. The addressee on the front of the envelope wasn't recognized by anyone, but the town of Santa Ynez, which was legible, got it to the postmaster. He knew who it was for and personally delivered it.

When the postmaster drove up the entry drive, Sarah met him outside and invited him for a lemonade. "This must be important if you delivered it personally." Sarah smiled as she took his hat and ushered him into the kitchen, where Tommy was sitting in their nook overlooking her garden.

The two men shook hands as the postmaster sat across from his host and handed him the letter. Tommy was careful as he opened the delicate envelope and took out a note pad sized piece of paper, and read the text. As Sarah sat down next to him, he handed her the note, and she chuckled as she read the invitation. Tommy's younger brother William Sitting Bull was marrying Scout Woman at the Pine Ridge Reservation on the first of July. Tommy and his family were invited to attend. His sister, Standing Holly, would be present.

After the postmaster left, they shared the news with Naomi and the children. Tommy and Naomi came from the Standing Rock Reservation, though Tommy had been to Pine Ridge many times. His son and daughter were excited and constantly interrupted their parents, asking if they could go.

Three days later, the family decided to go and take Naiwa and Raoul, Sarah's daughter and son-in-law, and their two children with them. Naiwa had lived at the Pine Ridge Reservation for several years with her first husband before he died. Sarah saw her daughter living in poverty and convinced her to come to Rancho Del Prado. Unfortunately, Sarah's son Juan, a practicing attorney in Santa Ynez, had a least three cases he was preparing for trial. Although he wanted to go, he couldn't take time off from his busy schedule.

The extended Sanchez family decided to go by train through Cheyenne, Wyoming, over to Chadron, Nebraska, and then by wagon to the reservation. It took them a few weeks to prepare for the trip, to decide who was in charge while they were gone, and what to take on the long journey. Tommy talked at length with Tomas and felt confident that Raoul's assistant could handle the day-to-day management as long as Juan stayed in the main house. Tomas had the loyalty of the ten Vaqueros employed at the ranch and felt honored that Tommy would consider him for the position of acting foreman.

They left on June 15th and made good time, reaching Cheyenne in three days. It was the trip to Chadron that took a week. They encountered a freak snowstorm in summer, a bridge that was down, and a train that had to be replaced. Luckily, the train conductor had planned for such a setback, and there was sufficient food to feed all on the train until they could get a replacement. Their misadventures weren't limited to the train. When they arrived in Chadron, the buggy they reserved wasn't available. The only conveyance they could find was an old stagecoach with the Butterworth emblem on each side. The family was enjoying the adventure, so they took the old standby. Everyone worked to clean it up, and they were on their way twenty-four hours later.

Tommy and Raoul shared the driving while the three women and four children were packed inside the coach. The first day out was beautiful, but around four in the afternoon, they could see a squall line approaching. They'd been paralleling a river, but once the rain started, they drove to a high spot. There was a tarp on top of the coach that covered their luggage and supplies. They passed the bags and supplies down and put them under the coach. Then the four children climbed on top of the coach and covered themselves with the tarp. The three women stayed in the coach, and the two men found shelter under the wagon with the baggage.

Three hours later, the rain moved on, and the twilight sky was clear. The men were soaked and had to change, but the women and children were fine. Sarah, Naomi, and Naiwa prepared dinner. Everyone sat around the fire and laughed at the experience. Raoul told them about his early life in Mexico. The village he came from had twenty families, and horses were scarce. Luckily, his grandfather had one of those horses, and he taught Raoul to ride.

Tommy told them how he infiltrated an enemy Indian Village and subdued the three sentries so they could capture the village without any loss of life. Sarah told the group her eyewitness view of the Battle of the Little Bighorn, while Naiwa spoke of her father and Sarah's first husband, Crazy Horse, the hero of that battle.

Naomi recounted her fight to stay alive and earn enough to feed herself. Sarah found her on the streets of Cheyenne and took her in.

Everyone slept on the tarps that night, rose at dawn, and, after a quick breakfast, were on their way. They arrived at Pine Ridge a day early and were received as honored guests. The legend of Tommy Sanchez started while he was a Sioux Brave. Everyone at the Reservation knew of his exploits, while many at the reservation remember Sarah from the days when she was the wife of Crazy Horse. The children, Naomi, Raoul, and Naiwa, were housed with other families, but Sarah and Tommy were given Chief Red Cloud's Teepee while they were there.

On the second day of their stay, Tommy was reunited with his younger siblings, Standing Holly and William Sitting Bull. Later in the day, they met Scout Woman, William's intended. She had seen Tommy and Sarah when they visited the reservation some years earlier. When she was alone with Scout Woman, Sarah reminisced about her wedding day with Crazy Horse, the dress she wore, and the beautiful ceremony they had. Much of what Sarah experienced would occur the day after tomorrow when Tommy's brother would take a bride.

During the later stages of his life, Sitting Bull became friends with Buffalo Bill and performed in his Wild West show. William Sitting Bull took his father's place after the great warrior was killed, and now, he was a featured performer in the show. He planned to continue with Buffalo Bill after the wedding, but Scout Woman would remain at the reservation.

Standing Holly presented Tommy with a picture of Sitting Bull when he was a member of Buffalo Bill's show. When he looked at it, a tear formed in his eye, and Sarah grabbed his hand. The legend never had a picture of his father.

On the day of the wedding ceremony, the Sanchez Family was dressed in traditional clothing they borrowed from their relatives and friends. The four children were very excited and ran with the other kids in the village, playing

games and just being children. The festivities started with an all-women's dance which lasted into the afternoon. Half of the women participated, and the other half spent their time cooking for the guests.

Late in the day, the bridal couple visited their new lodge. Shortly after that, the medicine man appeared, as well as four warriors, who held a blanket high above as the bridal couple walked under it and proceeded to where the marriage ceremony would take place.

After the ceremony, the groom went to their new lodge and started a fire. The bride went to her relative's home and was wrapped in a blanket and carried to the new lodge by her family. When they arrived at the lodge, which had its flap open, her family entered and unwrapped the bride and laid her at the feet of her new husband. He playfully slapped his bride and said, "you are mine."

The new bride rose and began to prepare food for the guests, who were relatives and close personal friends. Naomi put the four children to bed, and the other four adults stayed up late into the wee hours partying with Tommy's brother and new bride. All the children were up early the following day, looking for something to eat. It was Naiwa who volunteered to cook and let the other three sleep. The family was planning to leave in a day and still needed to spend some time with their relatives.

The following day Sarah and Tommy had another reunion. The three brothers of John Smart, convicted of killing four ex-soldiers in the Santa Ynez Valley, came to their teepee. Joseph Horn Cloud and his brother, White Lance, apologized for stealing two horses from their ranch and were willing to appear before the Sioux Council. If Tommy wanted to press charges, they would abide by the verdict. "I also apologize for my two brothers," said Dewey Beard.

"That was in the past. I'd almost forgotten about what happened. Where is your white brother now?"

"White Bird is back with his people. He's made peace with Rosita Riley and has accepted her child as his. I'd rather not say what name he uses in case there's still some hate in your heart." Dewey Bird responded.

The brothers shook hands with Tommy and Sarah and left the tent. "Well, you may have forgiven them, but Sheriff Rodgers hasn't forgiven you," Sarah said.

Red Cloud had some words for Tommy before they left for home. "I'm happy to see you again. I'm proud you're making your way in the white man's world and for what you've done for our reservation. I wish you a safe trip home, but the road to Chadron is filled with men who bear you ill will. Be cautious. I'll send a few braves with you. They'll stay out of sight but will be there if you run into trouble."

Tommy thanked him and said he'd be back for a visit. He and Sarah spent the remainder of their time with William Sitting Bull and Standing Holly, his half-sister. He had affection for his youngest sibling and suggested she come for a visit to Rancho Del Prado. She declined. "I know you mean well, but the language would be an obstacle, and besides, I like living with my people. I felt out of place when I visited a city. No, I think I'm happy where I'm at. But thank you for the invitation."

"If you should change your mind, you're always welcome."

Before he left, Tommy gave a cash donation of ten thousand dollars to help educate the young. The following day, they were off and camped on high ground near where they spent a night on the way to the reservation. Tommy heeded Red Cloud's counsel and had Raoul, Naomi, and Naiwa sleep in the couch with the four children inside; Raoul was armed with a rifle. Tommy and Sarah, who was an excellent shot, made their bed under the stagecoach with their rifles close at hand.

Around midnight, the horses became agitated, and Tommy woke Sarah. "Keep your rifle handy; I'm going south and working my way around."

"Be careful, Tommy, don't take any chances."

He changed into his moccasins, grabbed his rifle, crawled about fifty yards until he was in medium-high brush, and then made his way further south. He found a spot that was shielded by some boulders and waited. He wasn't there long before he heard movement to his right; there were two. He took his time and made his way toward them. The two were about twenty yards from the stage coach when a shot rang out, and someone yelled that he was hit. He wasn't sure, but he thought the shot had come from the coach. The two in front of him were distracted by the sound for a few seconds, and that was all Tommy needed to neutralize both white men.

Sarah saw the man crawl toward her. She wasn't about to ask about his intentions, so she shot him in the shoulder. He dropped his weapon and crawled away from her. The assailants would be more careful now after realizing that the people in the coach were armed and waiting for them. Another shot rang out, and another person yelled out. Tommy wondered how many were in the group that was attacking. As he maintained his distance from the coach, he saw one man behind a rock about fifteen yards away. Rather than shoot him in the back, Tommy crawled behind him, hit him over the head with his rifle butt, and then tied his hands behind his back.

The three Indians who were trailing the family walked into the campfire, pushing two men ahead of them and dragging two others who appeared to be wounded. Tommy gathered up the three he'd subdued and marched them into the small clearing near the coach. Seven men had been rounded up; none of them would talk. Soon he heard someone speak in the Lakota dialog that they had the last two. In Lakota Language, Tommy asked the Indians if they could take the seven to Chadron. He and his family would arrive later in the day and press charges.

The Indians escorted the seven to Chadron, including the two Sarah had wounded. The family slept very little the rest of the night and were up before dawn, had coffee, and made their way to Chadron.

With very little sleep the night before, they took their time and arrived late in the afternoon. After checking into the hotel, Tommy and Raoul went to the sheriff's office to be sure the bandits had been jailed and to formally press charges. The two wounded had been patched up by the local doctor; the entire seven were behind bars.

"This is a bad lot you tangled with. They've been tried for several burglaries and two attempted murders, but no one has come forward to press charges, or if they did, there were no witnesses to corroborate their story. One of the ones you shot was Craig Pickens, the younger brother of Clay Pickens, who leads the gang. He's over at the saloon. I know he will tell you to drop the charges or else. I'll do what I can, but he's a mean one. Just watch out and keep a gun handy", the sheriff told them.

That evening, Naomi picked up dinners for the children, and the five ate in their room. The two couples decided to have dinner downstairs in the small space that functioned as a dining room with eight tables and a bar. They'd just finished dessert when a tall blond man followed by two heavy-set cowboys approached their table. "Are you the ones who pressed charges against the seven in jail?" Tommy nodded.

"If you know what's good for you and these women, you'll drop the charges and leave town as fast as possible. Let me make it clearer. You won't get on that train unless you drop the charges." The blond man said his piece and walked away. The other two glared at the four at the table, then turned and followed the blonde man outside.

The waitress brought Tommy the bill. "That's Clay Pickens. He's a killer, pure and simple. My boyfriend tangled with him and was never heard from again. If he says he will kill you, he means it."

The four were silent as they paid the bill and went to their rooms. While they were undressing, Sarah asked Tommy what he would do.

"Nothing. We'll see how it plays out.' "Will the sheriff help?"

"I think he'd like to, but he lives here, and we're strangers. My best guess is that we must figure this out ourselves. Maybe with the children, we'll have to give in to them."

Sarah looked Tommy in the eye and said, "Not a chance."

The train left at eleven the following day, and the family was up early to have breakfast. Tommy took Raoul aside and spoke to him candidly. "I'll handle this. You stay with the women and children. If anything happens to me, you make sure everyone gets home safely."

"But Patron, I'm not afraid. I will stand with you."

"I know you're brave, but you must stay out of this if I go down. Please do as I ask."

The family came out of the hotel at ten that morning and made their way to the station when the tall blond man and his two friends blocked their way. "I told you that you're not leaving town without dropping the charges, and I meant it," the blond man said.

Tommy looked around and motioned his family to move back out of the way. "If you're looking for the sheriff, he will not help you. He's out of commission", his adversary said.

When Tommy was sure his family was out of the line of fire, he turned to face the three and moved back his jacket, exposing the gun and holster on his right side. "You're going to take on all three of us." The blond man laughed.

No sooner had he taunted Tommy when a rifle shot rang out, and the man on the far right of Tommy gripped his shoulder and slumped to the ground. Out of the corner of his eye, Tommy saw Sarah standing next to him with a rifle pointed at the three. "It won't make any difference to me if I kill you both." Clay Pickens said.

The blond man reached for his gun, two shots rang out, and the two men in front of Tommy fell to the ground. Each had been hit in the right shoulder. Their guns were still in their holsters. Just then, the sheriff ran up.

"I'm sorry, someone locked me in a closet, but I got out. I assume you want to press charges?"

"As long as we make the train by eleven, I'll fill out the paperwork and come back for the trial."

The town doctor treated the three men, and when they could walk, he had some of the town's people take them to the jail. They didn't go peacefully. The tall blond man vowed vengeance against all who participated in his capture. To Tommy Sanchez, he said, "I'm going to kill you."

"If you try again, the result will be the same." Tommy smiled. "Who do you think you are?" Pickens asked.

"I'm Tommy Sanchez, the son of Sitting Bull." "Oh my god" was all that the blond man could say.

Sarah hugged and kissed Tommy. "I thought I told you to stay out of the line of fire?" Tommy told Sarah.

She responded with a smile on her lips. "They weren't going to shoot you while I'm around. Besides, you forgot how good of a shot I am."

He hugged her and told her he loved her. His two young children ran up and hugged Tommy. His foreman shook his hand and said, "I heard about the legend of the fast gun, but I would never have believed it had I not seen it with my own two eyes."

Young Tommy asked his father if he'd teach him to draw like that. "No. Those days are over. When you grow up, men won't be wearing guns." Tommy put his hand on his son's shoulder, and the family walked to the waiting train.

CHAPTER 3

*T*he Boston Athletic Association was the main sponsor of charity events for older professional fighters. Over the past ten years, the BAA had raised over one hundred thousand dollars and used the funds to build a home for aging boxers. The proceeds for tonight's bout between two local fighters would be used for medical services with a local General Practitioner. The two participants had trained for a couple of weeks to prepare for the exhibition, and seven hundred tickets had been presold. Over the past five years, Hiram Bookers has been traveling in Europe and to the West Coast of the United States. Since selling his shipping line, he'd devoted himself to charitable events and philanthropic causes, but ever since his college days, he loved to box.

His opponent tonight was but twenty years old and had twenty fights under his belt. Hiram, at the age of twenty-eight, was in his prime. It was at Yale where he found the passion, but it was in the back bay of Boston where he honed his skills by sparring with all the up-and-coming locals. When asked to participate in an exhibition with such a young fighter, he told the event organizer that he'd take it easy on the lad and make a bout of it. Physically, the two men were similar in build and experience.

There were nearly four thousand fight goers packed into the tiny arena; many were up in the rafters of the old building. The fire department tried to limit the number to two thousand, but the mayor overruled his chief and allowed the overflow.

Many local dignitaries were in attendance, and at least ten more prominent were introduced at ringside. There were cheers from the raucous crowd as the two fighters walked through them and entered the ring.

After the two fighters were introduced, the referee called the two combatants together and went over the rules. After he was finished, the two men touched gloves, and Hiram's opponent said to him. "I'm John L. Sullivan, and I can lick any man alive."

They walked to their corners and Hiram thought the young man was full of himself and he'd give him something to think about as soon as the fight started. As the bell rang, Sullivan rushed his opponent and landed six or seven blows before Hiram could leave his corner; the crowd cheered. Each blow felt like it'd been delivered by a jack hammer. Hiram reached out with both hands to shove the young man away but he didn't move. What he received in return was the hardest punch he ever felt. Although it was to his upper arm, he thought his shoulder was separated.

The night ended early in the first round. John L. faked a left but threw a right that hit Hiram above his eyebrows and he toppled over. When he regained consciousness, it took him several minutes before he was aware of his surroundings. There were no hard feelings with Sullivan; he helped pick up Hiram and invite him to the "Ye Olde Oyster House" for a beer and a cup of clam chowder. It was several hours before Hiram was ready to go out. Sullivan didn't mind. He had a few beers in his dressing room while he was waiting for his opponent to recover. That was the last staged fight of Hiram's career.

Later, as he looked back on that night, he was delighted that the Great John L. talked him into retirement.

Three years after the fight, Hiram decided to attend the battle between John L. and Jack Burns. It was a short fight, with Sullivan dispatching the overmatched Burns in one round. Hiram went back to the dressing room and renewed his acquaintance with "The Boston Strong Boy", as the newspapers dubbed him. John remembered Hiram and the two went to dinner with four of John L's female friends. They made a night of it with Hiram waking up with one of the ladies in a low-class hotel in South Boston. He reminded himself never to get that drunk again.

They became close friends. Hiram followed the great fighter's career, attending some of his bouts and going out for a brew afterwards, which Sullivan liked to consume. Hiram didn't attend all the bouts but managed to see him knock out Harry Gillam for his twenty-second win and his forty-first win against Al Greenfield. At that point, Sullivan had won all his bouts except two, which were ruled a draw. Hiram was amazed at John L's stamina when he went seventy-five rounds before ending Jack Kilrain's night with a knockout.

The two would get together periodically over the next few years and Hiram could see a gradual change in his friend. Sullivan was putting on weight, drinking too much and staying out late at night. In addition, there were too many barroom fights with some of the rowdy patrons who wanted to test the aging champion.

John L. didn't look good when he started training for the Jim Corbett bout, which was to be held in the

Boston Gardens three years after his donnybrook with Kilrain. That bout took too much out of Sullivan. The great fighter confided in Hiram that he was going to retire after he knocked Corbett out.

Hiram visited with Sullivan in his dressing room the night of the fight; they made plans to go to a victory dinner afterward. John L. got him a ringside seat and seemed confident that he could dispatch the younger and smaller Gentleman Jim, who had a large entourage at the arena. The cheers were enormous for Sullivan as he walked through the crowd and entered the ring. He paraded around the ring, stirring up the crowd before Corbett climbed through the ropes to a warm applause. There had to be twenty thousand patrons in attendance.

Sullivan started the fight with the same tactics he used in other wars. He'd rush his opponent, set up in a crouch and try to bully his adversary. Generally, he would wear down the other fighter. Corbett had trained for those tactics; he was wary and maintained his distance while scoring points with a lightning jab, which didn't hurt Sullivan but annoyed him. By the tenth round, Hiram could see that the tide had turned, and it was only a matter of time before Corbett would win. The smaller, more agile fighter was frustrating the champ with constant jabs to his face, while John L. was swinging and missing and getting tired; his stamina wasn't what it used to be. Hiram didn't want to see his friend humiliated, but the profession he chose made that inevitable.

Between the thirteenth and fourteenth rounds, Hiram excused himself and went to Sullivan's dressing room to wait for the outcome. An hour later, John L. staggered into the room, and with disbelief in his tone, he told Hiram he had lost. He didn't cry, but he sat on the dressing room table with his head slumped in his hands. "I never lost before" was all he could say. It was an hour before Sullivan felt well enough to shower, dress and get ready to go out.

The place they chose for dinner had the victorious Corbett and his group taking over an adjoining dining room. Sullivan had his world championship belt with him. When he saw Corbett, he got up from the table, ignored the excellent wishes of some of the patrons, and walked up to the celebrating Corbett. He handed him the belt, shook his hand, and said, "I was beaten by a better man tonight."

He returned to the table where Hiram was waiting and said, "Let's go someplace else for dinner. This is a sad evening for me, and I don't want to share it with that crowd."

They had dinner from time to time after the bout with Corbett. The Boston Strong Boy had officially retired, and although he periodically fought an exhibition and picked up some needed income, he never fought professionally again. Although Hiram maintained his close friendship with Sullivan, he was squiring several women around the Boston area and didn't have enough time for his friend. There were a couple of ladies Hiram liked, but not in the same way, he felt about Jane Thornhill.

A few years after the Corbett fight, Hiram met a twenty-year-old woman of English ancestry; her name was Lucy Madison. Her entire family emigrated from London because of her sister's health. He was forty years old and entirely obsessed with the young lady. She enjoyed his love of sailing, his dry sense of humor, and the fact that he was well-known in the Boston Area. He liked to walk into a restaurant with the pretty young thing on his arm and shake hands or say hello to his many admirers. On the surface, it looked like an above-average match. Still, Hiram was to learn that even though her family understood he had considerable wealth, they felt the disparity in their ages was unacceptable, as well as his association with the fight crowd.

He tried to win over the family by introducing her parents to some of his political and social friends. Although they enjoyed meeting these prominent people, they weren't won over to his side. Finally, he asked Lucy to elope with him. He promised to buy her the home of her choice, and she'd never want anything. "Hiram, I can't go against my family. If I do, I'll be excluded from my siblings and relatives. I love you, but I'm not willing to be shunned by my entire family."

This was the second time he'd lost his beloved. He wondered if there was a woman that would be his. For months afterward, he spent most of his time with his close friends and tried to decide what to do next. He started to assess his life, assets, and way of life. Although Hiram had some investments on the east coast, most of his assets were liquid. Therefore, he wasn't tied to the Boston Vicinity. He'd been to California before and liked the warm, dry weather. As he aged, the cold, damp winters weren't something he looked forward to. The Great Blizzard of 1888 made up his mind to move to a warmer area in the United States.

For two days, the telegraph and any transportation on the east coast were shut down. Winds got as high as forty-five miles an hour, and snow drifts reached 50 feet tall. The snowfall continued for two days, and everyone was homebound. Luckily, he had three cords of wood that he burned all day and night to stay warm. He invited several of his neighbors, without any heat, to stay in his home until the storm lifted. Many poor and aged died of lack of warmth and medical attention.

There was nothing to keep him in the Boston area since the young woman wouldn't marry him. He was to learn shortly that his uncle William had also passed away. He took the train west and arrived in Los Angeles seven days later. Before leaving, he permitted his attorney to sell his tangible assets and forward the proceeds to him in California.

CHAPTER 4

$\mathcal{T}$he engineer of the Southern Pacific Railroad could see two lights flickering down the track, and immediately, an alarm went off in his head to the train approached the lights. The crew could tell that two lanterns were being waved back and forth perpendicular to the tracks. He was being signaled to stop. Jerry Martin, the sixty-year-old engineer, who'd been with the company for thirty years, was aware of the bridge just ahead over the Ventura River south of Oxnard, California. The first thing that entered his mind was that the bridge was damaged and he had to stop the train before it reached the river.

It wasn't an easy task to stop a six-car express train. It was four days before Christmas, and the three passenger cars were filled with happy travelers trying to get a head start on the holidays, and the engineer was aware of their welfare. In addition, there were extra deputies in the express car, between the engine and the passengers. Significantly, the train was carrying almost thirty thousand dollars in cash, bank notes and gold destined for the new Commercial Bank in Santa Barbara. There were five armed deputies in the express car assigned to protect the safe carrying the money.

The founder and chief executive officer of the new bank, William Keneally, spent nearly a month in Los Angeles raising most of the money. He was a man of forty-five from a wealthy family in St. Louis. He'd come to Santa Barbara ten years earlier, married a local girl, and made his living investing in land. It was one of these investments where he became acquainted with Mr. Thomas Sanchez of Santa Ynez. It was Mr. Sanchez who provided the initial ten thousand dollars of the funds he needed.

Although he'd given his guarantee, as well as that of his family, to the investors, it was Tommy Sanchez's recommendation and list of potential investors that made the venture plausible. Keneally was determined not to let anyone down, so he was in the express car with the five deputies.

Engineer Martin pulled back on the power so it would be a smooth deceleration for the five cars they were drawing. Even so, many celebrating in the passenger car stumbled and fell into the plush seats; luckily, no one was hurt. As Martin braked to a halt, two masked men carrying the lanterns boarded the train on opposite sides of the engineer's cabin. Each was carrying a weapon pointed at the two railroad men; one of the two ordered the Engineer and fireman to raise their hands. "Move the train just to the other side of the bridge and do it now," he called.

The engineer put on just enough power to move all the cars to the other side of the bridge and then pulled back on the throttle to the stop position. "Both of you climb down and sit on the gravel, and don't move," one of the masked men ordered.

The engineer and fireman were tied up as four other men wearing black masks appeared; two were carrying explosives. They moved toward the bridge and started attaching the munitions to the structure. The other two entered the nearest passenger car from opposite ends and systematically disarmed the passengers. They repeated this action in the next vehicle. The two who stopped the train banged on the door of the express car and ordered the occupants to open it. When there was no response to their demand, one of the masked men yelled to those inside. "I'll give you two minutes to come out with your hands up. If you don't, we'll blow the door off its hinges."

The discussion inside the express car needed to be fixed. The bank founder didn't want to lose the money he raised, but the senior deputy saw that they had no other choice but to open the door. The rest didn't know what action they should take and, therefore, didn't help come to a decision.

Meanwhile, when the train failed to reach the next checkpoint on its route, a red flag went up in the Los Angeles Headquarters of the Railroad Company. Automatically, a special two-car train to include workers, horses, food, and supplies was dispatched immediately.

The engineer of the special train was briefed to fear the worst and to run at top speed. He estimated that he'd reach the other train within two hours.

When those inside the express car failed to open the sliding door, the robbers placed a charge on that door and blew it off its slide. As soon as the smoke cleared, the bandits rushed the visibly stunned occupants and overwhelmed them. Two of the deputies guarding the money were on the floor with blood oozing from cuts on their hands and heads. The robbers confiscated all their weapons, lined up those who could walk, and had them carry those still unconscious from the car and lay them next to the engineer and fireman. Dynamite had been attached to the bridge, and the two men joined the other bandits. While two stood guard over those sitting or lying on the ground, the other two continued to disarm those in the passenger cars. The remaining pair of bandits carried dynamite to blow the safe.

The express car messenger was one of those who was injured and lying on the ground outside the car. He was the only one who had the combination to the safe. After several failed attempts to wake him, two doctors, who had been in one of the passenger cars, volunteered to help the wounded.

The bandits decided they'd wasted too much time, and their only option was to blow the safe. None of the masked men had ever blown a safe before. None of them could determine how much of a charge was needed. The one bandit who knew something about dynamite overcompensated and blew the door off the safe. But that wasn't half of it. Both ends of the express car as well as the roof and the other side, were completely blown apart. Currency and banknotes were lying on the floor of the express car. Many bills were torn, and the gold took on a black tint.

The group's leader sent two bandits to the bridge to ignite the dynamite. Despite the problem with the cache, the bandits removed and picked up all the gold, banknotes, and cash. As soon as the bridge was blown, the bandits' horses were brought around. Six rode off, leaving several of the railroad guards in serious condition. The passengers, confined to their cars during the robbery, emerged and sought to assist the doctors in attending to the injured. As the riders rode off and disappeared, another rider joined them as they headed to the hills south of Santa Barbara.

CHAPTER 5

*O*nce the two physicians cleared the injured security men to travel, the conductor loaded all the passengers, and the train made its way to Santa Barbara. Before that, all the debris from the explosion inside the express car was picked up and piled on the floor of that car. Upon arrival in Santa Barbara, the engineer relayed the details of the robbery to Southern Pacific Railroad Headquarters in Los Angeles. Next, he gave the local sheriff a limited description of the bandits and ensured the wounded were transported to the hospital.

Rewards were posted immediately. The railroad, express company, and the US Government each contributed five hundred dollars per robber. Since there were six bandits, the total reward was nine thousand dollars. Law enforcement personnel from Los Angeles and the state militia arrived in Santa Barbara within forty-eight hours. With local authorities, fifty men gathered in the fairgrounds would make up the posse. One of the groups brought bloodhounds.

For two hours after they arrived in Santa Barbara, Martin, the fireman, the express car messenger, and many of the train's deputies were interviewed, and descriptions of the bandits were compiled. Although all the bandits wore masks, the consensus was that four were in their late thirties or early forties; two were much younger, perhaps in their mid-twenties. Four were of average height; two were shorter. There were no distinguishing scars or characteristics that anyone would remember. Jack Rodgers, the Santa Barbara County Sheriff running for reelection, stated that the bandits would be caught within the week.

The express train dispatched from Los Angeles reached the damaged bridge in less than two hours. Among the people on board the train was an emergency crew who immediately assessed the damage to the bridge and started the repairs. Two days later, the bridge had been repaired to the point where trains could safely pass. The special train continued to Santa Barbara. With the bridge now usable, more law enforcement personnel, including agents from the Pinkerton's Detective Agency, joined the investigation. All the men aboard joined the group assembled on the fairgrounds. Along with their horses, they were prepared to be part of the posse.

Local toughs were rounded up, and initial suspicion centered on Samuel Saturday, a notorious bank robber and leader of the River Gang. Saturday had been in prison, serving fifteen years, for the robbery of the Main Street Bank in Santa Maria. He was pardoned by the governor after completing only five years. In return, Saturday promised never to participate in any robbery in California. When he was found, Saturday professed his ignorance of the theft. Still, the local sheriff kept him under surveillance for the next thirty days.

The heist was well-planned and carried out with precision. Authorities suspected that known outlaws committed the crime. Physical descriptions of the thieves further substantiated that opinion. The Pinkertons were sure some of the Wild Bunch was involved. Butch Cassidy's name came up more than once in any conversation. One thing worked in the authority's favor. The express messenger, who had regained consciousness, had a list of the serial numbers of the stolen bank notes and currency. The list was circulated to law enforcement personnel and banking institutions throughout the southwest.

Two days after the train robbery, the posse started their search. With over fifty men ready to be sworn in, the posse was divided into three fifteen-man groups. Those not selected would be held in reserve to supplement any of the three groups if necessary. The appointed leaders of the three possess were Sheriff Ben Jones of Ventura County, Sheriff Bill Paxton of Los Angeles County, and Tommy Sanchez of Santa Ynez. However, Sanchez was in Los Angeles, selling a consignment of his wine and, therefore, wasn't available then. Sheriff Jim Gray was appointed the leader of the third posse. Two of the posse started after the bandits before Sanchez was notified. Kaneally pleaded with Sheriff Rodgers to wait for Sanchez, but the sheriff felt they needed to move quickly, and Gray was selected to lead the group.

The first break for the posse came when they found a spot at the junction of several trails where seven riders separated into three groups. Initially, all three of the escorts had difficulty in catching up with the bandits because the outlaw's used relays of horses stashed along their escape route and, therefore, maintained their two-day advantage over the law enforcement officers. Sheriff Ben Jones, one of the posse leaders, suggested that it made sense for the bandits to divide up the loot at this location before splitting up. Two men interviewed from the train robbery were sure the money was carried off by just two robbers. Jones felt that dividing up the loot made the posse's task more difficult by forcing them to chase three groups instead of one.

Jones was a tall, lean man with hawklike features, with over thirty years of law enforcement experience. Ten years earlier, he led a posse that captured the McKenzie gang after they robbed a Wells Fargo Depot. The posse surrounded the robbers in a narrow canyon in Southwestern Nevada. Two of the team were killed in a shootout, and three posse members were wounded, one critically. The remaining three bandits surrendered after a two-day firefight. Feelings ran high among the posse over the death of one of their members. After a spirited argument, the captured bandits were hung on the spot. Jones's reputation suffered for allowing the lynching, and he retired. But he had friends who admired his tenacity; he was contacted soon after the Oxnard Robbery and asked to join the chase.

From their tracks, three Oxnard train robbers traveled directly north, two went northeast, and two went east. Up until this point in time, all three possess thought they were chasing only six bandits. They now knew that the person who saw a seventh man join the bandits was correct.

The posse headed by Sheriff Jim Gray gained ground when the three bandits who had gone north stopped at a ranch along the trail and tried to steal a horse. A bandit's horse had thrown a shoe, and the outlaw couldn't keep up with the other two. A short gun battle with the owner of the ranch ensued. After the bandits shot out the farmer's front windows, he told the bandits they could have a horse if they left without harming his family. The train robbers agreed, and after swapping horses, they were on their way.

The Gray posse stopped at that ranch to water their horses, and the farmer told them about the shootout. While the farmer's wife was feeding the posse, the farmer gave Gray a general description of the three bandits. One was of medium height and lean; the other two were short and of average weight. The owner didn't get too close to the three, but he reported to the posse that the medium-sized bandit seemed to be in charge.

In his eagerness, perhaps, to collect some of the reward money, Sheriff Gray pushed his group hard. He eventually led them into a small ravine that lacked cover. They were ambushed by the three bandits hidden in the rocks on one side of the canyon. Gray and his men were pinned down behind some rocks. He sent five of his group to the right trying to circle the bandits, and five to the left, with the same intent. He felt that if they could encircle the bandits, they'd give up.

When he was sure his two groups were in place, Gray and the other four members rushed the three bandits from the front. The gunfire was heavy from the bandits, forcing Gray and the four to retreat. As they ran from the bandits, Gray was shot and killed. With their leader dead, the other members of his posse were reluctant to pursue their prey aggressively. The thieves escaped as the posse debated on how to proceed. Several torn bank notes were found on the ground near where the bandits hid. The posse carried the dead sheriff back to Santa Barbara and waited until someone with experience was found to lead the group. Each of the three entities that established the rewards increased the total amount by two hundred dollars per robber, raising the aggregate to twelve thousand six hundred dollars.

Over the next several months, the remaining possess chased the outlaws through harsh terrain, several small towns, and even neighboring states. Some of the torn currency was turned in by a local bank. Two men, namely Crazy Joe Hitchins and his brother Harvey, were identified by a store clerk as the ones who were spending the loot.

The posse headed by Bill Paxton trailed the brothers into Southern Nevada to the town of Crane. It was believed that the two fugitives had lived in this town when they were young and had some kin folk still living there. The population was less than two hundred people, and most were suspicious of strangers.

A number this significant wasn't hard to spot, and two citizens alerted the brothers of their presence. There were only ten members left from Paxton's posse of fifteen. Attrition, illness, and lack of interest were the cause of the decrease.

The brothers had been holed up in an old shack in the hills overlooking the town for a couple of weeks. The posse surrounded the small cabin, and after calling for the brothers to surrender, they fired about twenty shots into the structure. When there was no response to their demand for surrender, the posse rushed the shack and smashed through the only door. They'd been on the trail of the brothers for over two months, and they were tired. Their lack of success caused frustration, and they needed to let off some steam. They left the cabin and went to a cantina in town, and after two hours of heavy drinking, they shot out most of the windows in the village and burned the shack that the brothers had used.

Feeling fortunate that they'd escaped capture, the brothers realized they couldn't continue to pass the currency taken from the train. Sooner or later, they'd be caught. They assumed the posse would continue to track them north, so they cleaned up, shaved, had their hair cut, bought new clothes, and went south to New Mexico.

Two years earlier, Joe Hitchins became friendly with an attorney in Southern California named Arliss Summers. The brothers sent him a telegram and asked him to meet them in Santa Fe. They met in the Plaza across from San Miguel Mission and on the site of the Palace of Governors four days later. Joe Hitchins asked Summers if he was interested in laundering their share into spendable money. Summers had experience in exchanging hot money and assured the brothers he'd be able to help. Within a week he exchanged their   share of the stolen currency, including the torn bills, into usable money. After settling their account, the brothers returned to Nevada with over forty-five hundred dollars in useable cash.

Unfortunately, the agent that Summers used to launder the funds sent the money to one of his associates in the mid-west, who put it into circulation immediately. Soon, many bills were turning up all over the Central United States, thus complicating the pursuit of the robbers. The Pinkertons put their best agents on the case and eventually traced the bills back to Summers. When confronted with affidavits that he was involved in the laundering operation, he gave up the two brothers to avoid jail time.

The posse headed by Bill Paxton was disbanded for their role in shooting up the town of Crane. The assignment of capturing the brothers was turned over to the posse led by Sheriff Jones. Instead of taking the posse into the town of Crane, he sent in two spies to see if the brothers were still holed up there. Even though the city of Crane had supported the brothers in the past, several town members accepted money from the spies and confirmed the brother's presence. Jones smiled when he realized the brothers' arrogance; they used the same shack. It hadn't been burned that badly.

The posse waited until midnight before making their move. With their horses tied up about a quarter of a mile from the shack, they crept slowly up to the cabin. It was three in the morning when they were in place. Imagine the brother's surprise when ten men burst through the door and aimed rifles at them in bed. Jones' posse captured the brothers without firing a shot and escorted them to the Ventura County Jail.

With five bandits still at large, the Pinkertons sent out flyers to banks and law enforcement agencies throughout the West, identifying the numbers on the bank notes and torn currency. Soon, some of the bills turned up in the town of Pueblo, Colorado. The authorities suspected three former members of the Wild Bunch, namely Snake Eyes Frank Porter, Jesse Helmon, and Larry Jefferies, were involved in the Oxnard holdup. Agents working for the Pinkertons went into Pueblo and saw Porter in one of the saloons and followed him to the outskirts of town, where they lost him. Luckily, one of the other agents learned that Jefferies' brother owned a small spread outside Pueblo and that Larry was a frequent visitor to the ranch.

With confirmation from another source that the three bandits were in town, the Pinkertons assumed the three were using Jefferies' brother's spread. Local deputies and seven Pinkerton Agents surrounded the barn on the property around midnight. An agent called out the three bandits by name; no one answered. The agents and local authorities crept up to the cabin and broke down the door. The house was empty. Despite their hard work, it was apparent the bandits had been tipped off.

Spending three days in Los Angeles to sell his wine contracts was more than Tommy Sanchez could bear. He disliked the crowds at the auction, and he hated the smoke-filled restaurants and taverns. However productive the trip was, he looked forward to his annual hunting trip.

There was a spot southwest of Santa Barbara in a lush valley where he went each year. Generally, he'd bag a deer at that location within the first two days and then head home. Most of the time, his adopted son Juan joined him, but Juan was in the middle of a jury trial; they'd have to do it another time. His goal this year was two deer.

After he got off the Train in Santa Barbara, he picked up his horse, mule, and gear he'd stored at the livery. He was gone five days, and the hunting trip would take at least ten. Sarah droves down with Tomas yesterday. They were going to spend the evening at the Arlington before he went on his journey.

Word must have traveled quickly that he was back in town because the next thing he knew, Sheriff Rodgers stopped by the livery and asked to talk to him. "I assume you know about the train robbery in Oxnard."

Tommy nodded yes.

"You were my first choice to track one of the groups who robbed the Train, but you weren't available then. I know you have many business ventures, but Sheriff Jim Gray, who led one of the groups, was shot and killed by the bandits. I need you to take over that posse and chase down the three that did it."

"Why me? Others are capable. I have a lot going on right now."

"I need a strong leader. The men in the posse want to hang the three we're after. They'll probably be hung, but I want it done by a jury. Your pal Keneally has pleaded with everyone that you be appointed to head one of the possess. Besides, everyone knows that one-third of the stolen money was yours. That should be enough incentive for you to go."

"My wife is waiting for me at the Arlington. If she has no objection, I can be ready to go tomorrow morning. Why don't you stop by the hotel around six, and I'll give you, my answer."

After they made love and cleaned up, he told her what the sheriff wanted. "I don't know how long it'll take, maybe a month, maybe less."

"I know you want to go. Nothing is pending at the ranch except that I don't like to be away from you for any length of time."

When the sheriff arrived, they had drinks sent up to their room, and Tommy told the sheriff he was available. "I want to meet with the group at nine in the morning and possibly be on our way tomorrow afternoon. Where were the three men last seen?"

Rodgers pulled out a map and showed Tommy where they'd been last week. It was a small town about fifty miles south of Cheyenne. They may try to hook up with Butch and The Kid. I know you know them. Do you have any problem if they're involved?"

"None. We should take the train to Cheyenne, check out the town, and see if we can find the three. Have any of the three been identified?

"All I have is their descriptions." Rodgers handed Tommy a piece of paper with the three descriptions given to him by the members of Gray's posse.

"One hombre could be Snake Eyes, Jack Porter. I never met him, but from what I hear, he's a stone-cold killer." Tommy said.

"I've heard of him. I'll take care of provisions for two weeks, the necessary federal warrants, and some money you may need to supplement the provisions while you're out. I'll have everything ready by noon tomorrow. I suspected you'd use the train. There's one leaving for Los Angeles at two PM tomorrow and one from LA to Denver the following morning at seven. I'll see you tomorrow morning at my office. I'll have what's left of the posse there to meet you."

The Sanchez' had a nice dinner at the Arlington and retired early. Tomas, their new foreman, was staying with his brother in town. Sarah sent word for him to pick up Tommy's gear and the mule he left at the livery and bring it back to the ranch.

After breakfast in their room and a passionate goodbye, he took a carriage to the sheriff's office. Twelve men were gathered in the small office. Tommy knew two of them, and they were good men.

He made a short speech and emphasized that they weren't a vigilante group but a federal posse, and as such, there won't be any lynching. "I'll shoot any man who tries to take the law into his own hands. Do we understand each other?"

There were several murmurs of acceptance, but Tommy would only leave once each man said he would act within the confines of the law.

The train to LA had a particular car for their horses and gear. Travel to Cheyenne took two more days, but it was faster than by horse. When they arrived in the city, they arranged for a livery to take care of their horses and walked across the street to the Plains Hotel, where they had reservations. All the posse went to the Mayflower Saloon in downtown Cheyenne and ordered their giant steak. Tommy had just finished when he saw someone from his past, and he decided to go over and say hello.

Three men were sharing a table and looked up as Tommy approached. Butch Cassidy smiled, rose, and stuck out his hand, but the Sundance kid frowned. The third man was Phil Boyle. "I've not seen you in a long time. Could you sit down and join us? What brings you here?" Butch asked.

Tommy remained standing. "I'm heading a posse looking for three men who robbed the Oxnard California Train in December. You don't know anything about that, do you?"

"You know me, Tommy, I don't travel too far from home. Besides, I did five years and was pardoned by the governor. I'm a legitimate businessman now.

Tommy looked at the other two. Sundance shook his head, no, but the third man stared at Tommy. "You have a lot of nerve to come over here and ask that question. I think you've overstayed your welcome."

Butch turned to Boyle. "That's Tommy Sanchez you're talking to, and, besides, he's my guest, and he can stay as long as he wants."

Butch turned to Tommy, "Phil's been up north and doesn't know who you are. He didn't mean anything by it." Tommy smiled.

"I'll be getting back to my group. I'm going to catch those three. I hope they're not friends of yours. I don't want any interference."

"Anyone who worked for me is a big boy and would know who they're up against. Good seeing you." Butch rose and shook his hand; Tommy tipped his hat and returned to his table.

Boyle turned to Butch." Why are you and the kid taking that garbage from this guy?"

"He's probably the fastest gun alive."

Boyle turned to Sundance. "Faster than you?"

"Let's say I don't want ever to find out. I saw him take on someone very fast, and this guy barely touched his gun before he hit the floor. When you face him, you're looking at death in the eye. I wouldn't run away from him, but if I knew he was across the street, I'd stay on my side. My advice to you is, let it pass."

The posse got together for a short meeting after a cold breakfast and hot coffee. Tommy went over their plans to capture the three bandits, and that some of the "Hole-in-the-Wall Gang" may be involved. "Does that give any of you pause?"

When no one responded, he left the room. The posse saddled up and rode south to the little town of West; it took them four hours. It was obvious that the three they were tracking weren't there. The questions the posse asked were, had they been here and, if so, how long have they been gone, and in what direction? The consensus was they left two days ago and went north.

Several of the posse members asked Tommy where he thought they were headed. "My best guess is they're headed for the Hole-in-the-Wall in Northern Wyoming. These guys were probably part of Butch's gang, so why not go someplace, you know."

The posse returned to Cheyenne, resupplied, and left the next day for the Grand Teton Mountains. Tommy knew a retired Pinkerton man living in Cheyenne who'd been to Butch's stronghold.

When they met, the old-timer took out a map with the hideout's location and gave it to Tommy. "As you can see, it's in a long narrow canyon. They may have guards posted inside, so be careful. Getting in may be easier than getting out," The old timer said.

"Do you think we can surprise them?" One of the members of the posse asked Tommy after he briefed them.

"I think everyone in Cheyenne knows where they are and where we're going," he responded.

It was a good thing they brought enough food for two weeks and extra tarps. It snowed the day after they left Cheyenne and for the next two days. They found an old line shack they broke into, but any wood for the fire was buried under a couple of feet of snow. The extra blankets, food, and tarps made the difference. By the fourth day, the weather had changed, and they could continue, though the going was tough.

Seven days later, the posse was at the entrance to the hideout. "Let's take this easy, and maybe we can talk them out of there," Tommy said.

The posse tied up their horses, stowed their provisions and made their way by foot inside the hideout with Tommy in the lead. When they were about three hundred yards inside the canyon, they saw smoke from a cabin perched behind some large boulders, acting as a shield for the structure. When they got close enough, one of the posse members yelled and called for those inside to surrender.

That request was met with intense gunfire. The three in the cabin enjoyed a distinct advantage until a more significant number of posse members outflanked the men in the shack and started firing their rifles indiscriminately into the hut. For over two hours, there was a standoff. When Jesse Helmon took a bullet to the head and Jeffries was shot twice, once in the right leg and once in his right shoulder, Snake Eyes put a white flag out the front door; the posse ignored the request to talk and stormed the shack.

Snake Eyes barely shut the door before the posse broke the door down and barreled into the single room. Snake Eyes threw his gun on the floor and dove under the only table. He was quickly handcuffed, and the posse examined Jeffries and Helmon, who was dead. Some of the train loot was on the table in the center of the room; some more was in the pockets of the three bandits.

The posse buried Helmon and bandaged Jeffries. He and Porter were transported to Cheyenne. Butch, Sundance, and Boyle saw the posse enter town and stop at the railroad station. The three walked down the main street to see who the posse brought in. Snake Eyes looked directly at Butch but didn't say a word. Tommy watched the silent exchange and knew Butch was involved in the robbery. But his job was to bring in the train robbers. If Butch were concerned, he'd leave that to the Pinkertons.

As Tommy looked at the three, Phil Boyle started to move toward him. Tommy knew the move and got ready for the confrontation. But as soon as Boyle took his first step toward Tommy, Butch reached out and pulled him back. There was a short exchange between the two until Sundance grabbed Boyle's gun hand, and Butch forcefully pulled him across the street into the Plains Hotel. As he walked away, Butch nodded to Tommy, and Sundance touched his hat.

After a doctor examined Jeffries and said he was okay to travel, they boarded their horses and gear in a particular box car and made their way to California. They arrived in Ventura two days later and turned the two over to the county sheriff. Tommy returned to the ranch, and the rest of the posse disbanded.

Before their trial, Porter and Jeffries were broken out of jail. Someone pulled the bars out of the back wall of their cell and left two horses for the bandits. Eyewitnesses said the two-headed southeast into the mountains.

The sheriff wired Tommy at his ranch, and Sanchez rode back to Santa Barbara the next day. Some of the possess were still in the area. Sheriff Rodgers rounded up six of the group, and they gathered in his office the next day. Tommy was the best tracker of the group, and he picked up the escapees' trail quickly. Two days of rain didn't help the posse follow the two. The bandits had a two-day head start, but they lacked the supplies they needed to survive in the mountains.

When Tommy's posse came upon them, it looked as though they were happy to be caught. They were cold and hungry and gave up without a fight. Tommy asked the two who had assisted them, but they wouldn't give up whoever it was.

Porter and Jeffries were tried, convicted, and hung in Ventura for their part in the killing of Sheriff Gray.

Tommy attended the trial but left before the sentence was carried out. He was to learn that Porter had given the Pinkertons some information on who planned the heist and who was involved. It didn't matter; he was still hung. Neither Porter nor Jeffries gave up the persons who helped them escape. Tommy suspected Butch and Sundance, but no one saw them in the area. Knowing how Butch operated, he probably sent one of his gang members to do the jailbreak.

Tommy said goodbye to the other posse members, thanked them for their work, and took the train to Santa Barbara. The sheriff met him and thanked him for capturing the two jailbreakers. There were still two that hadn't been caught, but nearly half of the money, gold, and notes had been recovered.

If the authorities were correct, one of the original six still on the loose was Charley Joe Richards, a former member of the Wild Bunch and a good friend of Butch Cassidy. Snake Eyes confirmed Richards was involved just before he was hung. The name of the seventh member who joined the group after the robbery was still a mystery. Even though Jeffries and Snake Eyes could describe him, they never heard his name. Tracking the last two bandits over rough terrain would be difficult. Even though the posse, headed by Sheriff Jones, lost their trail many times, they never gave up.

One night, months later, after everyone except those on the lookout retired, they could hear a mountain lion close to camp. When the two sentries went to investigate, they stumbled over a decomposing body in a thicket ten yards from the creek. It wasn't until daybreak that they could see that the body's face, arms, and hands had been torn apart by animals. Identification found in what was left of the man's shirt pocket indicated he was Charley Joe Richards, who they suspected was one of the train robbers. It was impossible to tell what the actual cause of death was, and none of the money was recovered. The posse searched the area for another two weeks before returning to Santa Barbara. If there was still one more bandit eluding capture, they'd lost his trail in the mountainous terrain and didn't have any leads.

Law enforcement had effectively captured the six Southern Pacific train robbers and recovered over one-half of the stolen funds. Only the seventh man, who probably joined the gang after the robbery, was still at large. With nearly eight thousand of the train's loot still unaccounted for and at least a two-week head start, they wondered if the seventh man would ever be caught. Speculation among the posse was that he was the ringleader. If that was true, then who was he? Butch Cassidy's name came up, but he was in Bolivia and may never return.

Sarah was at home when he arrived after delivering two of the bandits to the sheriff in Ventura County. After nearly a month with the children, he suggested she accompany him on his hunting trip.

"I appreciate the thought, but I'd be in the way, and you wouldn't have any fun."

"I would at night."

"If you want me along, I'll go. It may take me a few days to get ready. Are you okay with that?" Tommy had a big grin on his face.

CHAPTER 6

Lenny Harris had been in and out of jail since he was sixteen. Up until that time, his education was minimal. It wasn't that he disliked going to school; he wasn't in one place long enough to complete even half a year. He and an older brother, Jerome, grew up on several farms in Southwestern Missouri. The family was moving, on average, every six months. Lenny and his brother didn't know why; they knew it was reality. Their father was an abusive drunk, and when things didn't go his way, like being fired, he'd take his frustration out on his wife. As the two boys grew older, they became his first target instead.

When Lenny was fourteen, Jerome left one night and never returned. Lenny heard later that Jerome was killed in a stagecoach robbery; he was shot dead by the guard. Consequently, Lenny had to pick up the work his brother had done, or he'd suffer the wrath of his drunken father. Two years later, after another beating by his father, Lenny came up behind him in the barn and hit him over the head with an axe handle. The man lay on the ground bleeding from his scalp, and Lenny didn't care if he survived.

He bummed around for a few years until he was caught trying to rob a traveler outside Jefferson City, Missouri, and went to jail for a year. During his incarceration, his mother died. The warden told Lenny that she had fallen and hit her head, but Lenny knew better, and he knew he didn't kill his father.

His next stint in jail was followed by three other terms in jail or prison.

At the age of thirty, the only thing he could point to was his relationship with the Sundance Kid, a member of Butch Cassidy's Hole-in-the- Wall Gang.

The two became acquainted when Lenny was twenty. He'd just been released from county prison after serving a year for petty theft and was employed cleaning stalls at the livery in Jefferson, Missouri. Sundance needed a fourth man for a stagecoach robbery he was planning. The man he selected fell and broke his leg the day before and couldn't ride; someone recommended Lenny. This wasn't a job for a greenhorn, but The Kid was pressed for time and accepted Lenny as a last resort.

The stagecoach robbery went off without a hitch. Lenny's only job was as a lookout. Four outlaws split the five thousand in gold, with Lenny getting five hundred for his part. Primarily because he didn't complain about not getting a total share. Sundance used him on two other small jobs. When they parted, Sundance said he'd help Lenny if needed.

Over the next ten years, Harris spent most of his time trying to survive. He liked women but couldn't afford them. Those he associated with had reached the same point in life as Harris and were looking for a safety net, which Lenny was not. Half of the time, he lived in a six-by-eight shack or on the ground in the woods   the other half. Besides an occasional woman, he had no acquaintances.

Recently, Harris spent most evenings in a saloon outside Ventura, California, playing poker and drinking. When he was short of cash, he'd waylay some traveler and escape with a few bucks. Other times, the saloon owner let him tend to the bar for a couple of nights and sleep in the backroom. Tonight, he lost at cards and was sitting alone at a table in the back corner, consoling himself with a beer and thinking about what he could do to get some quick cash.

At the following table were three well-dressed men who had a few drinks and were talking louder than usual. He couldn't help but overhear their conversation about a special train carrying thirty thousand in gold, notes, and currency. Every once in a while, one of the men would look over at Lenny to see if he was paying any attention to them.

Harris faked being asleep. He pulled his hat down low and slumped back in his chair, trying to be as inconspicuous as possible, while listening to the three men discuss the special train and its shipment.

Soon the three men left their table; two walked to the bar, and the third, after saying goodnight, went out the front. Lenny remained in his seat until the two at the bar finished their beer and left. What was he to make of the information he had just overheard? He had the date, he had the train number, and he knew the cargo it was carrying. His mind was working overtime. Who did he know that could help pull this off? He'd pulled jobs with the Sundance Kid several years ago, and the Kid said if he'd ever come across something big, to let him know. Well, it was worth a shot. What other prospects did he have? He'd robbed too many travelers along the road to do that again. The authorities would be looking for him for sure. It had to be something else.

The first thing he had to do was verify the information. He needed the correct information to go to someone like Sundance. He hopped the train the next day to Santa Barbara since that was where the special train was headed. It took him two days before he was able to verify that the train was leaving Los Angeles on December 22, 1989, at four PM and was carrying a particular cargo.

Lenny was sitting in the storage room of the saloon where he bartended, trying to figure out how to pull all this together. He was desperate with very few prospects. He knew Butch Cassidy and the Sundance Kid had been seen recently in Denver; maybe Sundance could help. There was no choice; he'd go to Denver and seek out the Kid. He took everything from his pocket, including his handkerchief, and placed it on a broken bar stool; he had fifty dollars and some change.

Harris arrived in Denver a week later, but Sundance wasn't there. He found a guy in a saloon on Larimer Street he'd met some time back. Lenny had to buy him three beers before he passed on the information that the Kid and Butch Cassidy had gone to Cheyenne. The next day, he got a ride on a supply wagon going north to Cheyenne. He found them having lunch in the Mayflower Saloon in downtown Cheyenne.

Sundance was sitting at a wooden booth near the front of the restaurant, just behind a stationary bar. When Sundance saw Harris enter the Mayflower, he waved him over and introduced him to Butch Cassidy. "We have liver and onions. There's too much here for me."

The Kid put half of his portion on a bread plate and slid it over to Harris. Lenny hadn't eaten in a day and was grateful for the food. "You look like you've come a long way. What do you need?" Butch asked.

In between gulps, Harris laid out his plan to rob the special train shipment to Santa Barbara. The Kid and Cassidy listened intently until Lenny was finished. "Did you verify any of what you've told us?" The Kid asked.

"Most of it." There's a new bank opening in Santa Barbara, headed by William Kaneally. He's been in Los Angeles for a month trying to attract investor money for the bank. I learned he's raising thirty thousand dollars from some venture capitalists and has contracted with the Southern Pacific Railroad to transport the money to his new bank. I got a copy of the train schedules, and this train is going to Santa Barbara on December 22, leaving Los Angeles at four PM."

"Getting a train to stop isn't an easy task. You must create something unusual." Butch said.

"There's a bridge over the Ventura River near Oxnard that could be blown to slow down any help coming from the south. I don't know how many men it would take, how much dynamite is needed, and how to set up a workable escape plan."

"Butch and I can't be involved. The authorities are watching us like a hawk. I think those two guys at the table over there are watching us." The Kid nodded at two well-dressed men sitting at a table next to the wall. When Lenny looked over, they immediately turned their heads.

The Mayflower was a meeting spot in Cheyenne. It was located on a corner in downtown Cheyenne and boasted a good-sized dance floor, a liberal bar, and tall wooden booths on either side of a long rectangular room.

Today, several couples were dancing to a three-piece cowboy band banging out western melodies. Any conversation the three were having was lost in the noise.

"What we can do is give you some tips on how to set up everything and the names of boys who can do the job. What's the split on the thirty thousand?" Butch asked.

"Equal shares seem fair," Lenny responded.

"For this size of the job, you'll need six men. I can furnish the names of six that I'd trust. Dynamite is easy to acquire, and one of the guys I'll give you has a working knowledge of explosives. A posse or multiple possess will come after you fast. They'll be well supplied but will only have one horse each. The best way to get away is to set up fresh horses at intervals along your escape route. I would think two sets would be enough.

"Dividing up the money early after you pull off the job between seven guys is a plus. Everyone will have his own money and a greater incentive not to be caught. This also splits up the posse into three groups. Initially, you'll have a natural head start because the posse must be organized and its members rounded up. My guess is you'll have a two-day head start. Oh, there might be one or two characters chasing after you, but I wouldn't worry about them. You'll need food, water, and at least two changes of horses before they catch up. If you're not caught before the first change of horses, you've got a better than even chance of getting away with it."

Lenny wasn't entirely naïve. "What will I owe you for your help?"

"The kid and I get a thousand a piece off the top, plus another five hundred were advancing for the explosives and extra horses you'll need, which leaves twenty-seven five or around four thousand a piece for you and the others. You buy into that?" Butch asked.

"How will I get you your money?" Lenny asked.

"Snake Eyes Jack Porter will be one of the names we give you; he'll get it to us. The guys we give you will work with Jack. I gather you don't have a place to stay?"

"No."

"Here's a place you can stay and be fed. Tell her Butch sent you". He handed Harris a paper with an address and a woman's name. Before they split up, Butch passed Lenny five hundred dollars.

Rather than meet with the kid and Butch again, who were under constant surveillance, the prospective train robbers met at the boarding house where Lenny was staying. Sundance sent ten prospects, and Lenny picked the six he wanted from that group. Since he wasn't going to participate in the robbery, he needed someone to carry out his plan and get the others to go along with it. A guy named Snake Eyes Jack Porter fit the bill. He'd been in on a train robbery before and offered a few suggestions. After everyone was comfortable with the arrangements, Lenny told them where they would meet to finalize plans. It was up to Harris to lay out the escape routes, buy the extra horses, and determine where those horses would be stashed along the escape route.

It was October and snowing hard when Harris departed Cheyenne. He left fifty dollars with Kate Mosley for the two weeks of board and for keeping an eye out while he met with his new partners. He'd previously found an abandoned line shack outside Ventura that would be his hideout and the rendezvous for the other six. He mapped out three escape routes and six small farms where he'd place horses. Harris visited each of the six farms and made a deal with the farmers that if they kept their mouths shut, they could keep the horses his partners exchanged. He delivered the horses to the six farms a week before the robbery.

Trying to stay out of trouble and be inconspicuous for two months wasn't something he'd done in the past. But this was the new Lenny. He had a job that would pay more money than he ever had, and the job was doable. About a week before the gang met at his shack, he was drinking at a saloon he frequented. A guy came into the pub and sat at the bar. It was a rancher who'd won some money in a poker game one night and given it up to Lenny at the point of a gun. The rancher picked up his drink and looked around the room. Lenny was sitting at a table in the rear with his back to the wall.

He pulled his hat down over his eyes and slumped forward in his chair. Occasionally, he'd look up to see what the rancher was doing. Soon the man finished his drink and left.

Lenny waited a half hour before he carefully went out the front door. He decided never to go back to that saloon.

Everyone arrived a day or two before the robbery. There wasn't much room in the shack, but they made the most of it playing cards. Harris was nervous, but the others were seasoned criminals and were relaxed. Harris went over the plan, the escape routes, where the money would be divvied up, at which farm the horses were staged at. Snake Eyes made a few suggestions, and Harris agreed. Each rider was given his map in case he got separated from the others. Everyone was in place two hours before the train was scheduled to leave Los Angeles.

Snake Eyes told Harris the men weren't happy that he wouldn't be part of the group that would rob the train. Harris responded that he'd never robbed a train before and would be a liability if things went south. His main job would be as a lookout in case some law enforcement personnel arrived unexpectedly. The plan was for him to join them soon after they left the scene. Snake Eyes told the others Harris had a good plan and would be their lookout. No one complained again.

All six were excited as they left the robbery scene. Snake Eyes Jack Porter was in the lead. After three hours of hard riding, the bandits stopped at the first farm on their map and exchanged horses. Lenny caught up to the group there.

They filled their canteens and grabbed the food the farmers had waiting for them; within ten minutes, they were on their way. The second change of horses occurred around noon on the third day. They were in and out within fifteen minutes, filling their canteens and gulping down the food the farmer provided. Three hours later, they stopped at the preplanned place and divided the loot. Some groups preferred gold; others wanted currency, while three chose bank notes. It wasn't an even split, but no one voiced any concern. They were happy the heist went off as planned, that they had more money than they had ever had, and they had a substantial head start on any posse. Twenty-five hundred was taken off the top and handed over to Snake Eyes. He gave it to Butch Cassidy and the Sundance Kid about two weeks later.

Snake Eyes, Jeffries, and Helmon took the north route; the two Hitchins Brothers went northeast, while Harris and Richards went east. Everyone was on their own and wouldn't see any of the other two groups again.

After three days of constant traveling, Harris and Richards decided to camp for the night. The food the ranchers had given them was consumed.

All they had left was some beef jerky to share. Both were tired and decided to turn in early without a fire to attract unnecessary attention.

Harris was the first one to rise the following day. He had a fire going and made a pot of coffee. Richards joined him and shared his cigarettes. "I think it's time for us to go our separate ways, especially if a posse is still on our trail. It'll make it more difficult to keep up with us," Richards said.

"You're probably right. This is my first time being chased by a posse, and the harder we can make it for them, the better off we'll be. Which way are you traveling?" Harris asked.

"I'm originally from Central Georgia. I was with Butch and the Kid when we successfully robbed a train a few years back. I thought I'd head home, find a nice little girl, a piece of land, and farm it. The land is still cheap after the Civil War, and what I have in my pocket will give me a head start. I advise you to stay away from populated areas and not flash your bankroll around. You'd be surprised who your enemy is when you have money. The answer is everyone wants your money and will do what's necessary to take it from you.

As Richards set down his coffee cup, Harris shot him in the heart. Lenny could see the "Why?" question on the dying man's face.

Lenny looked at Richards and said, "Thanks for the advice."

He dragged Richards toward some tall bushes and scrubs and laid him on his back. He looked around to see if he had missed anything. He went through his pockets and found his money, a watch, and a letter from Butch Cassidy telling him about a job robbing a train in Oxnard; Lenny tore the letter into a dozen pieces, cut some brush, and put it over the body.

He made sure the fire was out, counted the money, and tied Richards' horse to his saddle after he discarded Richards' saddle. He was on his way with the most money he'd ever seen in his entire life.

CHAPTER 7

It didn't take a week in Los Angeles to make up Hiram Booker's mind that this wasn't a place he'd like to spend the remainder of his life. He would have left sooner, but there was a mudslide north of the city that precluded train transportation. The raucous style of living in Central LA turned him off immediately.

His next stop was Santa Barbara, a city he'd visited in the past ten years. The weather was comfortable, and the view was outstanding. He booked a room at the Arlington and was satisfied with the choice. That night, he rented a carriage and went down the coast for about two miles. He found a small restaurant on the beach and had shrimp and clams for dinner. The waitress was amiable since the patrons were few. To his question about some of the points of interest, she told him about the aquarium and Stearns Wharf. Though he enjoyed his first day, he was determined to take his time before making this his home. He planned to visit the Santa Barbara Bank and Trust to seek their guidance.

Other than listening to the manager's pitch to use the bank as his financial institution, the best suggestion he received was to contact the owner of the Land Company in downtown Santa Barbara. "Jed Harkins has been in the area selling land for thirty years and knows where the good parcels are."

He arose later than usual, skipped breakfast, and walked down State Street before having a leisurely lunch on Stearns Wharf. He had a two o'clock appointment at the land office on lower State Street. Harkins was a few years older than Hiram and gave him an overview of the town and the surrounding area.

Since Hiram was still determining exactly what he wanted, they arranged to meet in the morning and spend a few days looking at all types of land, with and without improvements.

On the first day, they visited the Santa Ynez Valley. Although he liked a five-hundred-acre parcel with an existing structure outside the town of Santa Ynez, Hiram decided to look further. The two stayed overnight at the Central Hotel on Sagunto Street, and after breakfast, they walked around the town. When they were checking out, Hiram looked around the lobby and saw four paintings hanging on the walls that depicted scenes from Indian life. All were different. Hiram spent about ten to fifteen minutes gazing at each one.

Being a student of history, Hiram was intrigued. The oil painting that intrigued him the most was Crazy Horse. "Who's the artist?" he asked the clerk.

"Mrs. Sanchez painted those," came the response. "Are they for sale?"

"Yes, Sir. The price is in the lower corner of the paintings. Mrs. Sanchez is a white woman who was the wife of that Indian." He had a smirk on his face as he relayed the information.

"Does she live around here?"

"She and her husband own Rancho Del Prado about three miles east of here. He's the legendary gunfighter and the son of Sitting Bull. Both are well known around here. The couple is a minority owner in this hotel."

Hiram wanted the painting and paid the listed price. He had the bellboy load it in the wagon. "I thought you were going to buy all four?" Harkins said as they got in the carriage.

"The colors are magnificent. Perhaps I'll come back someday and buy the others, but I want to meet the artist someday."

They returned to Santa Barbara, and Bookers picked up his carriage at Harkins office. One of the associates in Harkins office had been trying to sell a thousand-acre parcel, without improvements, fifteen miles southeast of Santa Barbara. Before returning to Arlington, Harkins showed Hiram a map of the property, and after his client showed some interest, he suggested they look at it tomorrow.

Access to the property was limited, but Hiram was intrigued that it had a stream and a small lake in the middle of the parcel serviced by the stream. Harkins wasn't in as good a shape as Hiram, and they went by covered wagon with seven days' provisions. On the second day out, they came over a rise and saw the parcel in an enclosed valley. The trail was nonexistent, and it took them nearly half a day to make their way down the valley.

Most of the next day was spent verifying that this was the property. Hiram was able to find three of the steel stakes marking its boundary. The lake was about five acres in size, and Hiram could tell there were some fish in it. He walked the property perimeter the next day and was sold on it. Land and man were made for each other. Hiram asked how much the owner wanted, and rather than have a protracted negotiation; he accepted the owner's terms, conditions, and price.

The way back to Santa Barbara seemed more straightforward and quicker. Following their return to Santa Barbara, Hiram completed his side of the transaction and waited for the telegram from the seller confirming the sale. The remoteness of the new purchase gave him pause, but only for a short time.

His adrenalin was rising, and he didn't want to wait around in Santa Barbara. He didn't know how long it would take the owner to get back to them, so he bought a good horse, purchased a week's worth of provisions, and rode back to the property. Any supplies he didn't use this time could be stored near the lake and used in the future. He took his time and let everything come to him. What he saw this time made him comfortable that this was where he wanted to spend the remainder of his life.

Since he had all the time in the world, he sketched out where the main house should be, the location of a small barn, and what other buildings he'd need to make this a livable homestead. On the third day, he rode to where Harkins told him an Indian Family lived. It was nearly a mile away.

There were two men and a heavy-set woman sitting outside a rundown shack. Only one of the men could speak some English, but they could communicate that they would work for money or supplies. The Indians weren't sure whether other families or people were in the vicinity.

When he returned to the Land Office in Santa Barbara, Harkins met him with a firm handshake. "I've good news. The owner approved the transaction, your funds were transferred, and the deed is recorded in your name."

With that part of his future in motion, he returned to the bank and arranged to transfer all his assets from his New England Financial Institution. He made this banker very happy. Next, he put the banker in touch with his attorney back east to receive the balance of money when the sales of his east coast properties were completed. Hiram estimated that he'd have nearly three hundred thousand dollars in his account when those assets were liquidated.

Building wasn't his forte, so he visited the local lumber yard and talked to the manager/owner about his plans. The owner suggested a sequence for the project, provided some techniques he could use and outlined the type of lumber Hiram would need for each of the structures he contemplated. He listened intently and agreed to start with an outhouse and then a utility shed that could store grain and farm equipment and would also serve as a place to cure meat and store vegetables.

His next stop was the local livery, where he purchased a used wagon, two sturdy horses to pull a heavy load, and a mule. At the farm supply store, he was outfitted with clothes, hand-held farm implements, saws, a hammer, a plow, and a harrow. He made several trips to the property, trailing his horse and mule behind the wagon. The first day after he arrived with a load, he rode to the Indian Homestead and hired them to unload his equipment. He tried to communicate with the Indians to be at the homestead when he arrived with a load, but it was a waste of time; they didn't comprehend. So, each time he brought supplies, he left it in the wagon and rode over to get the Indians. This was a pain in the neck for him.

Finally, he figured it out. Suppose he provided enough food for the Indians. They'd hang around his homestead until he returned with another load.

This way, he could leave his riding horse and mule to graze, and the Indians would keep an eye on his equipment. Once he had all the lumber on site to build the outhouse and storage shed, they completed construction within six weeks. Weather was kind to him, and having the Indian woman cook probably kept the other Indians happy.

The building went much quicker as soon as the roof was on the small barn because they had shelter at night. The Indians didn't mind camping out, but Hiram was tired of sleeping on the hard ground. It was okay for a few weeks, but after that, he wanted a roof over his head. It took him a year with the Indians working every day to finish all four buildings, including a two-room house.

CHAPTER 8

*F*rances Kelly was born in 1869 to James Jay and Elizabeth (Lizzie) Kelly in Charleston, Massachusetts. Her mother, a protestant by birth, was a housewife known for her wit and lively personality. She'd come from Belfast, Ireland, when she was sixteen and immediately went into the service of the Callahan's on Beacon Hill, starting as the assistant upstairs maid. Mr. Kelly, a practicing Catholic, came to South Boston from Dublin via Cincinnati, Ohio. He was a strapping lad of seventeen when his uncle, a fireman in South Boston, wrote him a letter telling him he could get him a position with his fire brigade. Young James was delighted to follow in his relatives' footsteps, as was the custom of the Irish; he immediately left Cincinnati and never looked back.

Lizzie, number four in a line of five girls, met James through another girl doing a balancing act with him and two other suitors. Theirs was an instant attraction; they were married six months later. Within eight years, they had four children.

Although he had a steady job, it was still a financial hardship to support a wife and four children. James and Lizzie encouraged their girls to meet young men. Frances, the youngest, liked the opposite sex; but she was more interested in a career. She'd seen what happened to her siblings, who married early, had numerous children, and lived on the poverty threshold their entire lives.

One of Frances' uncles, William Kelly, had bypassed the typical male Irish professions of Policeman and Fireman and put himself through law school at night.

He and his wife had no children; Frances was their favorite, and she'd often accompany them on Sunday picnics or motor rides. When Frances expressed an interest in being a nurse, William and his wife Mary arranged for her to travel by train to Massachusetts General Hospital. One of William's clients was the hospital administrator, and he owed William a favor.

She was twenty-four years old when her father died; her mother had passed two years earlier. All the siblings were married, and she was lonely. When she was younger, she shared her closest thoughts with her mother and sisters. Now that wasn't an option. About this time, Winthrop Smith expressed an interest in her. His father was on the hospital board, but lately, Winthrop was assuming those duties. They met one day in the hall on the first floor of the hospital, and Winthrop was fascinated with the petite woman with the engaging smile. The following week, after he attended a board meeting, he sought out Frances. He had one of the resident doctors introduce her. She was flattered that he would seek her out and readily agreed to lunch the following week.

The luncheon invitation was followed by a dinner invitation the next week; intimacy would come three months later. They kept their relationship a secret for months before he suggested she meet his parents. They'd confessed their love for each other and started talking about marriage; it never dawned on her that his family might object to a union between the two. He introduced her to some of his family at a garden party in honor of his father. Subsequently, he invited her to a family dinner where his two sisters, their spouses, and his two bachelor brothers were present.

Although everyone was cordial and friendly, his mother passed on the disappointing news to Winthrop. His lady friend wasn't suited to join the Smith family. Winthrop didn't tell her directly. He began to make excuses for canceling dates. Frances was busy, so it didn't seem like anything was wrong between them. It was months later when Frances read the society section of the Boston Globe. That's when she discovered that Winthrop was escorting Miss Sally Ferguson of Beacon Hill to a charity ball. Frances read the notice at least three times. It was the exact ball that he'd promised to take her to. She was devastated. Gathering her nerve, she went to his office downtown, but his secretary told her that Winthrop was too busy to see her.

She asked the secretary what day Winthrop would be available. "I'm sorry, miss, but Mr. Smith is booked up the entire week, and I haven't set his schedule for the next week."

Frances lost her temper and summoned enough courage to shout, "Tell the prig that he has a small penis and is a lousy lover." She left on that chord.

She was crushed and embarrassed in front of her co-workers, who knew about the relationship. Avoiding her friends and family so she wouldn't have to answer any questions about Winthrop became the norm. She would spend most of her free time in church praying for guidance or at the public library reading the newspaper. She tried to be around the meeting room when the hospital board adjourned. Smith either didn't attend the sessions or he exited another way.

One day she was thumbing through the Boston Globe Newspaper and found an ad from a former Boston ship owner looking for a bride to share his ranch in California. She decided to write him a letter and send several pictures. After many letters and photos were exchanged between the two and four visits to her priest for counseling, Frances accepted his offer to pay for the train ride to Santa Barbara, California, to meet her future husband.

Seven days on the train was no picnic. Keeping herself fresh and maintaining her appearance was a necessity. She had to make a good impression when she arrived. When she stepped off the train in Santa Barbara, a distinguished-looking gentleman, about fifty years of age with gray hair, carrying a bouquet of roses, approached her in a chauffeur driven carriage. "Miss Kelly, I'm Hiram Bookers. Welcome to Santa Barbara. I've made reservations for us at the Arlington Hotel this evening. I thought you'd be tired after your exhausting trip and need a few days to ponder our marriage. I know it's late, so if it's okay with you, I'll escort you to the hotel and meet you for lunch in the dining room at noon tomorrow, where we can discuss our future."

Hiram was introduced to several eligible women in Santa Barbara by his banker, but none of them seemed to attract him. When he moved to his property, he couldn't commit to a specific time to squire the young women. Consequently, he reluctantly decided on a mail-order bride.

He'd been apprehensive since he sent her the fare to come to California. Pictures were fine, but they're no substitute for the natural person.

The first thing Francis did when she arrived at the hotel was take a nice hot bath and washed her hair. She traveled for over a week to get here, and she was going to do her best to impress Hiram. Frances was five foot three inches tall, with a round chin, upturned nose, and hazel eyes. Hiram expected a redhead, and here she was with dark wavy hair and high cheekbones. If her disposition was as sunny as it appeared, he'd made a good choice.

Her room was exquisite, and Hiram was charming. At lunch, he told her about his ranch, showed her some pictures of the cabin and barn, and told her about his plans. That evening, after dinner, he rented a carriage and drove her through the lighted streets of Santa Barbara. Afterward, they returned to Arlington for a nightcap. The next day he rented the same rig and took her to the pier, where they had a seafood lunch followed by a walk along the beach. She felt warm toward the former ship captain and, after two days, accepted his offer; they were married in the hotel dining room the next day.

They spent their honeymoon night at the hotel, and after a few awkward moments, they consummated their marriage. The next day Hiram rented the same rig. They rode north and stopped for lunch at Kinevan's Stagecoach Relay Station atop San Marcos Pass. They returned to Santa Barbara in time to watch the sunset over the Pacific Ocean. The next day, he introduced her to his banker and transferred five thousand dollars into an account for her. She would have access to these funds if something happened to him or if she decided that this marriage wasn't for her. She thanked Hiram, kissed him on the cheek, and promised him that she'd try to be the wife he wanted.

It was a two-day trip by wagon to his thousand-acre ranch southeast of Santa Barbara. They slept on the ground along an active stream the first night out; it was a first for Frances. It was uncomfortable and somewhat embarrassing for her to make love outside and not in a bed, but Hiram was patient and easy to please; besides, they were husband and wife now. Although her passion for Winthrop had never diminished and probably never would, the warmth of Hiram Bookers was winning her over.

He was a patient and caring lover and had an unusual wit. So far, she liked   being with him.

Around three o'clock the next day, they came over a rise and saw the cabin he built nestled in a grove of cottonwoods, lying fifty feet from a small stream. The inside of the two-room, one-bedroom house had been decorated with nautical items and things from his home in Boston. There was, however, one exception. On the far wall, so it would be the first thing you saw upon entering the cabin, was the colorful painting of Crazy Horse. Frances was immediately drawn to the image and walked over to see it more clearly. She turned, looked at Hiram, and asked about the painting. "I bought it in Santa Ynez. It was on the wall in a hotel where I stayed while looking for property. I hope you enjoy it as much as I do?"

"I do," she responded.

Although the cabin was small, she immediately felt the warmth of the furnishings. While she was putting her things away, he told her about his plans to enlarge the cottage, cultivate ten acres, and buy a bull to increase their herd size.

Over the next week, he told her about the funds he received from the sale of his schooner. "Right now, there is no beneficiary to the three hundred thousand dollars I have in the account. After five years of marriage, I'll make you the beneficiary. "Is that acceptable to you?"

"I have no right to anything you had before our marriage. But if we have children, I'd like them to be the heir to those funds. Perhaps you could also set aside a small amount to carry me into my later years. "

"I'll take care of that the next time we visit Santa Barbara."

He paid the Indians to handle the cattle and maintain the garden during the next six months of their marriage. She was eager and a good worker; soon, she could assume some of the duties of the ranch. Rather than overwhelm her with the responsibilities of ranch life, he taught her to ride and tend a horse.

Teaching her to milk the cows was the most challenging task; she squirted the milk on the ground. One time she sprayed herself in the face and fell over the pail. Hiram happened to be walking by and roared at the sight.

At least twice a week, they went on a picnic or fished in the small pond. She giggled when she caught her first fish but couldn't handle taking it off the hook. Within a few months, she felt comfortable and looked forward to their life. The climate was a definite upgrade from New England, and the quietness of the country was soothing. She hadn't thought about Winthrop in months.

"We can grow most of our vegetables, but I like meat. There's a good hunting area about fifteen miles east of here with many deer. I go there twice a year and bag one or two deer. I usually bring them back here to clean and cure. Although I'm gone three or four days, you're safe here. Still, I'll have the Indian woman who lives with her family about a mile from here stay with you while I'm away. That way, you won't get lonesome."

The Indian woman had come over two days before Hiram left, and though she didn't speak English, Frances and she bonded. There was plenty to do, so by the end of each day, Frances was exhausted and fell asleep early. Normally, Hiram would feed and water the cattle. While he was gone, she took over that task and, after a couple of days, found it wasn't difficult.

CHAPTER 9

*H*arris would think about the robbery and his share of the loot every few hours and smile. Through thirty years of slim pickings, he was wealthier than he ever dreamed. He knew that Butch and Sundance wouldn't be happy that he killed their pal Richards, but he didn't plan on seeing them again. Besides, they had their problems. Lenny heard the two went to Bolivia to get away from the sheriff who'd been tracking them. It was possible they'd never come back.

Only the Indians, native to this area, knew the hills southeast of Santa Barbara. They were steep, and the ravines narrow with few streams. The footing was treacherous throughout the region. He wasn't prepared for the thought that he might have to hide out here permanently. Yet the game was plentiful and water easy to find, so he could stay away from any populated area for an extended time in case the posse was still on his trail. But sooner or later, he'd want to go where the action was. He also had a distinct advantage. Besides the Sundance Kid, the gang had yet to learn about Lenny, where he was from, or where he might go. He used the name Larry French when dealing with the other members of the robbery team. Snake Eyes may have learned his real name from Sundance, but he didn't challenge him.

On the fifth day after he said goodbye to Richards, he came over a rise and saw smoke in the ravine below just as the sun set. The hills were too steep to navigate at night, so he kept a cold camp and decided to investigate tomorrow. As he walked his horses into the camp where he'd seen smoke the previous evening, he called out, "Coming in."

No one answered, so he continued into the camp. A deer was hanging from a tree that hadn't been skinned. There was a saddleless horse, a mule, and a small fire.

He called out again, but still, there was no response. As his eyes took in everything inside the camp, he saw a coffee pot sitting on a rock in the middle of a small fire. He decided to help himself. He tied the reins of both horses to a bush and stretched as he got out of the saddle. When he grabbed a mug sitting next to the coffee pot, he heard the click of a rifle and a voice, "put your hands up and don't move." Someone had come up behind him.

He did as he was told. "I wasn't going to steal anything. I didn't think you'd mind if I had some of your coffee", Lenny responded.

"I see that you're carrying. Drop your revolver on the ground, kick it to your left, and sit on the log next to the fire. I want to take a good look at you", the voice said.

Harris did as he was told. Soon a hearty-looking man in his mid-forties or early fifties, standing five foot ten with snow-white hair, came into view. He had on a nautical hat and was carrying a Sharps rifle. "Tell me what you're doing here?" the man asked.

"I was looking for game. I've been out about a week and saw your smoke from the ridge last night. I don't mean any harm. I just wanted to talk to someone," the older man smiled.

"Help yourself to some coffee. I had already finished breakfast and cleaned up everything. If you're starving, I can give you some bacon. There's still enough fire for you to cook it. I'm Hiram Booker. I have a ranch about fifteen miles from here. You can pick up your gun and holster it."

"Just coffee is enough," Lenny responded as he picked up his pistol and put it in his holster.

Lenny introduced himself and told Booker he was from San Francisco and was looking for some property. He wanted to get away from populated areas.

"That's interesting. I left Rhode Island four years ago to escape the big city. The cold weather got the best of me, so I came to California and purchased property southwest of here.

I stocked the farm with ten heads of cattle and a mule. After two years, I was lonely and sent for a mail-order bride. It took about a year of writing letters back and forth before she came out. My wife is twenty-eight years old, small, with average looks, been a nurse and never was married; she's a good wife; it turned out pretty good for the both of us."

"I can see why you wanted the woman. Did you ever build a cabin for you and your wife?"

"Before she came, I'd go to the lumber yard in Santa Barbara with a sketch of what I wanted to do. The owner would figure out how much material I needed and show me how to build it. I started with an outhouse, storage shed, barn, and cabin. I use the storage shed for my grain and any game I bag."

"Do you have any help?" Harris asked.

"There are a couple of Indians about a mile away. They work for me from time to time. Communication is a little difficult, but eventually, they figure out what I want."

"I purchased a plow and had the Indians cultivate three acres. They planted corn, tomatoes, and lettuce. Come to think of it, I know of a parcel about two miles from my spread that may interest you. I have a thousand acres; this one is a little smaller, but it has access to water", Bookers told Lenny.

"What do you do with the excess produce?"

"That's the part I haven't worked out yet. I should sell it, but the closest place is Santa Barbara; it may not be profitable for only three acres. I may have to cultivate ten to make it productive enough to sell the crop."

"I see you have a sailor's hat. Did you sail?"

"We carried supplies back and forth from Rhode Island to Africa and then to the Caribbean. It was a miserable life at sea. The first chance I had to sell after my father died, I did.

What I longed for was a piece of land where I could grow things. I'd been to California twice before and thought Santa Barbara was a beautiful place to live, so after a heavy snowstorm back east, I came here."

"Do you have any relatives?"

"I was an only child and missed growing up without siblings. My wife is young enough to have children. I hope I'm not too old to father them. We'll see if that's going to happen soon."

"What's your wife like?"

"She's something of a homebody. She likes our place and hasn't nagged me about going to the city. She hasn't been there since we married. She's a good companion."

"Just where is your spread?" Lenny asked.

"It's over that line of hills to the west, in a valley at the end of a small creek." Bookers pointed to a line of hills to the west of them.

"If you're interested, you could ride with me, and I could point out the parcel for sale. I'm ready to leave; what do you say?"

"That won't be necessary. I think I can find it; your directions are great." As Bookers kicked some dirt over the fire, Lenny shot him. The older man fell over the log Lenny had been sitting on and landed on top of the embers. His jacket started to burn and then fizzled out. Lenny took a wallet from the man's pocket and tore up the contents except for his identification card and the two hundred dollars he carried. He let the pieces scatter in the wind. He'd discard the identification later.

The question was, what would he do with the man's horse and mule? He already had Richards' mount and his own. He threw Booker's saddle in the bushes, broke the stock of the man's Sharp, and tossed the pieces in several directions. He swatted the mule and the man's horse with a towel; both ran off. If they found their way home, that'd be okay, but he couldn't be seen with them.

It was an effort, but he tied the deer over the back of Richards' horse. He wrapped a rope around Bookers' legs and dragged him behind some rocks; animals would probably take care of the corpse. The bedroll and provisions were tossed into some high bushes.

Bookers' place sounded fine; he might even keep the woman after he tried her out. As he was getting ready to leave, he had an idea. He took some torn bills from the robbery and stuffed them down his victim's boots.

CHAPTER 10

Lenny was an adequate horseman, but he was a failure in every other facet of life. His primary motivation was looking out for himself. He set out to find Booker's Ranch and see if he could hide until the posse gave up. He had enough money to get out of the country, but the ranch sounded too good to pass up. He reached in his pocket and found Bookers' identification. He tore up the paper and threw the bits into the bushes. Initially, he thought it might come in handy while on the run, but he couldn't chance someone finding it on him.

Intuitively, he knew there was wild game in the area because Richards' horse was being spooked by something. He'd traveled slowly for two days and sensed that he was near the ranch. He decided to camp out one more night and get his act together if he came upon Bookers' wife. At midnight, he was awakened by a soft growl spooking the horses; he got up to see what was causing the problem. Just then, he was knocked sideways by a medium-sized animal, and he fell helplessly into some rocks. He assumed it was a cat going for the deer on the back of Richards' horse.

When the animal leaped on the horse's back, it reared and broke away with the predator in pursuit. The thought occurred to him that the animal would come back for him. He'd be no match for the predator. He reached for his rifle but couldn't retrieve it because of the intense pain in his shoulder. He assumed his shoulder was broken; he wasn't sure about his ankle, but it was numb. He lay between the rocks until dawn, then passed out.

Frances Booker was worried. She was full of optimism. Hiram was always back within four days. It'd been two weeks since he left on his hunting trip, so she took the wagon to look for him.

Perhaps he was on his way, and she'd meet him on the last mile or two. About three miles from the ranch, she heard Lenny's horse and stopped to investigate. It was cast against a rock outcropping and thrashing to the point where it was about to give up.

The horse was so dehydrated that it hardly moved when she grabbed its ear. She tied a rope around its rear legs and then to her wagon. While holding onto the reins of her horses, she gradually pulled the horse to a position ninety degrees from where it initially lay. She tried to entice the horse to get up with some hay and water she carried in the wagon, but the horse appeared too far gone. She grabbed a stick and hit the horse on the rump, and it got its feet under it. With some prodding with hay and a couple of whacks with the stick, it rose and shook itself off. She let the horse drink about a quarter of a small bucket of water and then tied it to her wagon.

Much of its side was bleeding where it had thrashed about on the ground; some of its skin had peeled off. She removed most of the dirt and washed several severe scratches. The legs near the hoofs where she tied a rope were also skinned; she applied some cream to all the skinned areas.

As she was about to head back home, she heard a human moan pierce the stillness. She wasn't spooked, but she still retrieved the rifle from under the wagon seat and carefully looked around the area. It took her fifteen minutes before she located Lenny Harris. He had fallen between two medium-sized boulders and was lying on his back. She went back to the wagon and fetched the bucket of water. She squeezed some water past his lips, washed his forehead, and tried to assess the damage. Trying to help him sit up only aggravated the situation, and he lost consciousness when she probed to find out if anything was broken.

There wasn't much choice; she was a tiny woman, and he was lying pinned between two boulders. Somehow, she had to pull him out of there. She grabbed a long lead out of the wagon and tied one end tightly around the fallen man's calves and the other end to her wagon. It took a few minutes, but he was free of the rocks and lying on the ground on his back. He woke up, screamed, and then blacked out again. Since he was on his back, she could put an emergency sling around his right shoulder.

Her nurse's training paid off as she probed his body and located a break in his right foot. She ripped off some of her dress and fashioned a compression bandage for the fracture. The only problem now was how to get him back to her place. She didn't want to fetch the Indian woman and leave this man alone; anything could happen. She retrieved an old tarp from the

back of the wagon, spread it out on the ground, and placed a blanket in the center. It took some time, but she rolled him onto the combination tarp and blanket. She created an envelope of sorts by tying the bottom two ends of the tarp together and the top two ends together. The front ends were connected to the back of the wagon. The trail back to the cabin was rough, but she believed they'd make it without seriously injuring him. His horse had recovered somewhat, and she gave it more water.

The smell of smoke from the oven the Indian woman used to make dinner told her they were nearly home. She pulled up before the cabin and called out to the woman. Lenny had regained consciousness about a half mile from the house. She could hear him yell out whenever he and the tarp went over a rock. It wasn't that she was insensitive to his suffering; it just wasn't going to help if she had to stop continually along the way to tend to him.

Lenny put some weight on one foot as Frances and the Indian woman half- carried him into the cabin and lay him on her bed. They always had soup in the kitchen, and the Indian woman fed Lenny a few spoonsful until he fell asleep. Frances covered him with a blanket and sat down near the fire. It had been a long day, and she fell asleep immediately.

Tomas prepared the animals and gear Tommy and Sarah were taking on the hunting trip while Naomi got about a week's worth of food ready. The couple left the ranch at seven AM and traveled over the pass, stopping for lunch at Kinevan's Stagecoach Stop. They traveled south to Santa Barbara, staying the night at the Arlington. After an early dinner, they retired, were up at five, and were on their way again. Sarah hadn't camped out in some time. The next day was awkward, and it took her some time to get acclimated to cooking over a fire and sleeping on the ground.

For Tommy, the trip after they left Santa Barbara was fabulous. The weather was crisp, and the ride casual.

He fished in a small pond where they camped that afternoon and caught some brook trout for dinner and enough for breakfast the following day. As he was placing the last fish in the basket, he looked up and saw his wife, without any clothes, sit down in the small stream and start splashing water at him. He got the message, and it wasn't long before he sat beside her.

Sitting Bull had been an inspiration to Tommy in his formative years. He remembered how his father would shoot pheasants, pluck off their feathers, and roast them over an open fire while telling him tales passed down from his ancestors. He couldn't help but reminisce about his younger days because his father impacted his early life. He missed his father and wished he'd spent more time with him. When his son Thomas was born, he promised Sarah that he would try to be the father Sitting Bull was. His wife wasn't a stranger to living off the land. Her life with Crazy Horse was no picnic. Many nights they would sleep hungry on some prairie because there wasn't any food or shelter. On other nights they scavenged and ate what others may have thrown out.

They were getting back to their roots, and Sarah was starting to relax and enjoy the outdoors. He skinned the birds he shot that afternoon, and Sarah put her skills as a cook to the test. They had a feast of pheasant and their wine the second night out. They drank two bottles of wine, made love outdoors, and fell asleep in each other's arms. It started to rain about midnight, and they rolled under the wagon.

They found his hunting spot along a small creek bed two days later. He unloaded the gear and tethered the two horses and mule such that the animals could walk around and graze but couldn't run off. They planned to be here for two days. That night the temperature dropped into the forties. He'd cut enough kindling and firewood to last the night and laid their bedrolls close to the fire. Sleep came quickly; they didn't wake until daybreak. After he rose and washed his face with cold water, he made a pot of coffee, and they ate some left-over trout his wife prepared. Though they were rich now, he couldn't separate his current self from the brave who lived off the land. He knew that Sarah felt the same way and was grateful they had met.

He planned to bag two deer, clean them, and transport them back to his ranch in Santa Ynez. Sarah had learned to shoot when she was married to Crazy Horse, but under Tommy's instruction, she became an expert.

It was going to be a competition to see who would bag the first deer. They'd walked a couple of miles away from their camp when he shot the first deer. That's when Sarah saw someone's cold camp a short distance away. Something seemed out of sorts to her, so they decided to investigate. Tommy wasn't a stranger to danger or to entering a strange territory. On two occasions, as a young brave, he infiltrated an enemy camp and subdued the sentries. He might be getting older, but he hadn't lost his skills or instincts. "Sarah, you cover me while I look around."

"Just be careful. Something seems ominous about that place."

As he entered the camp, he first noticed broken pieces of a Sharp's rifle and a bed roll that had been torn apart. He grabbed his rifle out of the sheath and circled the burned-out fire. Thirty minutes passed before he found a body. "There's a man's body over here," he called to his wife. Sarah stiffened.

Tommy knelt, checked the man's pulse, and was stunned to feel that there was one. "This man is alive," he called out. Sarah rushed to him.

With Sarah keeping a sharp eye out for someone watching them, Tommy pulled the body from the bushes and laid the man on his back. A bullet hole in the back of his shirt had come out near his heart. Since he couldn't feel the bullet either in the front or the back, he assumed it might have gone clean through. Tommy carried a tarp with him that he used when he bagged a deer. He placed it on the ground, rolled the man onto the tarp so he lay on his back, and slowly took off his shirt. After he washed and bandaged the wound, he tried to get some water down the man's throat, but it was no use. "We have to keep him warm and try to get him to drink," Sarah said.

"We have to get him to a hospital, Tommy." after Tommy wrapped the man in some clothes they carried, he gathered some firewood, started a fire, and moved the man nearer the fire, but not too close. Sarah took a wet cloth and wrong it out over the man's mouth, and water trickled down his throat.

"Who do you think did this," Sarah asked.

"I don't know. Maybe it was a robbery that went bad or had something to do with the Oxnard Train Robbery."

The major news in Santa Barbara over the past year was the Oxnard Train Robbery, the subsequent capture of five bandits, and the finding of a dead body believed to be the sixth member of the gang. The sheriff told several members of the county council that there were only six men who robbed the train in Oxnard. However, speculation was rampant that a seventh man joined the bandits after the train robbery and was still out there, especially since about eight thousand dollars of the loot was still unaccounted for. The fifty-member posse had been disbanded, and any further investigation had been turned over to the Pinkertons.

Tommy could tell that the unconscious man was about fifty years old, his clothes were high-end, and he was well-groomed. Except for the wound, he appeared to be in good shape. They couldn't tell how long the injured man had been lying in the bushes, but it was apparent he needed immediate medical attention.

This is where his early training as a Sioux Brave paid off. He cut some medium-sized branches and made a travois to transport the injured man. He wrapped the man in one of Sarah's dresses and then in the tarp and placed him on the travois.

Tommy walked around the camp to see if he could find anything else belonging to the man. Obviously, the man didn't throw away his bedroll, break up his rifle and then shoot himself in the back. He saw where a deer was hung and skinned; he also found small pieces of paper torn apart. He picked up all he could find and put them in his jacket pocket. He'd try to put them together later. He could tell that three horses and a mule were in the camp before his arrival. A horse and mule went off to the east while two horses went southwest. Tommy's best guess was that the man he found was on a hunting trip and met with foul play.

The tiny deer he shot earlier was only two hundred yards away, and their camp was less than two miles. Tommy brought the deer back to the cold camp while Sarah kept a lookout lest they meet the person responsible for the shooting.

"I don't want to leave you alone. Why don't you accompany me to our camp and help bring back the horses and mule."

"Tommy, we can't leave this man unattended. A predator could come in and find him and the deer. I have a rifle, and I can shoot if someone approaches me. Besides, you won't be gone long. I'll be okay."

Reluctantly, he agreed to leave Sarah to watch both the wounded man and the deer while he hustled to their camp and brought back the horses and mule; he was gone only forty-five minutes. "I can't believe you made it so fast," Sarah said.

"I wasn't going to take any chances where you're concerned. I'd never forgive myself if anything happened to you."

Tommy tied the deer to the back of the mule and the travois to his saddle, and they were on their way. It took two hours to reach their camp, about half an hour to clean up their base, and they were on their way to Santa Barbara.

The Indian Woman fed Lenny and cleaned his bedside pot daily until he could use the crutch she made. Gradually he took his meals with Frances and the Indian. He didn't say much; he seemed to be assessing the situation. He did tell her his name was Lenny Harris, and he was from San Francisco. Frances treated his broken ankle and separated shoulder; both were healing normally. After two weeks, he could transition to a small sling, and with the compression bandage, he could put some weight on his damaged ankle. Soon Frances was taking him for buggy rides around the ranch. After a month, he would take the buggy out alone and remove the sling from around his shoulder.

Hiram's absence was bearing on her; Frances didn't know what to do. They lived in a remote location without any neighbors other than the Indians. She hadn't ventured very far from the ranch since she came to live here or sought out any neighbors. Going to Santa Barbara seemed out of the question, though she needed to tell the authorities that her husband was missing. She thought that Lenny could do that when he recovered.

There was enough food from the three-acre garden to feed her and the Indian Woman, and some deer meat was still left. In an emergency, they could always butcher one of the cows. She remembered that Hiram had set up funds for her in Santa Barbara.

Right now, she was okay, and besides, he always kept about four hundred dollars in the cabin. When Lenny was better, he would take her to Santa Barbara so she could get some money out of her account and report Hiram missing.

The man she'd found on a trail was puzzling to her. He seldom spoke and didn't try to help with the chores; he seemed to be taking everything in as though he was trying to decide what to do. When he was able, he'd walk around outside. A few days ago, he started riding his horse. Frances didn't know where he went, and Lenny wasn't forthcoming.

This morning he asked Frances if she'd like to picnic at the small pond on the ranch; she didn't think Hiram would mind, so she accepted. They left the following day after the Indian Woman prepared a lunch basket; they stopped under a shady tree. Frances laid out a blanket and retrieved the picnic basket. "Why don't you sit down, and I'll serve you some chicken and potato salad," she told Lenny.

He took a big bite of chicken, and with his mouth full, he said, "This is the best meal I've ever had. Thank you."

After lunch he lay back on the blanket and closed his eyes. Frances gathered the remaining food, dishes, and utensils and put them back in the basket. As she was about to rise, Lenny grabbed her arm and pulled her to him; she tripped over the basket and spilled the contents on the ground. His hands found her breasts, and he kissed her longingly. She pulled back, but he was too strong. "Stop it, I'm a married woman, and I don't appreciate your advances."

Lenny wasn't sympathetic to her protests, and gradually he pulled off her dress and undergarments. When she resisted and pleaded for him to stop, he slapped her hard in the face and forced himself on top of her; she screamed as he entered her. "Shut up, or I'll beat the hell out of you," he snarled.

He remained on top of her long after he was spent. She thought he had fallen asleep and tried to get up, but he slapped her again, and she lay quietly under him. He wanted to kiss her, but she turned her head. He began playing with her breasts, flipping her nipples with his finger. She begged him to stop, but he just laughed.

Soon he rose but told her to lay there until he said it was okay to get up. "You and I both know your husband isn't coming back, so I'll be your man until it's time for me to go. The Indian woman must go. You and I will sleep in your bed. Get up, put your arms around me, and tell me you'd like to have sex again. If not, I'll take the buggy whip to you."

Frances was sobbing as she got to her feet and stood before him. He raised his arm to strike her, but she closed the gap and put her arms around his body. "I'd like to have sex with you," she sobbed hysterically.

He told her to kneel in front of him. "Please don't make me do this." She begged.

Lenny grabbed her hair and pulled it until she screamed. "Get to it and make sure I enjoy it."

When she satisfied him, he pulled her to her feet, turned her around, and slapped her hard on the rump. "That's my girl."

Frances picked up her clothes and started to dress, but he wouldn't allow it. I want to play with you on the way back. We're going to have such a good time." He laughed.

About a mile from the cabin, he allowed her to dress and told her what to say to the Indian woman. The bruises on Frances' face were evident to the Indian woman. She'd grown up in a male-dominated society, and the abuse of women was the norm. She picked up her blanket and told Frances she'd be back in two weeks.

Tommy and Sarah made good time, but the condition of the unconscious man dictated caution. They knew the dead carcass of the deer would attract some predators, and it did. As soon as they heard sounds around them at night, they fired warning shots, which seemed to silence the predators. The result was that one or both were awake most of the night.

They arrived at the Santa Barbara Hospital three days later and met with the head of the hospital.

Tommy guaranteed payment for the stricken man; the hospital superintendent assured him that he would be notified immediately once the patient regained consciousness. Before heading home, they stopped by the sheriff's office to report the condition of the man they found and where they found him. The sheriff went through his missing person's reports, but nothing was on the man. "Did he have any identification on him?" the sheriff asked.

"No, but here's some torn pieces of paper I found at the campsite. There may not be enough left to tell us anything, but you're welcome to it." Tommy handed him an envelope containing the pieces.

"I don't know if you're aware that we found the sixth man involved in the Train Robbery. That leaves about eight thousand dollars unaccounted for."

"What about the rumor that a seventh man joined the gang just after the robbery?" Tommy asked.

"If you believe there was a seventh man, could the man you found be part of that gang?"

"I hadn't given it much thought. He's well-dressed and looks like he was on a hunting trip. And then there's the fact that he was shot in the back. He didn't do that to himself."

The twins were taking riding lessons from Tomas as Tommy and Sarah rode down the access lane. When the kids saw them, they rode directly toward them. "We missed you, mom and dad. We hope you stay home for a while now."

He turned the mule with the deer on its back over to his ranch foreman and told him to dispose of the travois. "I didn't have time to skin it. We found an injured man on the trail and had to transport him to the hospital. Have one of the Vaqueros skins it and hang it in the smokehouse."

The man they found hadn't regained consciousness before they left Santa Barbara. And though they spent an hour at the hospital talking to one of the attending physicians, no one was optimistic about his chances for recovery.

"Who do you think he was?" Sarah asked her husband as they walked into   their house with the twins.

Tommy put his arm around his wife's shoulders. "I think he was on a hunting trip. Someone came into the camp, shot him, and stole everything he had. Trashing the Sharps is a puzzle unless the shooter feared someone would recognize it."

CHAPTER 11

$\mathscr{S}$heriff Rodgers, who'd been a good friend of both Sarah and Tommy, had broken off their relationship. The incident where the two brothers rescued their younger brother, John, after he'd been convicted of four murders was the turning point. The convicted younger brother was imprisoned in Santa Barbara while awaiting transportation to state prison. The two men overwhelmed the jailer, stole a horse, and escaped with the prisoner. Rodgers felt confident that Tommy orchestrated the jailbreak since the brothers of the convicted felon had been guests of Tommy Sanchez at his ranch just before the jailbreak, but he couldn't prove Sanchez was involved. There was a general feeling among many county leaders that Rodgers and Tommy were close friends and, therefore, the sheriff wouldn't arrest the man. The sheriff greatly admired Sanchez, but a jailbreak under his nose was embarrassing. He'd be arrested immediately if he found proof that Tommy was guilty.

Two weeks after Tommy returned, Sheriff Rodgers arrived, unannounced, at the ranch. Tommy was tending to some cattle in a nearby pasture, but Sarah was home. Their meeting was cordial and polite but strained. "Come in, sheriff. Can I fix you a cup of coffee?" Sarah asked the man as they sat down at the kitchen table.

"I'd like that."

"Is this a social or business visit?" "Social."

As soon as Sarah saw the sheriff coming down their entrance lane, she sent Tomas to find her husband. Tommy went into the kitchen as Sarah, and the sheriff finished their pleasantries. The sheriff rose and shook Tommy's hand. "It's been a long time since you visited us. Good to see you", he said.

Dinner was ready, and the Sanchez' invited Sheriff Rodgers to join them and stay the night. As was their custom, they always offered the guest house when it was too late for someone to return home. After dinner, they sat by the fire in the living room and enjoyed a glass of wine from the Sanchez Vineyard. The sheriff was relaxed and told them the reason for his visit.

"The man you found on the trail has regained consciousness, but he can't remember who he is or why he was where you found him. The hospital knows you guaranteed payment. The problem is, what happens to him next?"

"Sarah and I planned a shopping trip to Santa Barbara the day after tomorrow. We'll stop by the hospital and talk to him. There's got to be a way we can make sense out of this tragedy", Tommy responded.

"I couldn't make any sense out of the pieces of paper you gave me. It looks like some invoice, but it doesn't indicate who the buyer, the seller, or the product is", the sheriff said.

"I found the scraps in about a ten-foot circle. Some may have blown away." Tommy responded.

When the sheriff retired to the guest house attached to their barn, Tommy and Sarah sat in the breakfast nook having a glass of Sauvignon. "What are you thinking, Tommy?" Sarah asked.

"I can't leave him to fend for himself. Why don't both of us talk to him? We can always bring him back here until he's recovered. This might be the medicine he needs to sort things out and regain his memory. What puzzles me is why the sheriff rode out here to tell us about the man we found. He hasn't been that friendly to us since the jailbreak. It makes me think he has something else on his mind."

Naomi and the housekeeper were glad to look out for the twins while they were in Santa Barbara. The sheriff left before they rose, so Tommy couldn't ask him what his visit's real purpose was. After he hitched up the buggy, Tommy and Sarah drove toward Santa Barbara, stopping for lunch at Kinevan's, just short of the pass. The husband-and-wife team that ran the stage coach stop always had a warm spot in Tommy and Sarah's hearts. Mrs. Kinevan nursed Sarah until she was able to go home after she was kidnapped and beaten by Brown, the bank robber.

They had a light lunch and promised their hosts they would return and spend more time with them. Three hours later, they arrived at the Arlington, where they would spend the night. Tomorrow they'd visit the man they found near a stream fifteen miles outside Santa Barbara.

The two visited Hiram's doctor the following day and asked about his condition. "His injury has healed, and he can be discharged anytime. Psychologically, he's depressed because he can't remember his name and doesn't know where to go after he's released. Additionally, he's had some restless nights. The nurse on duty reported that he awakes in a sweat", Doctor Alexander told Sarah and Tommy.

"What kind of personality does he have?' Sarah asked.

"He seems like a pleasant sort, well-spoken and courteous."

"If he's amenable, we'll take him home with us until he recovers. We feel responsible for him." Tommy said.

Hiram Bookers was sitting on the veranda of his second-floor room in the Santa Barbara Hospital. Half of a cup of coffee was on the table in front of him. He didn't recognize Tommy and Sarah as they introduced themselves and asked how he felt.

"I seem okay, but I can't remember who I am or what happened to me. Do you have anything to share?" he asked the couple.

Both Tommy and Sarah immediately recognized the thick accent of a New Englander. He was wearing the same clothes that he had on when Tommy found him, yet he looked like a man who commanded respect.

"We found you about fifteen miles from here in a small valley with a running stream. You'd been shot in the back and were lying in some heavy bushes. Your gear had been discarded, your rifle stock broken and thrown in the bushes, and your Horse and maybe a mule was missing. I guess that you'd been shot the day before. Can you remember how you were shot?" Tommy asked.

"No. I have no recollection of being shot. Did you find any identification on me; do you have any idea who shot me?"

"No to both questions. It's possible that the shooting was random and that this could be a robbery that went bad. Do you have any idea why you were at that location?"

"None at all."

Could you have been on a hunting trip? Your clothes are those of a hunter."

"I don't know."

"I saw remnants of a deer. Could you have shot a deer and were in the process of skinning it when you were shot?" Tommy asked.

"Not that I remember?"

"Could you have been traveling with someone? Three horses and a mule were there before I found you."

Hiram put his head in his hands. "I just don't know."

"The care I'm receiving at this hospital is superb and must be expensive. How am I going to repay them?" Bookers asked.

"I'm a member of this hospital's board and responsible for you. We'll worry about reimbursement when you're on your feet."

"I wish I knew where to go, but I don't. I don't even know what I'm good at, if anything."

"My wife and I have a large spread in the Santa Ynez Valley, about thirty miles north of here. We raise cattle and have a medium-sized vineyard. We want you to be our guest until you can recover your memory. If you're embarrassed by our offer, don't be. We have plenty of work on our cattle ranch and vineyard; you'll earn your keep."

"Thank you."

"I can't keep calling you 'hey there.' What name would you like to use until your memory returns?"

"I understand what you're saying. How about Silas Smith? Is that okay?"

"Well, Mr. Smith, I promised my wife a day of shopping in town, and she's anxious to get going. We're staying at the Arlington Hotel tonight. I'll send a carriage for you this evening, and the three of us will have dinner. Let's say six PM."

"I appreciate your generosity, but these are my only clothes. I would embarrass you."

"You're slightly bigger than I, but about the same height. You'll be fine. I'll send a suit of clothes with the carriage. Now if you'll excuse us, we're off to the stores."

Shopping was not his favorite pastime. He'd rather fight a grizzly bear than parade around the shops all afternoon while Sarah sampled everything. But this was his wife, and he was committed to this chore twice a year. Around four in the afternoon, he was exhausted; Sarah was disappointed there were no other stores.

They sent a carriage at 5:30 PM with a new outfit for Smith. Tommy and Sarah were waiting for him when he arrived in the lobby. They could tell by his demeanor and how the staff addressed him that he was a quality individual. "Let's go to dinner," Tommy said after he shook hands with his guest.

They ordered a bottle of wine and toasted each other for their newfound friendship. "The staff at the hospital couldn't stop talking about you and your wife, Mr. Sanchez. You're a legend in this town. Is it true that you're a former Sioux Brave and the son of Sitting Bull, the great chief?"

I am only half Sioux. My mother was Elizabeth Kelly, a red-haired white woman my father captured."

"But it's the gun they all talk about. Are you the fastest man with a gun?" Smith asked.

"It's academic these days. Seldom do I wear a gun. Occasionally, I help the sheriff track down someone, but I haven't used my guns in a long time." Sarah smiled at Tommy.

"Mrs. Sanchez, I hope you won't be embarrassed if I ask you about Crazy Horse. You don't have to answer if you don't want to."

"Everyone knows the story, and I'm not embarrassed. I was a Sioux captive and married Crazy Horse when I was eighteen. I had two children with him. My son lives in Santa Ynez, is an attorney, and is very close to my husband, who adopted him. My daughter is married to our ranch foreman; they live in the spread next to ours. But the question for you is, how do you know about Crazy Horse? Your accent is that of a New Englander, probably somewhere around Boston.

"I don't know how I know, but it seems natural coming out of my mouth."

We can work on that and find out who you are. Did they tell you you're suffering from some form of amnesia?"

"They did, and I read the hospital's book on the two forms of amnesia. At present, the doctor doesn't know which form I have. He will consult with a specialist from Los Angeles and get back to me. I appreciate everything both of you are doing for me, and I'll do everything to honor your trust." Smith was near tears, so Tommy broke the spell and ordered dinner for the three.

During the meal, their server kept looking at Smith, trying to remember who he was. Tommy noticed the interest and asked the waiter if he recognized Smith.

"I could be wrong, but you remind me of someone. I am trying to remember who. I hope I didn't embarrass you?"

The following day, the three drove over the pass, stopped to talk to the Kinevans, and made it home by five

PM. They could tell by the look on Smith's face that he was very impressed with the ranch. They moved him into the guest room in the barn and told him dinner would be at six in the main house.

This was a reunion of sorts. Juan arrived just at dinner time, and Sarah's daughter, Naiwa, and her husband, Raoul, brought some vegetables they'd grown on their spread next door. Smith spent most of the evening asking each family member about their background. Silas was fascinated with Juan's resurrection from a renegade to a prominent attorney. "You must be proud of your accomplishments?"

"I'm not the one you should be talking to. Tommy Sanchez saved my life by rescuing me from adolescence and being an embarrassment to my mother. He laughs now, but it was a project. Thank god he had the patience to help me through that time of my life."

The women cleaned up when the meal was finished, and Smith retired to his room. Juan went to the kitchen to talk to his sister, and Raoul asked if he could speak privately with Tommy.

The two men went out on the front porch. The evening was comfortable, with the temperature in the mid-sixties. Tommy offered his foreman a cigar and a glass of wine. Raoul accepted both, and the two men sat down.

"Patron, I owe you everything. You saved my life last year; I thought I would be convicted of those four murders, yet you stood up for me. My wife and I are grateful for the wedding present of the five-hundred-acre spread next door. I don't know how we'll ever repay you."

"You are family. Naiwa had a difficult life, and we're glad you and she found each other. You can't image how worried my wife was."

"The problem is that I can't be your foreman anymore and run my spread as well. I'm not ungrateful for your generosity but I need to spend more time on my spread. We added thirty heads of cattle, and our garden produces vegetables we sell at the market. Naiwa has been doing much work, but she's with   a child. I don't want her to work anymore."

"How much time do you need to train your replacement?"

"Two months should do it. Tomas is almost ready, but he's young and must   earn the respect of the Vaqueros."

"I like Tomas. I want you to train him to take over, but I also want you to teach Smith. He may not be the rider Thomas is, but he can run this place.

"I can always come back for a few days if things get out of control," Raoul said.

"Let's start tomorrow. Tell Tomas he must be able to give orders if he's going to be the foreman."

CHAPTER 12

*T*ake off your clothes and get over here," Lenny commanded. He waited until the Indian woman left before he walked into the cabin. Frances was at the kitchen sink.

Frances turned to face him. She had a large butcher knife in her right hand. She'd rather have a gun, but Hiram took the pistol and rifle with him, and this was all she could find. Unless you want me to stick this in you, you'd better get out of here and never come back. If I see you again, I won't hesitate to kill you."

Lenny walked closer to her, but Frances didn't move other than to extend the knife out in front of her. "You think I'm nervous, but I'm not. I know how to use a knife, and after what you did to me, I'm willing to go to jail for killing you", Frances said.

He'd inched a little closer to her as she was talking. He feinted with his left hand, and when she went to parry that blow, he swung out with his right hand and hit her as hard as he could along the side of the head, and she fell to the floor. The knife dropped out of her hand, and Lenny kicked it away.

He circled her, but she didn't move. Blood was coming from her nose, mouth, and cheek. She appeared to be dazed as she lay on the floor. Lenny picked up the knife, poured himself a cup of coffee, and sat in one of their two rockers, waiting for Frances to get up. He didn't offer to help her.

She came around twenty minutes later and started to get up.

The beating she took had some lasting impact, and she could barely rise as she pulled herself up while holding onto the kitchen countertop. She turned slowly when she heard him speak. "You had enough, or do you want more?" he sneered.

"I've had enough. "She was barely audible, but he heard her. "Well, get over here."

She was unsteady on her feet as she walked toward him. "Take off all your clothes," he demanded.

"Without thinking, she disrobed and stood in front of him. "Turn around," he ordered.

Frances turned around; Lenny slapped her hard on her rump, and she yelled out. "Now get to bed, and when I say do something, you do it, or I'll give you another beating."

She hurried to the bed and got under the covers. Lenny smiled. She was sufficiently cowed and shouldn't give him any more trouble in the future.

Frances lay crying in bed. She was disadvantaged, but she knew she would kill Lenny Harris as God was her witness. Soon, she fell asleep. Luckily, he didn't bother her the rest of the night. She got up early, dressed, fixed breakfast, and left it for him on the warm stove. She'd have to wait him out. There had to be a way.

Hiram Bookers, alias Silas Smith was amazed at the size of the Sanchez spread. It took him two weeks to learn some of the basic chores around the ranch, but under Raoul's tutelage, he began to understand the duties of the Vaqueros and the people Tommy had tending the vineyards and making wine. He understood that Tomas was being groomed to take Raoul's place, so he deferred to Tomas in most cases.

Although he caught on much quicker, he didn't embarrass Tomas but assisted him in reaching the correct decision.

That wasn't lost on Tommy and Raoul. "Silas is especially adept at fixing most of the equipment, but he also analyzes problems and comes up with practical solutions. What about his riding skills?" Tommy asked Raoul.

"He's competent, but he will never be the rider the Vaqueros are. They're instinctive; he's mechanical."

Sarah and Tommy hoped that, as Silas became more involved in their operation, he might recover some of his memory. Tommy decided to learn a little bit more about Silas. He invited Silas and Juan to go fishing in the stocked pond at the southern part of the ranch. They planned to be away for two nights. Juan had just come off a lengthy trial and needed a breather. And Tommy's hunting trip had been interrupted when he rescued Silas along the trail. This seemed to be an excellent time to get away.

Raoul and Tomas provided the bait. They packed up three fishing rods with the gear while Naomi and Sarah prepared food for three days. When they arrived at the pond, Silas unloaded everything and immediately tried out the three rods. The other two were fascinated as he tested the three rods, adjusted the reels, and set the tension on the lines. "Where did you learn to do that, Silas?" Tommy asked him.

"I don't know. It just seemed natural to me."

Tommy had stocked the pond with some brook trout and bass. The three caught eight fish and decided to cook them for dinner. Juan usually handled this chore when he and Tommy went fishing, but tonight, Silas was the self-appointed chef, and the meal was superb. "You not only know how to fish, but you cook better than any fancy chef in this area," Juan told Silas.

After dinner, Tommy broke out the cigars, opened a couple of bottles of wine, and the three men relaxed. "I haven't had much time to talk to you about your trial; how did you make out?" Tommy asked Juan.

"You probably weren't aware that the county prosecutor's office was down to one lawyer. The county hired my firm to prosecute the Jenson Brothers for stealing two supply wagons from the county yard in Santa Maria.

I was the prosecutor in this case. It looked like it was open and shut, but the witness we had went missing the day before he was to testify. Without any concrete evidence or testimony, the jury found the brothers innocent."

"Wasn't that a little awkward to switch sides?" Tommy asked.

"It was, but the concept was the same. If I were the defense attorney, I'd try hard to trip up the key witness as the prosecutor, I'd pump up the key witness."

"I thought you had enough of a practice that you didn't have to fill in for the prosecutor?" Tommy asked.

Juan smiled. "Being a half-breed has some drawbacks, as you well know. I get all the minorities for clients I can handle, but the larger and more lucrative cases go to my Caucasian brethren. It's just reality, nothing more."

Tommy knew what he was talking about and decided to change the subject. "Can you tell us who the witness was?"

"It was John Trotter, the deputy sheriff for this area. I think he was scared off by the Jensons and left the county. I went by his home when he didn't show up for the trial, and the house was cleaned out. The landlady said she looked out her window about midnight the night before he was to testify and saw him get on his horse and ride away."

"What's the sheriff going to do?" Tommy asked Juan.

"I know what he wants to do."

"What does that mean?"

"He wants to swear you in as the Deputy Sheriff for this area and have you chase after the gang."

"I thought he was still mad about the jailbreak at the Santa Barbara Jail."

"Well, there's that, but he's coming up for reelection, and he knows your capability. I don't think he wants to stay mad. He asked me if I would intercede for him. I told him he had to find the courage and put it directly to you."

All this time, Silas Smith was taking everything in but being quiet. "This is the third time I've heard about this jailbreak. Can you fill me in?"

Juan smiled. "We had a series of murders in the valley that appeared to be committed by someone of Sioux Ancestry, mainly because the rituals performed on the victims were of Sioux origin. There are very few people with Sioux blood in this area. There's Tommy, me, and one older man. Although no one would come and say it directly, Tommy and I were the first suspects.

Tommy sensed the ritual killings were made out of revenge since all four victims were ex-soldiers who served together at an Army Post near The Standing Rock Reservation. We learned this from the four who worked at the ranch for a short period. Three of the ex-soldiers became good friends with Tommy and Sarah. One tried to get too friendly with my mother, and my stepfather dealt with him.

Tommy decided to conduct an independent investigation of the murders and went to the fort where the four ex-soldiers served. He learned about their participation in the Battle of Wounded Knee, where perhaps, three hundred Sioux were slaughtered.

To make a long story short, Tommy suspected the killer was a young man who worked at a general store in Santa Ynez. Since the massacre happened close to the Pine Ridge Reservation, Tommy met the young man's three brothers. His name was White Bird, but he wasn't Indian. He'd been taken by the Sioux when he was a young baby. White Bird survived the massacre by burrowing under the bodies of the dead; two were his Indian parents, and another was his Indian bride- to-be. Tommy asked the three brothers to come to Santa Ynez and help in the investigation, but only two agreed. When the young man saw his brothers at the ranch, there was a confrontation with Tommy, and the young man confessed. He was tried and convicted of all four murders.

The brothers stayed at the ranch as my parent's guests during the trial. While the young man was waiting in the Santa Barbara Jail before being sent to state prison, the brothers borrowed two of Tommy's horses on the pretext of going for a ride. They subsequently stole another horse and broke their brother out of jail. After Tommy turned white bird, The sheriff believes that Tommy had regrets and assisted the brothers during the jailbreak.

"Where are the brothers now?" Silas asked.

"The two who stayed at the ranch are back on the reservation in Wyoming. The elders at Pine Ridge Reservation tried the young man who was ostracized and banished from the Sioux Nation for ten years. He lives with his wife and child."

Silas was intrigued. "It seems like a coincidence, but then again, I can see why the sheriff suspects Mr. Sanchez is involved."

Again, Tommy decided to change the subject. "Where is the Jenson gang hiding out?"

Juan turned to him. "They're using the old Stillman Ranch in Los Alamos. They're a bad lot. There was a shooting the other night at Joe's Saloon in Santa Ynez. One of the brothers was in a card game and accused another player of cheating. There was a confrontation, and that brother shot the other card player in front of about twenty customers. Everyone said it was self-defense. Whether it was or not would be hard to prove. No one is going to dispute the brothers."

"I think I have too much on my plate to get involved," Tommy said.

"You're already involved," Juan responded.

"What does that mean?"

"Why do you think Raoul wants to quit? He had thirty heads of cattle go missing. He needs to be on his ranch and protect what's his and your daughter- in-law's."

"You can't be serious. Why wasn't I told?"

"Raoul looks up to you and doesn't want you to think that he's not brave enough to hold on to the property you and mom gave them."

"This conversation has gotten too heavy; I want to enjoy my cigar and a glass of good wine. I meant to ask you about the young woman you've been seeing in Santa Barbara. Is this serious?"

"I don't know. I love her, but her family is a little cool to a match. They see me as a half-breed and aren't sure they want me in the family. And then there's you", Juan laughed.

"What does that mean?"

"They're scared to death of you. They've heard all the stories of the gunfights, especially the one in Santa Barbara where you didn't shoot back. And then there's my mother. Some see her as a fallen woman since she took a Sioux Chief as her husband."

"I better not hear anyone say that about your mother."

"I'm just telling you that we're different, and it may take some time before we can assimilate into society. Linda is a beautiful woman, and I would be proud to be her husband when I'm ready."

Silas took in all the conversation but didn't ask any more questions. He didn't think it was his position to question them.

Tommy had a restless night. He started to talk to himself. Somebody out there is crazy if they think they can rob my kin, and I'd look the other way. What made it worse was Silas was also having a bad dream and woke up in a sweat. When Tommy asked him what was wrong, he said, "I had a recurring dream. I see black men in chains in a dark hole."

The following day, the three rode to the southeast corner of the ranch to check on the access gate from the south and the one between Raoul's and the Sanchez Ranch.

Multiple cattle tracks led from Raoul's spread through Tommy's Ranch and out his southern gate. They found both gates down. "Let's fix these gates. I have a couple of new locks in my saddle bag."

Silas reached into his saddle bag, retrieved his tools, and went to work on both gates. With Juan and Tommy acting as helpers, Silas had the gates up and secured within an hour. "Silas, put these gates on your list to check at least twice a week or until the cattle rustling stops," Tommy said.

That night, after another fish fry, Tommy asked Juan about the Jenson brothers. "Where'd they come from?"

"I understand they're farm boys from Missouri, somewhere around Jefferson City. There are three of them, Jed, Mike, and Hollis. They're equally mean and vicious, but the gun hand is Mike. He's the one who shot the cowboy in Joe's saloon. I don't know the names of the other four members of the gang. They've become aggressive, rustling cattle, stealing supply wagons, and the occasional murder. They probably scared the deputy sheriff out of town, and there's no one to stop them."

"Do they come to town often?"

"They hang out in Joe's saloon when they're not robbing someone."

"When do you think Raoul's cattle were taken?"

"It was two weeks ago when he told me about it. Naiwa asked him not to tell you."

"Do we know for sure the Jenson Brothers took them?"

"No."

"It's too late to track the cattle. They've probably been sold off by now. I can wire the stockyards in Santa Barbara and see if the Jenson's sold some cattle, but that's probably all we can do now", Tommy responded.

Frances was even more determined to rid herself of Lenny. What he had done to her was inexcusable. She had never hated anyone as much as she hated this man. There had to be a way to rid herself of this individual. She made biscuits and gravy, left them to warm on the kitchen stove, and got ready to do her early morning chores. She put on her boots and jacket and fed some grain to the cattle. The mule received hay, and the chickens some pellets. Hiram had planted tomatoes, lettuce, and corn, and she was expecting a good crop. The problem was that they needed some help to harrow the rows and keep the weeds from killing the crop. She planted potatoes, corn, and peas separately in an acre plot the Indians cultivated for her.

Her chores were completed when Lenny came up to her; she cringed. "It looks like you've planted enough to survive. Do you have any help picking the vegetables?"

"Hiram planned to hire a couple of the Indians to do that work." She replied.

"Well, Hiram's not coming back. If he were, he'd be here by now. No. I don't think we can plan on him. Where do the Indians live?"

She couldn't control her temper. "Hiram is coming back, and when he does, he will kill you for what you've done to me."

Lenny smacked her alongside her head, and she fell to the ground. "I told you to hold your tongue. Do you want some more?"

She was sobbing, but the words came out firmly.

"No."

"Take all your clothes off."

This time she didn't hesitate. She took all her clothes off immediately. "Now, that's a lot better. If you start obeying me, we're going to get along fine.

If not, I'm going to teach you the lessons of life." He rubbed one of her breasts, and she flinched. He tried to kiss her, but she turned her head.

While rubbing her breast, he asked, "What do we do for meat?"

"We still have a quarter of the beef that Hiram smoked. It's wrapped and hanging in the shed. We need a bull. We planned to build a herd of cattle and bag a few deer each year for meat. Can I put my clothes back on? I'm cold."

"Go ahead. Do any neighbors have a bull they'd lease to us?"

"None that I know about." She responded as she dressed.

"I think I'll go over to see if the Indians know anyone who has a bull. I expect you to be here when I get back. Don't have me chase after you. It'll make me angry, and you know what that means."

"Where would I go? This is my home."

Sheriff Rodgers reluctantly made the trip up to the Sanchez Ranch again. He didn't want to come, but he had no choice. He was up for reelection, and the number of supply wagons that had been intercepted, plus the number of cattle rustled, would make him unelectable. He needed Tommy Sanchez, and he needed him now. Besides, Sanchez owned him one. He knew that Sanchez orchestrated the jailbreak; if he didn't, he told the brothers how to do it.

Sanchez was in his study when the sheriff arrived. Sarah escorted the lawman into Tommy's office and asked if the men wanted coffee or brandy. Both thanked her but said they were fine.

"Nice to see you, sheriff; what's on your mind?"

"Deputy Trotter has left the area and his job as well. I don't know where he is, and the number of robberies has increased. Thieves made off with a supply wagon and wounded the driver and shotgun rider yesterday in broad daylight. It's got to stop. The county needs you to put on your guns and stop this lawlessness."

"I don't know, sheriff. I've helped in the past, but I have a business to run, and I don't know if I can devote enough time to the job. Then there's the matter of help. I need at least two men to put the crime wave down."

"I can agree to those terms. You can have two deputies, and you can pick your men. What do you say?"

"Give me a couple of days to think it over. I want to talk with Sarah and see what she has to say. Then there's Juan."

"I know our relationship is strained, but the community needs you. I hope your answer is yes."

Tommy wasn't interested in putting on his guns again. He had a good life, a great family, and enough money to maintain a high standard of living for himself and his family. Even if he was interested, he knew that Juan had a good law practice and was seeing a girl from an elite Spanish Family. He didn't want to draw any attention to himself while that relationship was blooming.

A week later, Sarah, Naomi, and Naiwa went to Santa Ynez to buy clothes for their children. Tomas drove them in the buckboard. While they were in Stewart's General Store, one of the Jenson brothers, who seemed drunk, got fresh with the women. He tried to put his arm around Naiwa, and when Sarah interceded, he wanted to kiss her. Naomi hit him with her umbrella, and he released Sarah. The other two women started throwing some of the items in the store at him. He thought it was funny and left the store laughing.

Mike Jenson walked across the street and into Joe's Saloon. His two brothers were sitting at the bar, having a beer. There were very few patrons in the saloon. Mike couldn't stop laughing, even when he sat alongside his two brothers and ordered a beer." What so funny, brother?" Jed Jenson asked.

Mike told them the story, especially about the old Indian woman hitting him with her umbrella. Jed walked over to the window just as the three women exited the general store and got in the buckboard. "Hey Mike, is that the three women?"

Mike walked over to the window. "Yup, that's them. I wanted to kiss the pretty blond woman, but she stuck a hairpin in my leg."

"This isn't funny, Mike. That's Tommy Sanchez's wife. He doesn't take kindly to anyone who disrespects his wife."

"Oh, he'll get over it. Who's Tommy Sanchez, anyway?"

'He's a former Sioux Brave, the fastest man alive. He's a legend around here."

"Never heard of him."

"Well, he doesn't turn the other cheek; he gets even." That's tough for him. The three of us can take him."

It was Naomi who told Tommy about the incident. It wasn't that he didn't believe her; he just wanted to hear what Sarah had to say. "It wasn't much. He tried to hug Naiwa, and Naomi hit him with her umbrella. When I pushed him, he tried to kiss me, but Naomi and Naiwa threw pillows at him, and he left laughing. I smelled wine or beer on his breath. He probably got a good laugh out of it. You're not going to do anything, are you?"

"Not right now, but I'm considering pinning on the deputy's badge to clean up the gang that's been rustling cattle and robbing supply wagons. I know Raoul and Naiwa had thirty heads go out the back gate. What do you think about my taking the job temporarily?"

"You're not going to do this by yourself."

"I won't take the job unless Juan and Smith are my deputies."

Three days later, after Sarah told him that she didn't have any problem with it, Tommy, Juan, and Silas were sworn in as deputies, with Tommy as the lead.

They asked the sheriff for an inventory of the supplies taken the past month and whether any cattle were sold at the Santa Barbara Stockyards by any of the Jenson Brothers. The sheriff provided the list, but none of the cattle were sold in Santa Barbara County.

Before leaving to find the Indian shack, Lenny hid his bankroll inside a metal container under a tree about one hundred yards from the one-room cabin. He made sure that Frances didn't see where he hid the money. He saddled up and rode to the Indian camp, about an hour away. They didn't have a bull; they didn't have much of anything. Their whole existence depended on the work they could get at the farms in the area. For a dollar, one of the older men said he'd show Lenny where there was a bull.

The owner of the farm, John Jacobs, had fifty head of cattle and a small Hereford Bull. As he and the Indian rode up, Lenny could see several people come outside from a dilapidated cabin. There were two men, a heavy-set woman who Lenny assumed was the wife, and a couple of small boys running around. One of the men, whom Lenny thought was the owner, came to greet them. The cattle were scattered around the farm, but the bull was in a holding pen. A half- acre had been cultivated and was planted with vegetables.

Lenny told Jacobs that he wanted to borrow his bull for a few months, and he'd be willing to pay for the use of the bull, provided it was delivered and picked up.

"Are you willing to pay two hundred dollars for three months?" Jacobs asked.

"I'm willing to pay some, but two hundred is too much; how about fifty?"

"No deal. It's two hundred or nothing."

Lenny wanted to shoot the farmer and take the bull, but he knew he couldn't start killing people in this area and still hideout at the ranch. "I'll give you a hundred, but that's all."

It's fifty now and one hundred fifty upon delivery and no trickery. My   hired man, a good shot with a rifle, and I will deliver the bull."

Reluctantly, Lenny had no choice. "You got a deal. When can I expect the bull?"

"I have a few things to finish here, and then we'll bring him over. Five days ought to do it."

He knew he'd been taken, but there wasn't much he could do about it. When the bull was delivered, he could turn the tables. He was seething as he rode back and wanted to kill Jacobs. He hitched his horse to a post and went into the cabin; Frances wasn't there. He found her in the shed, looking through some old crates. "What are you looking for?" he asked.

She didn't hear him arrive, and she was startled. "These are my husband's things. I was looking to see what was here." Lenny laughed.

"Come here."

"My husband will kill you when I tell him what you're doing to me." she walked over and stood defiantly in front of him. He squeezed her breasts and then undressed her.

"Your husband's dead, and you know it. Of course, he could have run away."

"If he's dead, it had to be you who killed him."

Lenny lashed out and hit her in the mouth, and her lip split; blood ran from her nose. He pushed hard, and she fell on her back; he was on her instantly. She fought like a wild cat, but after a few slaps, she lay back and let him have his way. When he was finished, he got up. "Boy, did that work up an appetite? I hope you have dinner ready for your man."

"You're not my man."

"I am now."

Over the next four days, Lenny and two of the Indians he hired built an enclosure for the bull and its ten cows. It was about one hundred feet in diameter. They only had time to finish three-fourths of the section before the bull arrived. True to his word, Jacobs brought his hired man; he was carrying a Remington with him, and he kept Lenny in sight while Jacobs unloaded the bull. What was ironic for Lenny is that he paid Jacobs the two hundred dollars he took from Bookers after he shot him.

They tied the bull to a solid post dug six feet in the ground in the center of the enclosure. Lenny and the Indian finished it in another three days. Rather than determine when each cow came into heat, he let the bull decide. It took less than three months. The bull covered the cows more than once during the first forty- five days; afterward, Lenny let him loose to graze around the cabin; if he ran off, that would be Jacobs's problem. The first calf was born in sixty-one days, and they had seven new calves by the time Jacobs came to pick up his bull.

Lenny grew up on a farm and hated it, but that was because he was constantly being told what to do. If he didn't complete his chores on time, his father took the whip to him. Still, he knew what to do on a farm; besides, he was the master here. He had the two Indians stay on to pick the vegetables. He didn't want Frances tiring herself out picking them; he wanted her to prepare his meals and have sex whenever he wanted.

This morning, he told her he was going to look at another area on the farm to plant corn. They had one good plow horse, a mule, and a good plow. "I'll be gone until after lunch. I want you to bring my lunch and something to drink to the area beyond those trees out there." He pointed to the area.

"I want you to wear boots and a hat."

"I'm not going to do that. The Indians will see me. Who knows what they'll do to me when you're not around?"

"Okay. When you get up to the trees past the cultivated area, take off all your clothes except your hat and boots. They won't see you there, and we can have some fun."

"What makes you think this is fun for me?"

"You want me to beat the hell out of you?"

"No."

At noon, she carried his lunch toward the spot he said they would rendezvous. When she was past the tree, she looked around and didn't see the cabin. She took off all her clothes, put her boots back on, and walked to where he was sitting. "Put the lunch on the log over there and come sit on my knee."

She put his lunch down, walked back, and sat on his knee. He fondled her breasts and squeezed her bottom. When he tried to kiss her, she turned her head.

"Okay, have it your way. Kneel and give junior the works." "I told you I don't want to do that."

He grabbed her hair and pulled her down. It's your choice. It's either no hair or a good day for junior. She whimpered but did as she was told. God, she hated this man; Hiram had to have some weapon in those trunks of his. She had to find it soon, or she would be pregnant, and then where would she be?

She sat there on a rock near him while he ate his lunch. She ignored his rambling about increasing the herd every six months; she was too busy trying to devise an escape plan. When she came to pick up the dishes, he said, "leave them there and come here. She did as she was told and stood in front of him.

"I want you to bend down and put your hands on that rock over there, she walked to the rock and did as she was told. He came up behind her, grabbed her breasts in both hands, and had anal sex with her.

She cried out when he penetrated her and tried to throw him off, but he was too strong and had his way with her. When he was finished, he slapped her hard on the behind and laughed. "That a good girl; you might make a good companion yet."

After she retrieved her clothes, she hurried back to the shed and opened the remainder of Hiram's trunks. Two hours later, she was no better off than before. She had to think of something. Maybe the Indians could get her a gun.

CHAPTER 13

They'd taken the last two supply wagons at the top of San Marcos Pass. That was an ideal holdup spot. A wagon or stagecoach coming up a steep rise with tired horses would slow down as it reached the top and then stop to give the horses a breather. The Jensons thought that the shotgun driver would be more alert to bandits after several robberies at the top of the pass. On the two previous holdups, neither the driver nor his guard was injured. They let the northbound wagon go past Kinevans and travel through the valley before turning onto the main trail to Santa Ynez.

Mike and Jed were on foot while Hollis was astride his horse. He created a diversion by racing directly at the wagon as it slowed down, coming up to the crest of a slight rise just before turning onto the main road. With the driver and guard focused on Hollis, the other two brothers, hiding in the brush, jumped on the wagon, hit the driver and the guard with their revolvers, and shoved them off the wagon. While falling backward, the guard reached out with his left hand and hit one of the bandits in the face, drawing blood. As he landed on the ground, he reached for his gun and fired at his assailant. One bandit returned fire and killed the guard; the driver gave up immediately.

Mike Jenson dragged the guard's body into the high brush while Jed took the reins and moved the wagon to a remote spot off the road where theirs was hidden. Hollis tied up the driver and put him near the dead guard. After transferring everything to their wagon, they moved the driver to a spot where a passerby would find him. It was nearly nightfall when they reached the outskirts of Santa Ynez.

The brothers were familiar with all the dirt trails in and out of the valley, and that's one of the reasons why they were so hard to capture. They picked a dirt trail about five hundred feet north of the town and headed toward Los Alamos. Their lookout was alert as they entered the Stillman Ranch without anyone noticing.

After they unloaded everything into their barn, they returned to their rundown cabin; each had a beer bottle. "It looks like a pretty good haul, but I didn't like shooting the guard," Hollis said.

"I didn't have much choice. I had to shoot quick," Mike said. He hit the ground and drew his gun...

"With a killing, more attention will be paid to the robberies. Maybe we should wait before we hit another supply wagon." Jed said.

"That's okay with me, but what are we going to do with the stuff we have on hand?" Mike asked.

"We'll wait two days before we take it to San Luis Obispo and sell it. It'll probably bring a good penny at that big general store in the town." Hollis suggested.

Jed was the one the rest of the gang went to when they were unhappy. "The guys are complaining they haven't been paid this month."

"Do we have any cash on hand?" Hollis asked.

"Tell them to stop complaining. When we get money from the last haul, we'll pay them a bonus," Mike responded.

Tommy received a wire at his ranch about the holdup and killing. He was asked to investigate. Juan was busy that afternoon, and Silas was checking the gates on the south end. Both indicated they'd be available the next day. They decided to head out early, along with the driver who lived in Santa Ynez. It took them three hours to cover the distance to the robbery site. The sheriff left some markers at the scene and had taken the guard's body to the morgue in Santa Barbara.

When they reached the holdup site, the driver, Bill Reddy, recapped what he saw and where the guard was shot. "I gave up right away after they shot Frank. I got the impression they didn't want to kill him; he forced the issue."

Juan sketched the crime scene with particular emphasis on where the two robbers hid in the bushes and the location of the other wagon used in the transfer. Juan was taking notes while Tommy and Silas were looking for anything the bandits could've left behind. They weren't able to uncover any clues. "Who do you think did this? Tommy asked the driver.

"They had masks on, so I didn't see their faces, but their builds were the same as the Jenson Brothers. I wasn't on the other two wagons that had been robbed, but I've seen the brothers around town, and I'll bet it was them."

"Did they say anything?"

"Not a word. They knew what each other was doing all the time. It was well planned."

"Were there any physical characteristics or mannerisms that you noticed?" Juan asked.

"No, I was positive it was the Jenson boys, and I wasn't looking for   anything. I also think it was Mike Jenson who shot Frank."

"Other than masks, what were the three bandits wearing?" Tommy asked.

"Jeans, shirts, hats, boots, and holsters."

"Sleeves rolled up or down?' "Down."

"Were they wearing clothing that was torn or badly worn?" Juan asked.

"Not that I remember."

"Well, we may think it's the Jenson boys, but we don't have any proof that it was them. If we arrested them, their lawyer would win the case with what we have," Juan said.

Tommy turned to the driver. "You can head home, Bill. We're going to Santa Barbara and view the body."

They reached Santa Barbara at about two in the afternoon and went directly to the sheriff's office. They told the sheriff that the driver thought it was the Jenson Brothers. "Do you have any evidence that points to them?"

"No," Tommy said.

Their next stop was the morgue, located in the hospital basement. They rode over to the morgue to view the guard's body. They didn't expect to learn anything; they were filling the square. The doctor, acting as county coroner, allowed them to examine the body and the bullet taken from Frank Graves, the guard.

"It's a .44 caliber bullet which is common with gunshot wounds in this area," Doctor Rhodes, the coroner, said.

"Is there anything else you found that could help our investigation?" Juan asked.

"He may have been in a scuffle because there were skin fragments under the nails on his left hand. I understand he was thrown out of a wagon, then shot. Perhaps his hand scraped someone's arm or face while he was falling."

They recapped the crime and decided on a course of action. They stayed over at the Arlington, and the sheriff joined them for dinner. The sheriff provided them with a search warrant for the Stillman Ranch, enforceable for ten days from today. What was interesting was the number of questions the sheriff directed to Silas. It was as though it was an inquisition, but Silas handled himself well and didn't take exception to the scrutiny. When the sheriff left, Juan asked Silas what that was all about.

"I don't know. He seems to have taken an interest in me. I get the impression there's a crime out there, and he's trying to put my name to."

"I understand how you feel. I'll talk to him," Tommy responded.

The three left early the following day for Santa Ynez, stopping at the Kinevan Stagecoach stop. They arrived back in time for dinner and briefed Sarah on what had transpired in Santa Barbara and the crime scene.

They discussed the robbery, the killing, and the search warrant for the Jenson hideout at dinner. "I don't know if the warrant will do any good, but at least we'll have it. Notice the term is for ten days. I don't know when you'll serve it, but I suggest doing it quickly while some of the stolen goods may still be in their possession," Juan said.

"What about the stockyards south of Santa Barbara? Did the Jensons sell any cattle in the past sixty days?" Sarah asked the three.

"Not in Oxnard or Ventura. We need to look in Santa Maria and San Luis Obispo," Tommy responded.

Silas had been quiet during the entire dinner. "I'm curious about one thing." The other three turned toward him.

"If there were skin fragments under Graves' nails and the bandit's sleeves were all down, then whoever we're looking for has some sort of gash on his face," Silas said.

"Good point," Juan responded.

With a search warrant in hand, Tommy, Juan, and Silas set out two days later at four in the morning and arrived outside the old Stillman Ranch before six AM. Tommy and Juan got off their horses and handed the leads to Silas. Juan went left, and Tommy went right and circled the front gate in case of a sentry. Juan found one of the gang members asleep just thirty yards inside the entrance. Their old skills as braves had not diminished in any way.

He placed his knife at the throat of the gang member and asked, "how many are inside the house?"

The man didn't answer, so Juan slid his knife sideways, and a trickle of blood fell on the man's shirt. "There are six inside the one-room shack," the sentry said.

"Let's tie him up, gag him, and take his gun," Tommy said.

The three made their way to the cabin without alerting those insides. "Juan, you go around the back. Silas, keep your shotgun cocked and cover the front. Don't hesitate to shoot".

"I won't," Tommy answered.

The front door was unlocked, so Tommy pushed it open slowly, then walked inside cautiously. He fired two shots into the ceiling. "Get outside right now. If you hesitate, we'll shoot all of you right where you lay."

Tommy stepped aside, and six men bolted for the front door. They first saw Silas with the shotgun, and they stopped on the porch. Juan came around to the front and aimed his gun at them. Tommy brought up the rear.

"Who the hell are you?" one of the six asked."

"I'm Tommy Sanchez, the district deputy for this area, and these are my deputies. I have the warrant to search your premises for stolen supplies and to use whatever force is necessary to search."

"We didn't steal anything; we're peaceful citizens," one of the men responded.

"Who are you?" Tommy asked.

"I'm Mike Jenson."

Tommy stood in front of the six and ordered the three to Mike Jenson's left to move six paces away.

The two at Jenson's right automatically did the same. Tommy put his gun in his holster, feinted Jenson with his left hand, and when the man reacted, Tommy smashed him in the face with his right. Jenson fell to the porch. "That's for hugging my daughter-in-law and trying to kiss my wife. If you try again, I'll kill you."

Jenson looked up from the porch. "You wouldn't get away with this if I had my gun on," he said.

The sun was up, and it was a bright clear day. Tommy walked back into the shack and found a holster with a loaded revolver in it. He came out of the cabin and threw them on the porch in front of Jenson. "Here's your gun. I'll give you time to put it on."

Mike Jenson had gotten to his feet. Tommy had taken off his hat and placed it on his saddle horn. Jenson looked down at his holster and gun, then at Tommy, who was less than six feet away; he did this several times. Each time he saw the steel gray eyes; Jenson knew in his heart that he didn't want to pick up the gun. He looked death in the eye, and a shiver went down his spine. "Not today," Jenson said.

Tommy walked closer to Jenson and examined his face. "How did you get those scratches on your face?"

"I picked up the cat, and it clawed me. "Ask them," he said, pointing to his brothers.

Juan smiled. "We don't see a cat around here." "It ran off," Mike Jenson smiled back at him.

"While Juan and Silas guarded the other five, Tommy took Mike Jenson with him and inspected the barn, the outhouse, and a wood pile to see if any stolen items were there. When they were done, Jenson smirked. "I told you we didn't steal anything. Whoever told the sheriff we did is a liar."

Tommy looked directly at Mike Jenson. "This isn't going away. The guard was shot and killed.

We think it was you who pulled the trigger, and we're going to keep after you until we get enough evidence. Then I'm coming back for you." Tommy said.

Tommy saw five men lying on the porch as he and Jenson walked back to the cabin. "What happened here", he asked Juan.

"Just after you left, the five jumped us and knocked our guns from our hands. We fought with our hands. Well, that's not true. Silas fought with his hands. It seems our fellow deputy knows how to fight. While I was trying to hold my own with Hollis, he took on the other four and knocked them all down. All   I did was knock down Hollis, recover my gun, and tell them to remain on the porch until you arrived." Juan couldn't help but laugh.

Tommy looked at the five men holding onto their chins and turned to Silas. "You're more of a mystery now than when you first came to our ranch. How do your account for your skill as a fighter?"

"Tommy, I'm as surprised as you. It just seemed like the thing to do. One of the guys swung at me, and I ducked and hit him with my right. Everything after that was rote."

Tommy turned to the Jenson Brothers. "We're leaving now. If any of you follow us or fires a shot, we'll return and kill all of you." Tommy and his two deputies rode off. There was no further incident.

"I assume you didn't find anything," Silas asked.

"Yes and no. None of the supplies on the list the sheriff gave us were there, but in one corner of the barn, there was an impression left on the hay. There had to be heavy boxes there recently. They sold the stolen goods to someone, and he's not around here."

"Who do you think is accepting stolen goods?" Silas asked.

"I don't know. I think I'll have you go to Oxnard and Ventura, then to Santa Maria and San Luis Obispo.

We have the list, and I guess the receiver of the stolen goods probably still has some on hand. I believe the goods were sold to someone who has a warehouse and a general store. I was hoping you could go to Oxnard and Ventura the day after tomorrow and check out the major stores. When you're done, come back to the ranch, then leave the next day for Santa Maria and San Luis Obispo, if necessary. Do you have any problems with the assignment?" Tommy asked Silas.

"None whatsoever."

She was impressed when Tommy told Sarah what Silas did to the Jenson gang. "I wonder what else we'll find out about him?"

The train trip to Ventura and Oxnard was quick but investigating where the supplies might take time and effort. Silas was cautious when he approached the clerks at the general stores he visited. He assumed any stolen merchandise coming to this area was already in the stores or warehouse. He found four possible stores, but concentrated on Price and McMullen's General Store in Ventura; they were the largest. Of course, a smaller establishment could receive stolen goods, so he didn't pass them up either.

At Price and McMullen, Silas acted like he was supplying for a large farm. Before visiting them, he'd memorized the entire shipping list and the stolen goods' sizes and quantities. To avoid any suspicion, he ordered the staples of a farm, such as sugar, coffee, flour, etc., before he asked for the items on the list he had memorized. They either didn't have any items on the list or were unavailable.

The order was becoming quite large. When the clerk at Price and McMullen went into the warehouse to look for one of the listed items, Silas left the store and hid across the street. Soon, he saw the clerk come out of the general store in a hurry and run one way and the other looking for him. When Silas was sure the young man had given up, he returned to his hotel and took his dinner in his room. He left on the next train to Santa Barbara.

The town of Santa Maria, north of Santa Ynez, had two medium-sized general stores. Neither indicated they had any of the stolen items in their inventory. The goods might have been moved elsewhere. But Silas was determined, and he went by train to San Luis Obispo.

There was one large store and two small ones. He first visited the two small ones and then went to Hardesty and French on Main Street.

This is where he met with success. Rather than using a subterfuge of ordering everyday items, he immediately asked for the items on the list. After the clerk retrieved the first five items he ordered, Silas purchased them. The clerk put them in shopping bags, and Silas left the store with a contented smile, making the train ride back more comfortable. He picked up his horse at the Santa Ynez livery stable, tied the purchased items to the horn of his saddle, and rode to the Sanchez ranch. It was late when he arrived, so he unsaddled his horse, brushed him down, put him in a holding pen, and went to sleep.

They wired the sheriff that they found some of the stolen supplies. He was busy that day but rode up early the next morning and compared his list with the items that Silas purchased in San Luis Obispo. Since Tommy had installed a telegraph line to the ranch, they could wire the San Luis Obispo County sheriff with the information and ask for his help. After several telegrams back and forth, Tommy, Juan, and Sheriff Rodgers took the train to San Luis Obispo and met with the sheriff. Silas didn't go this time.

It took only a couple of hours before the owner of Hardesty and French, James Hardesty, told them the story. He and his partner had been approached by two men selling a wagonload of supplies at a substantial discount. "I know I should have been cautious, but it was a helluva bargain, and we stood to make a nice profit, so I bought everything they had," Hardesty said.

"How much have you sold?" Juan asked.

"About half of what we purchased," Hardesty responded.

"Where's the rest of the merchandise?" Tommy asked.

"It's in our warehouse next door."

"We'll send a wagon to pick up what's left. Don't sell more items on this list; they're stolen property.

The San Luis Obispo Sheriff handed Hardesty a copy of the list of stolen supplies he'd received from Sheriff Rodgers.

"Are we in trouble other than losing money?"

"That's up to the circuit judge. I'm not going to take you in, but when the judge comes to town, there will be a hearing. I'll let you know when you have to appear before him," the sheriff responded.

They hadn't come prepared to take the remainder of the stolen goods back with them. The two sheriffs would determine the disposition of the stolen goods. Since they found the stolen goods and had good descriptions of the two who sold the merchandise to Hardesty, they took the train back to Santa Ynez. Rodgers congratulated Tommy and Juan. Their work was done. He'd follow up with the SLO sheriff and get a warrant for the Jenson brothers.

"Silas Smith did the hard work and should be congratulated," Tommy said. "What do you know about Smith?" the sheriff asked Tommy with Juan present.

"He's a great worker, gets along with everyone, and has a good work ethic. Why do you ask?" Tommy inquired "I know you led one of the possess and captured two bandits, but how much do you know about who planned the robbery?"

"There had to be a leader, but I thought everyone felt it was Butch Cassidy since many of his Hole-in-the-Wall gang were involved."

"That may be true, but the Pinkertons spent much time investigating whether Butch or Sundance could have been involved. Their best guess is that Butch gave some advice to the ringleader and provided the men, but he wasn't involved in the actual robbery."

"It could easily have been Snake Eyes, Jack Porter. The men around Butch liked him."

"No, someone rode with Richards, and it wasn't Snake Eyes. You caught him and brought him back. The one that rode with Richards killed him and escaped with both of their shares. I think the leader could be Smith."

"That's a real stretch. Smith doesn't seem to be the type who'd rob trains," Tommy responded.

"I think we need to keep an eye on him until we catch the seventh man."

Silas is living in the guest room. "I disagree with you, but I'll honor your request. Why don't you stay in the house tonight?"

Juan asked Tommy if Silas might have been the seventh man. "I don't believe it, but stranger things have happened. The problem with the sheriff's theory is that it doesn't explain who shot Silas and left him for dead?"

CHAPTER 14

*I*t'd been six months since he arrived at Bookers' farm and taken Frances as his. A thought had started to creep into his mind. What if he stayed here indefinitely? And what if he took Frances as his wife? He didn't have any place to go; he had all the sex he wanted, and with a little effort, there was plenty to eat. In addition, no one came here to look for him, and none of the neighbors, other than the Indians and the guy with the bull, were within a day's ride. This was a better hideout than Butch and Sundance had.

Recently, he found himself admiringly looking at Frances. She was petite, kept herself clean, and was reasonably attractive. When she noticed him looking at her, she immediately looked the other way. Lenny didn't have much experience with pregnancy, but he was sure Frances was with a child. Her abdomen had started to swell, and she had an upset stomach most mornings.

Lenny didn't know how he'd feel about being a father. Domesticity wasn't in his makeup. But if she was pregnant, he was the father. Having a family had never occurred to him. The more he thought about it, the more intrigued he was. He wondered what she thought of the idea. She was probably still thinking about her husband and hoping he was coming back.

Things were better with her; she didn't try to kill him in the last two months, which was a plus. But she wouldn't open up to any dialog, which wasn't good. Of course, she'd respond if he asked a question. She probably didn't want to get hit anymore.

The fact was that Lenny hadn't hit her in about three months. The thought must be in her mind that she was going to have his baby; whether she liked it or not, he was the father, and, for all practical purposes, he was her husband.

The fact was that Frances had been thinking about her predicament. She hated Lenny, and she was pregnant by him. She still wanted to kill him but didn't have a weapon. She searched and searched, but Hiram didn't leave anything behind that she could use.

She wanted a child very much, but how could it be with Lenny Harris? Down deep, she knew that Hiram was dead. He was a good man and wouldn't have left her alone. No, he was dead. She had to think of her child and their future. Every so often, she'd catch Lenny looking at her. She wondered what that was all about. He was still making her do whatever he wanted and still having her do deplorable sexual acts. So why look at her as though he cared?

Running away was an option in the past, but she couldn't take a chance now. The baby was too important. A tear formed in her eye when she realized Lenny might stay here indefinitely. Over the last month, he'd taken more of an interest in the farm. He even got on the roof of the barn and fixed a leak. Then he had the Indians dig a hole closer to the house, so it wasn't too far to go to the outhouse. And he was always talking about the herd of cattle and how it had doubled since he'd been here.

She was peeling potatoes for dinner when he came up behind her and said, "I know you're pregnant. When the baby comes, we'll need more room. What do you think if I added a room to the cabin? The Indian woman can stay there when its time, rather than in the barn. After the baby comes, we can put the child in that room."

He was waiting for an answer, but she couldn't speak to the man who raped and brutalized her for six months. She knew he had a vicious temper and could rage over anything. The question was, what did he think of having a child? If he hit her and she had a miscarriage, he'd be a loser, same as her. She decided not to answer him. She put down the paring knife, walked into the bedroom, and lay on the bed. He didn't follow her.

Frances had four hundred dollars on hand when Hiram left. Lenny searched through all the drawers in the house and found the money. Two days later, he told her he was taking the wagon to Santa Barbara to buy some lumber. "I'm going to build an 8-by-10 room in the rear of the cabin. On the way, I'll stop by the Indian shack and ask the woman to come over and be with you while I'm gone. The trip should take up to three days. Is there anything you want me to bring back?" Frances turned around and didn't answer. Lenny walked out the door.

However, the first thing he wanted to do was see what the latest information on the Oxnard Robbery was. He hated his father, but his mother was a saint. It was she who taught him to read and write. Though his skill level wasn't that of a college grad, he at least could read and comprehend. Before going to the lumber yard, he stopped off at the library. He remembered December 22, the day of the robbery, and read all the papers that covered the train heist after that date.

It took him two hours, but he felt he was up to date on the robbery. Everyone but he and the Kitchen Brothers were dead. There was a story about Richards and where his body had been found. There was much speculation about a seventh man. The most common theme was that he got away and was out of the country. All the loot had been accounted for except about eight thousand dollars in marked bills. That last piece of information made Lenny pause. He couldn't spend the money and be caught, especially in the Santa Barbara area, if he wanted   to remain at Bookers Ranch with Frances.

He assumed that the authorities couldn't get to him in Mexico. Of course, he always had the option of going to Mexico and further south and being able to spend the money. But how long would the money last? No. He had to figure out how to stay at the farm.

He was armed with only a sketch of the addition he wanted. Lenny went to the lumber yard and talked to the owner. Within a few minutes, the man made a list of what was needed for a 10-by-12-room addition. He took a few minutes and showed Lenny how to build the room step by step and make it appear professional. "I assume the addition is for a child. Is this your first?"

"Yes, it is."

"Well, good luck. You remind me of someone else who came in here several years ago. He knew what he wanted to build but didn't know how. I gave him a sketch of a barn and a step-by-step list of how to do it. By the way, we have some nice cut flowers and boxes of chocolates that would please your wife."

The owner was a good salesman. Lenny not only bought flowers and chocolates but stopped in a department store and bought Frances a nice warm coat. All he could think about on his ride back home was what she'd say when he presented her with the gifts.

He had a smile on his lips as he entered the cabin and presented her with the flowers and chocolates. The Indian woman was at the kitchen sink. "What are these for?" Frances asked.

"I thought you'd like them. Here's something else." He smiled as he handed her the coat wrapped in gift paper.

She couldn't control herself. "You beat the hell out of me and treat me worse than a dog, then give me some flowers and chocolate, and that's supposed to make it better. You can go to hell and take your gifts with you." She threw the flowers and chocolates at him, but he ducked.

He stormed out of the cabin, saddled his horse, and went for a ride. Frances picked up the gifts, gave the flowers and chocolate to the Indian woman, and told her she could leave. She needed a coat, so she tried it on. It was a little large but would keep her warm. "That son-of-a-bitch has some nerve to think he could make everything better with a few gifts." She said out loud.

Lenny came back two hours later. He made sure she knew he was home by slamming the front door and kicking a pot on the floor. She knew she was in for a beating but other than some rough sex, he didn't say anything, and he didn't hit her. He told her not to wear anything to bed, but she was defiant, put on a long nightgown, and went to bed. What a surprise, what's going on? She asked herself.

Sarah Sanchez had been smiling more than usual the past few days. Her husband wondered what was going on.

He didn't ask her why she was in such good spirits; he knew she'd let it be known in due time. Silas usually ate dinner with Tommy and his wife every evening. Sarah made it clear that tonight was a special occasion, and dinner would be at six. When it was time, Naomi went into Tommy's office and told him they had a female guest tonight. She asked him to wear his coat to dinner.

So that was it. A guest for dinner wasn't unusual, but a female guest was. He wondered what Sarah had up her sleeve. He entered the dining room just as Silas came into the house. The female guest had already been seated. "Tommy, this is my friend, Marjorie Rawlins." Tommy shook the hand that was offered.

"And Marjorie, this is our new friend, Silas Smith." The matchmaker was at work. Silas was seated next to Marjorie.

The guest was a petite brunette, about thirty-five years old, with long brown hair and an engaging smile.

She wore her hair pulled back in a ponytail. They would learn during dinner that she was a widow and owned a small ranch off Refugio Road in Santa Ynez.

Tommy opened the wine, and Naomi served the ladies first. Usually, Naomi, Raoul, and his wife, Naiwa, would have dinner with the Sanchez'. They must have been given word that Sarah was trying to fix up Silas. The entree was steak with mashed potatoes and green beans. After dessert, Naomi served an after-dinner liquor, and they adjourned to the parlor. Marjorie was open and quickly engaged in conversation. She wanted to hear Silas' story of his near-death experience resulting in his memory loss.

"Do you find that you're doing something as though you've done it many times and don't know how you did it?"

"How did you know?"

"I read of a case similar to yours that happened back east. The patient had been a plumber before he was in an accident. After he was diagnosed with amnesia, he began to fix his neighbor's faucets and soon took up the plumbing profession.

One day on the job, his memory returned, and he realized he'd been in the plumbing business. I think there's a good chance you'll recover."

"I like your positive attitude, but enough about me. Sarah tells me that you had a heart-breaking experience when you and your husband visited Los Angeles."

"We went to the city to celebrate our wedding anniversary. We'd just come from having breakfast in the hotel, and my husband wanted to break some bills. He had just finished the transaction when three men yelled out it was a holdup. Eventually, they caught the robbers, and all three were hung. That's when   James was shot.

"Do you know why the robbers shot him?"

"Oh, yes. As one of the three robbers came near him, he grabbed the bandit's gun and knocked him down. He turned to shoot the second one when the third came up behind him and shot him in the back. He died instantly and lay on the bank floor during the holdup. When I tried to go to him, one of the robbers threw me to the floor and wouldn't let me near him. To me, he was truly a hero. He left me with a wonderful son and a nice income." A tear formed in her eye.

"I'm sorry; I get emotional when I talk about it." I don't know when I've had a better time, but it's time to go home. This was nice of you; Sarah, I'll have all of you over to my home shortly.

"How did you get here?" Tommy asked.

"Your son-in-law, Raoul, and his wife came for me. Tomas has agreed to take me home."

"If Marjorie didn't mind, I would be delighted to escort her home safely," Silas said.

Everyone smiled, and Marjorie accepted. Tommy knew in his heart that this was how it was planned.

CHAPTER 15

They had enough on the Jenson Brothers to arrest them for the supply wagon robbery north of Kinevan Road. The sheriff and two of his deputies came to the ranch, stayed overnight, and the three, along with Silas and Tommy, made their way to the old Stillman Ranch. Juan was in court and couldn't be spared.

When they arrived, they spread out and slowly approached the old shack the gang was using. They found the same sentry sound asleep again and tied him up. It was nearly seven in the morning when the sheriff, hiding behind a tree, called out to the gang in the cabin. "We have warrants for your arrest for armed robbery and murder; come out with your hands in the air. That demand was answered with a hail of gunshots fired from the two windows in the cabin.

When the five posse members returned fire, Jed Jenson and another gang member were shot dead. "Good god, they shot Jed," Mike Jenson said.

"We can't stay in here. There's no protection. I want to get my hands on Shorty. He was supposed to be guarding the front gate. Damn him", Hollis responded.

"Can we make a break for it?" Mike asked.

One member of the gang looked out the front window. "They're behind trees and rocks. We don't have a chance."

"Well, we can't surrender. Mike shot and killed the guard. They'll hang us for sure. Let's see if we can negotiate with them", a gang member said.

Hollis opened the front door and stuck a stick with a white cloth attached. "We want to talk."

"Go ahead and talk," Rodgers responded.

"We didn't murder anyone. The guard fired first, and one of us fired back in self-defense. If you take murder off the table, we'll surrender."

The sheriff responded. "I don't have the authority to do anything but arrest you. You can tell the judge and jury if it was self-defense. I'll see to it that you're given a fair trial. That's better than dying in that old shack."

Hollis Jenson, followed by his brother Mike, threw out their weapons, raised their hands, and came through the front door. The two remaining gang members followed them. "The two insides are dead," Hollis said as he waited for the posse to surround them.

Handcuffs and shackles were placed on the remaining robbers. They were put in a buckboard the posse brought and transported to Rancho Del Prado before being taken to Santa Barbara by the sheriff and the two deputies he brought along. Tommy and Sarah hosted the deputies that evening and fed the prisoners, who were kept under guard in the barn. Tommy's Vaqueros took turns spelling the deputies. Mike Jenson attempted to escape. Somehow, he was able to take off one of his handcuffs. When one of the Vaqueros checked the prisoners, Mike jumped him and tried to take his rifle.

However, another Vaquero was close enough to see the scuffle and hit Jenson over the head with his gun, and the two guards restrained him and tied him back up.

Whether they had a poor attorney or the jury was angry because of the number of robberies committed by the gang, Mike Jenson was found guilty of theft and murder and sentenced to hang. He appealed and lost. Hollis received thirty years, and the other gang members received fifteen years each. Silas attended the sentencing hearing, and the sheriff asked him if he had ever heard of the Hole-in-the-Wall gang, Butch Cassidy, or the Sundance Kid." I'm sorry, sheriff, I've never heard of the term or the two men," Silas said.

Later, Silas asked Tommy the significance of the questions the sheriff asked. "He's a funny guy. The two men are famous outlaws, and that was the name of their gang. Maybe he thinks you were associated with them at one time", Tommy responded.

"Am I under suspicion for some crime?" Silas asked.

"I don't know. I think the sheriff is up for reelection and looking for anything that could turn the tide in his favor."

Silas was no dummy. "So, there is a crime that hasn't been solved, and because I can't remember who I am, I'm a suspect. Is that true?"

Tommy told him the story of the Oxnard Train Robbery and the significance of where he was found.

"I don't think I'm a criminal. I know I don't think like a criminal. How can I prove to you I'm innocent?"

"You don't have to. I see a man of character, and I won't believe that, at a former time, you were a robber and murderer. Can we forget this?"

"I'll try, but it's challenging to be suspected of something you know nothing about.

Marjorie Rawlins became a frequent visitor to Rancho Del Prado. She'd either come on the spur of the moment and be invited for dinner or on a once-a- week basis. Occasionally, the Sanchez' would join Marjorie and Silas at her ranch and enjoy a fine meal. Marjorie was an excellent cook, and Silas started to put on a few pounds. If they had dinner at her farm on a Saturday, Silas didn't return with the Sanchez'.

Silas was proud of Ranch Del Prado and enjoyed showing Marjorie around the ranch. One Saturday, he asked Sarah if taking Marjorie to the lake was okay. She agreed and had Naomi make up a picnic basket. The two rode out to the lake in one of the rigs they had on the ranch.

They'd not been intimate, and Marjorie wondered why Silas was so shy. She'd at least like him to make a pass at her. Naiwa prepared the spread, and after a glass of wine, they relaxed on the blanket they'd spread for the picnic.

When Marjorie turned to smile at Silas, he took her in his arms, and nature took its course. The flush on

Marjorie's cheeks wasn't lost on Sarah when the couple returned.

A couple of days later, Silas notified Tommy and Sarah that he was going to marry the pretty brunette in three months. He planned to live on and work the Rawlins' spread and would leave the Sanchez Ranch just before the wedding. "I'm not a farmer, but I like growing things. You and Tomas have taught me much about ranching since I've been with you."

Lenny Harris was beside himself. He wanted to shout out, "I'm a father." Even Frances couldn't help but smile at the transformation in Lenny. He hadn't beaten her in months; now, he was there to provide encouraging words during the delivery and assist the Indian woman. Lenny finished the new room addition two days before Frances gave birth to a 6-pound, 5-ounce baby boy.

When he knew the birth was imminent, he fashioned a crib out of some left-over lumber and padded the bottom and sides with clean blankets. Frances was cautious. She couldn't be sure that this was an individual she could live with. How could she be nice to this monster, even if he did change? She would never refer to him as her husband, and that was a fact. She didn't know what triggered the change in Lenny, but suddenly, she thought about Hiram. What would she do if he suddenly came home? And more importantly, what would he do?

Three days after the baby was born, Lenny brought her breakfast in bed. The more he was nice to her, the more stubborn she became in her resolve to kill the son-of-a-bitch.

CHAPTER 16

*I*t was late in the afternoon. Sarah and Tommy were having a glass of wine in the kitchen; Naomi was cooking dinner, and the children, now of school age, were doing their homework. They heard a horse come up and then a knock at the front door. Sarah hurried to answer. She returned with a visitor; it was Sheriff Rodgers. "I know I should've told you I was coming, but I wasn't sure you'd want to see me."

"Nonsense, we've had our differences lately, but you are always welcome here. I will always listen to what you have to say. Come and sit down. Dinner is almost ready, and Naomi has cooked pork chops tonight. The family won't be here tonight; Silas is having dinner in town."

Naomi had pounded the pork chops and made a delicious gravy to pour over the entrée, served with steaming wild rice. The dessert was apple pie. The men adjourned to Tommy's study after dinner for cigars and brandy. Sarah helped with the dishes, put the twins to bed, and joined the men. They talked about the sheriff's reelection and the trial of the two Jensons. "There had to be something important for you to come up here. Why don't you tell us what's on your mind" Tommy suggested?

"You're right. It's about Silas Smith or whatever his name is. I know you like him, but the train robbery is constantly on my mind. I want to catch the one who got away if that's possible. Finding Silas proximate to where

Richards' body was discovered seems too much of a coincidence."

"You must have some evidence that makes you suspect Silas?"

"No more than what I told you. The possibility that there was a seventh train robber hasn't been investigated well enough to suit me."

"What do you want me to do about it?" The Pinkertons are the ones you should be talking to.

"You and I know you're the best tracker in this area. I'd like you to go to where Richards was found and see if the tracks lead to where you found Silas."

"Sheriff, it's been a year since I found Silas. Those tracks are gone by now. The rains certainly would have destroyed them."

"That's possible, but I don't think so. That area is mostly uninhabited. Except for an occasional hunter and some Indians, many of those tracks may still be there, or there's enough left for someone with your skills to see what others like me don't."

"Well, I did miss out on my second buck. I'll do it, provided you drop the investigation into Silas if we can't prove he was the seventh man."

"Agreed."

"I assume you want to go right away." "If you can spare the time."

"I'll have Tomas outfit us for ten days, and we should be ready to leave the day after tomorrow."

Sarah agreed that he should go. "I know Silas feels pressure from the sheriff about being involved in that train robbery. It'll take some heat off both him and Marjorie if you can clear it up. They're very much in love."

"Let's not tell Silas why I'm going on this trip. If you have to tell him anything, tell him the sheriff and I are going on a hunting trip."

While the women were preparing the food and Tomas was getting the gear ready for the sheriff and Tommy, the two men went to the south end of the property and fished for the day. They came back later that night, talked about the election, and the sheriff shared his thoughts about Silas with Tommy. "I'm not targeting Silas. I don't want to convict an innocent man, but it does seem that where you found him gives me pause. I want to do what's right and play this out to a logical conclusion. I appreciate your listening to me."

They took a mule along to carry back a deer. They figured it would take three days to reach the spot where Richards' body was found. The sheriff had a good map and marked the two locations on the map he was interested in. The men were friendly but not as close as they had been before the jailbreak by the Sioux Brothers.

They came upon the Richards' site at the end of three days and decided to camp there. They got up at first light and gave the area a good going over. They found some of his gear. His saddle was hidden in the heavy shrubs. While the sheriff searched for other items belonging to the deceased or his killer, Tommy concentrated on the hoof prints for three hours.

By noontime, Tommy was ready. He and the sheriff had a small lunch and told each other what they found. The sheriff found nothing significant.

"There were many horses in this area, and it's difficult to distinguish which horses were Richards and which were from another man had distinctive markings, and they seemed to be traveling together. Let's say that Richards and number seven had a falling out. The seventh man probably shot Richards and took his horse. I tracked the two distinctive marks toward the Silas site for a mile, convinced the two horses were together. In addition, I spent an hour backtracking to see if I could find these same two hoof marks coming into this camp, and I was able to do that. To the best of my ability, I was able to establish that two horses with riders came into this camp. Both horses went toward where I found Silas. I know one of the horses had a rider when they went toward this camp. Let's break camp, follow the tracks, and see where they lead us", Tommy said.

They lost two sets of tracks at least ten times the first day, but Tommy was working on the premise that if the sheriff were correct, the paths would lead to where he found Silas. Any other plan could have been a better use of time. That's how he kept seeing the tracks the first day out. The second day was a replication of day one. The going was slow, but the good news was they were tracking the same two horses directly to where he found Silas. They'd lose the track and then find them.

They lost the trail on the third day but continued going on until they reached the Silas location. Again, it was late, and they decided to camp and take a fresh look tomorrow. Tommy concentrated on the tracks and the sheriff on anything he could find at the site. They compared notes over a bottle of wine. "I found parts of a bedroll, some harness, and bits of skin. I believe someone killed and then skinned the deer here. I did find the initials H. B. inside a saddle hidden in the bushes. My guess is all of this could have belonged to Silas. Perhaps even the saddle, but I'm not sure."

"The light was better this morning, so I backtracked, and after an hour, I picked up the two sets of hoofs we were tracking about two hundred yards back along the route we took; I followed them here. So now we know someone came from the Richards camp to the Silas site, trailing another horse. My best guess is that there were three horses and a mule simultaneously. Two horses from the Richards camp were here. Two animals, probably a mule and a horse, never were at the Richards site. The horse and mule ran off to the south; perhaps they were run off. I tracked them for two hours. They were riderless about a hundred yards from here, and there was a lot of blood on the ground. Maybe a deer was on the mule, and a large animal attacked it."

"What's your conclusion?" The sheriff asked.

"We know for sure that one rider and a riderless horse came from the Richards camp to the Silas location; those two horses subsequently left here, traveling west. Whoever was with Richards came here after Richards was shot. Whether he shot Silas is just speculation. I don't believe Silas came from the Richards camp and shot himself.

Therefore, Silas could not be part of the Oxnard Robbery. He wasn't with the two at the Richards camp, and he didn't leave after the man with Richards came here and left."

"That is one possibility and a good one. Perhaps there was an argument with whoever was at this site, and Silas was shot." but it doesn't rule out the possibility that Silas killed Richards, took his horse, came this way, and was shot by someone else."

"That's a little far-fetched. The horse and mule that were here with Silas have different hoof prints than the ones that came from the Richards' site. Besides, how do your account for the missing money unless you think I took it?"

"I can't believe that you stole your own money. Silas could have hidden it before someone came into his camp and shot him. Or if he's the one who came from the Richards' site, whoever shot him could have taken his money."

"Why would he want to hide the money on the off chance someone would   come into his camp and shoot him in the back?"

"I don't have an answer for that."

"I came on this trip conditioned on your word that you would get off Silas' back if we couldn't prove that he was the seventh man. Well, logic says he's not your man.

I also believe my analysis of the hoof prints would stand up in a court of law. Silas was probably on a hunting trip when the real seventh man came into his camp and shot him. It would help if you went after that guy. He has the money and is probably hiding out in the area. I've done what you asked me to do, but you have a crime, and you have somebody you'd like to fit with the crime. I'm finished here, and I'm going home. You're welcome to join me."

"I think I'll look around some more." The sheriff said.

Two weeks later, the sheriff and two deputies came to the Sanchez Ranch and immediately went into the barn where Silas was working. Tomas alerted Tommy to the three visitors, and it was Tommy who sent his new foreman to get Juan.

When he entered the barn, there was a confrontation between Silas and the two deputies who were lying on the barn floor. The sheriff had his gun out, and it was pointed at Silas. Tommy walked directly up to the sheriff. "Put that gun down. Since when do you talk to my employees without clearing it through me?' Tommy said.

"This is law enforcement business. I don't need to inform you about my business." The sheriff was a little prickly and still had his gun leveled at Silas.

"I thought I was the deputy for this district, and Silas was my deputy."

"You are, but I'm the sheriff. I don't have to tell you everything."

"Get out of here now, and don't come back without a warrant."

The two deputies had risen and were dusting off their clothes; one was rubbing his chin. Tommy could see out of his eye that one deputy was reaching for his gun. Tommy pivoted quickly, drove a right hand into his midsection, and took his weapon. As he turned to face the sheriff, Silas punched the other deputy in the stomach with his right hand, then left-hooked him on the chin. The deputy fell and lay still on the barn floor. Rodgers, who'd holstered his weapon, reached for his gun, but Tommy was quicker and placed his hand over the sheriff's hand, who had his hand on the gun. "Your men were going to draw on another law enforcement officer in his home. How dare you? Didn't you train these men properly?"

"Okay, we made a mistake. We don't have a warrant. I just wanted to talk to Silas. I didn't come here to create a problem, but Silas is coming with me because he hit my deputy." The sheriff responded.

"He's not going anywhere with you without a warrant. Your deputy provoked Silas. Who the hell are these guys you brought with you?"

"They're new and shouldn't have tried to draw on you. I apologize for that."

"What did you find after I left you?"

"I can't divulge that."

Juan and Tomas had just ridden up, and both walked into the barn amid the heated argument. "What's going on?" Juan asked Tommy.

"I entered the barn and found the sheriff interrogating Silas without a warrant. These jerks tried to pull down on me, and I punched one out and took his gun while Silas took care of the other guy." Juan smiled.

"Okay, sheriff, I'm Silas Smith's attorney. What's this all about?"

"Since I'm not bringing charges now, I have nothing to say to you. My deputies and I are leaving. Here's a letter for you, Mr. Sanchez, and two more for Juan and Smith. Your appointments as my deputies are at this moment terminated." The sheriff and his deputies got on their horses and rode away.

"Tommy, what's this all about?"

He told Juan about his trip with the sheriff to try and clear Silas of being the seventh man that robbed the Oxnard Train. Silas was attentive to what Tommy said and immediately asked him and Juan about this. "Let's go into the kitchen, and I'll tell you everything I know."

CHAPTER 17

*F*rances named the baby James after her father once he reached six months old. Lenny refused to call the baby James, insisting he was Lenny Junior. She'd been waiting until the baby was old enough before she tried to escape. She was waiting until the time was right. She thought long and hard and came up with a plan.

Just after breakfast this morning, Lenny told her he was going to Jacobs Farm and make arrangements for the bull to be brought here. Working with Jacobs made Lenny irritable. The farmer always wanted more money, and the negotiations with him were tiring. Lenny was so angry with him that he thought of killing the entire family and burying them there. It might be years before anyone becomes suspicious since they have yet to go to their place.

This was the time. Over the year and a half that Lenny had been with her, she made a list of what she should take with her when she escaped. As soon as Lenny left, Frances hitched up the horse to the wagon, loaded it with the bare essentials, and she and the baby drove to the Indian shack. She knew enough of the Indian language now that she could communicate with the older woman. Luckily for Frances, the woman was there and could translate for her. She wanted one of the men to drive her to Santa Barbara. She had a few dollars left that Hiram had given her, and she'd see to it that he got five dollars if he took her.

After an hour of haggling with the man, they struck a bargain. She'd pay two dollars now, ten when they got there, and buy a horse for the Indian so he could return. She was worn out with the haggling but persevered; they were on their way.

"It took Lenny two hours to reach the farm but another hour to reach an agreement with the bull's owner. Out of frustration, if for no other reason, he agreed to Jacobs' terms and left. He couldn't wait to leave the Jacobs's place; he feared he might shoot the bastard at any time. He took his time putting up his horse before he walked into the cabin. The first thing he noticed was the silence. The baby wasn't crying. Perhaps he was asleep. Lenny walked into the baby's room and saw his missing blankets. He walked outside. That's when he realized the wagon and Sarah's horse was missing. "She's run away and taken my son," he shouted.

The question now was, where did she go? As far as he knew, she had yet to go to Santa Barbara since her wedding to Bookers. That's probably where she was going, but how? The only thing he could think of was the Indians were helping her.

Lenny saddled up his horse and rode to the Indian shack. The older woman and an older man were the only ones there. Neither would talk to him until he started slapping the older woman in the face. Finally, she told him the other Indian had taken Frances and the baby to Santa Barbara. His knowledge of their language was limited, so he couldn't ask them how long they were gone. His life depended on reaching her before she got to anyone. He assumed her goal was to call the sheriff.

He'd already ridden his horse for five hours today, but he didn't have time to go back to the cabin, switch mounts and still be able to catch Frances. He had to bring her back. He did think of going back, digging up his money, and making his way east. At the last minute, he decided to try to catch her; he could always make his getaway if he failed.

Frances held the baby tightly as she rode up with the Indian. He didn't speak much English, but he knew Lenny would be coming after them. He didn't want to face him; he wasn't sure if that man would shoot him if they were caught. Using the whip was not an option because they had at least a full day of riding to reach Santa Barbara. She nearly had a heart attack when the Indian stopped to rest the horse and give it some water after an hour. It was a hot day, so he took a wet cloth and rubbed down the animal. She knew he was correct, but she was still nervous.

They got back in the wagon and were on their way. They stopped for the second time at nearly two in the afternoon.

The Indian went through the same ritual, and they were on their way again after ten minutes. Frances had no choice but to nurse the baby in front of the Indian. Embarrassment would have to take a back seat. This was her life, and she was on edge. She was constantly turning around to see if Lenny was coming. She knew they were getting closer to Santa Barbara, but would they make it?

Lenny's horse was tired. He had to rest the animal and ensure it was hydrated, or he might as well turn back. He knew he was on the correct route because he saw wagon tracks now and then. He didn't know what to do if he found them. Frances and his son would return with him; he wondered if he should kill the Indian.

It was late afternoon when he came over a rise and saw the wagon up ahead. He wanted to push hard to overtake them, but probably for the first time in his life, he showed discretion and took his time. He fired a couple of shots to see if they would stop. All that did was scare them enough that they took the whip to the horse. His was spent, he couldn't push the animal anymore, or he wouldn't be able to escape. Lenny pulled back on the reins and slowed the horse to a trot and then a slow walk. As far as he was concerned, he wasn't going to catch them. He had to turn around and try to save himself.

As they came over another rise, Frances could see some homes in the outlying district of Santa Barbara. She knew she was going to be free. She looked back and could see Lenny pull back on his horse, and she smiled. The next thing she knew, the Indian stopped the wagon. "You can't stop. We're almost there. My baby and I are going to be free."

The Indian didn't respond; all he did was make the point. There was a large tree limb blocking the trail. The Indian got out of the wagon and assessed the obstacle. Frances laid the baby in a box on the wagon floor and rushed to the site. She didn't have to ask if it could be moved; she knew it couldn't. All this planning she had done and waiting for this chance disintegrated right here. Lenny didn't turn around. He was walking his horse toward them, and there was nothing she could do.

She expected a beating. She even wondered if he'd shoot. But all he did was look at her and say, "Let's go home. I'm tired."

"You can have the place and all the cattle. Just let me, the baby, and the Indian go. We won't tell on you."

Lenny tied his horse to a tree, got in the wagon, and backed it up to where he could turn around. He hopped down and hitched his tired horse to the wagon when it was headed back to the cabin. "My son is in the back of the wagon. I'm going home with him. You and the Indian are welcome to come back with me, or you can continue to Santa Barbara. That's up to you. Make up your mind; the wagon is leaving in thirty seconds."

She stood there trying to understand what had just happened. Her heart was heavy; she nearly made it to freedom. Now her jailer had returned and was telling her to come with him. With her head down, she walked to the wagon, picked up her child in her arms, and beckoned the Indian to get in the back of the wagon. She took her place next to Lenny and asked, "Do you want me to drive?"

Lenny and the Indian lay on the bed of the buckboard alongside his son. Frances drove them to their cabin. It was early the following day when they arrived. Lenny told the Indian to sleep in the barn, and he, the baby, and Frances went into the cabin. "We'll talk about all of this tomorrow. Put the baby to bed and come to bed with me. You have a lot of making up to do."

The baby was sound asleep, and she covered him up and went to bed. He fell asleep quickly, but she tossed and turned all night, regretting her failure to escape.

Would there be another opportunity, or would he be more alert to another escape? She expected to be beaten or slapped around, but all he wanted to do was cuddle.

He woke later than usual, went into the kitchen, and grabbed a cup of coffee. She just finished his eggs and put them on a plate before him. "Why don't you make some eggs for yourself and have breakfast with me? I want to talk to you."

Frances didn't know if this was some ploy on Lenny's part to lure her into a false sense of security and then explode. She made breakfast for herself and sat down at the table with Lenny. "When I realized that you were attempting to escape with our child, I was more than angry. I wanted to tear your head off. But as I walked up to where that tree limb fell, I realized I didn't want to hurt you; I wanted to live with you as husband and wife."

"You wonder how someone who could beat the hell out of you and abuse you sexually could want to spend the rest of his life with you?" Lenny asked. Her expression must have given her away because he smiled.

Frances was dumb founded and couldn't think of anything to say in a rebuttal. She just sat there, mute. It wasn't that he was asking her to contribute to their conversation; he was telling her the way he wanted it. He got up from the table, walked around to the other side, placed his hands on either side of her face, and kissed her longingly. Frances was stunned at the behavior change, and it took her a few seconds to pull away. "There is no way that's going to happen while I'm alive," she yelled.

Lenny walked back to his seat. "I've been living with you as husband and wife for a year and a half. You know that. I love our son. It's the first thing that's ever been mine that I'm responsible for. I won't let him go without a fight. Why don't you and I make the most of our lives and see this ranch prosper? I know why you hate me, and I'm sorry. I haven't hit you since our son was born, and I don't intend ever to hit you again. I won't give up the child, and I want you. Why don't you give me a chance to show you I can be a proper husband?" Lenny asked.

"You can go to hell. I'm married to Hiram Bookers, who I believe is still alive. Other than my child, the next thing I want the most is to have Hiram return and kill you in front of me. You can abuse me, but you can't be my husband. I'd rather be dead."

CHAPTER 18

*T*his was Raoul's last week at the ranch. Tomas would be taking over as foreman, and Silas was moving on with Marjorie Rawlins as soon as they were married. Initially, much of the load would fall to Tommy, but he had done it before and was sure everything would be fine. This morning, Raoul came to the house and knocked on the front door. Naomi opened the door, and Raoul asked to speak with Tommy. When Tommy was summoned, Raoul asked if he could have a few minutes. They decided to meet in Tommy's office and have coffee.

"With the Jensons out of the picture, I thought the rustling would end, but it hasn't. We had five more head taken this week" Raoul was serious.

"Are they being taken through the south gate?" "Yes, the lock on the gate was cut."

Silas was in the barn, so the two men joined him. "You've been checking the southern gate, haven't you?" Tommy asked.

"I checked it four days ago and planned to go down there again this afternoon."

"I'll go with you. Let's leave at about 2:30 and plan to be gone overnight. Get all our gear together and make sure we have two Remington's. I have a lunch appointment at noon at the ranch, so I should be done in time."

Sarah had made chicken salad and apple pie; she'd be joining the luncheon.

They hadn't met the man Juan was bringing to lunch, but they had heard of him. When they arrived, Juan introduced Jacob Thunder, a man of forty years and a fellow attorney. "This is my mother and stepfather."

The weather was nice, so they sat outside at the rear of the hacienda overlooking their vineyard and the mountains to the east. After dessert, Juan explained the purpose of his guest's visit. "Jacob is a member of the Chumash Tribe in Santa Barbara. His great-grandfather, a full bloodied Chumash Indian, had a prosperous livery stable and married into the Ortega family. Jacob is a Bar Association member, married to Louise Martinez, and is a friend of mine. He's announcing his candidacy for County Sheriff at noon tomorrow at the courthouse in Santa Barbara."

"What does this have to do with us?" Sarah asked.

"I know you don't know me and probably never heard of me, but I have of you and your husband. I'm here today seeking your endorsement", the candidate responded.

"Why do you want to run?" Tommy asked.

"I've been interested in law enforcement since I was young. Additionally, I've served on various groups supporting our police and sheriffs, and I'm not happy with how our minorities are being treated. If I'm elected, I will be the first of my tribe to hold a political office, which means a great deal to me. My family and relatives are numerous but not rich. We can't run an effective campaign without generous donors like you."

"It seems you could accomplish more using that forum than as a sheriff.

Why not use your legal status to represent your people?" Sarah asked.

"I have done much pro bono work for my people and many other minority groups, but my supporters feel we need to get into law enforcement if we're to make significant progress to help our people. Many people get caught up in the system too early and can't get out."

"What do you think of our current sheriff, Jack Rodgers?" Tommy asked.

"I think he was a good man early on, but he's too quick to arrest and takes too long to investigate. He's accountable to the group that has money, political influence, and runs Santa Barbara County."

"I wonder if you realize what an uphill fight it will be. There are three candidates in the field already. Each is well-known in the area and has significant backing. You'd be a long shot at best. What do you think, Juan?" Sarah asked.

"Do you realize how many doors are closed to people like us and how often we must insist upon our rights? Imagine it's like not having any money or knowing someone with influence to protect your rights. I think it's time to have a change in the power structure. What do you say, Tommy?"

Tommy turned to Sarah. "Everything he says makes sense to me. I'll let you know in a day or two if I want to support you; if I do, I'll make a significant contribution." Everyone shook hands, and the meeting adjourned.

"Silas and I will be gone overnight. Someone's been stealing Raoul's cattle, and I wouldn't say I like it. They're coming through our south gate and then entering his property. This is the second time this has happened. Perhaps some of that chicken salad could go with us."

After changing his clothes, Tommy met Tomas and Silas in the barn. "Who do you think is taking the cattle?" Silas asked. Everything was ready, and the two men made their way to the south gate.

"I suspect it's either a small rancher or a couple of guys trying to make a few dollars. We'll know when we catch up with them. I thought the rustling would stop once the Jensons were apprehended, but that doesn't seem to be the case. I'm pretty sure the Jenson boys took the first thirty cows but not the last five. We'll track whoever it is, and when we catch them, we'll turn them over to the sheriff."

They camped that night on his property. At first light, they were in the saddle and riding through the Los Padres Forest.

The sky was blue, and the air was crisp as they tracked the cows up a short grade, then a steeper one. It was apparent the five cows had come from Raoul's property, through the joint gate, and then into the preserve.

After two hours of tracking the cattle, they could hear them in the distance. When they were close enough to the sound, they tied their horses to some brush, got their Remington's, and walked closer. "Silas, you head toward the large rock to the south; I'll circle the left side. I know this area, and there's a small clearing nearby where the cattle can graze. Please don't take any chances, but I want to take whoever they are alive. No shooting unless we must."

Tommy went to the left, circling toward the rock he pointed out to Silas, who went straight to the rock. Tommy could hear voices when he was within fifty feet of the outcropping. He continued in that direction until he was within twenty feet of the sounds. Then he lay down on the ground and crawled toward the voices. When he saw their clothing, he rose, cocked his rifle, and yelled, "Don't make a move if you want to live. I'm coming in, and I wouldn't advise either of you to go for a gun or try to run."

"I have both of you in my sight, and you better not move," he said. Silas heard the exchange and hurried to the large rock. Soon he could see two young men sitting on a rock.

Tommy entered the clearing first. The two voices he heard belonged to teenagers. "We don't have guns, and we didn't do anything. We found them right here if you're here about the cattle."

Silas had come into the clearing, pointing his rifle at the two boys. He checked to see if they had guns on them or in their bedroll.

"There aren't any guns," Silas said.

"I told you so," one of the youths said.

"Who are you?" Tommy asked.

"I'm Jeb Winthrow, and this is my brother Billy." The taller of the two said.

"Where do you live?" Tommy asked.

"We don't have a home. Our parents are dead, and it's just Billy and me."

"Get the rope, Silas," Tommy told him.

While Silas went to get the rope, the older of the two wet his pants. "We didn't steal the cows. We found them. You got to believe us. Billy and I don't mean any harm."

The younger boy got on his knees when Silas returned with the rope. "Please, mister, let us go. We're hungry and don't have jobs. Take the cows. Don't hang us."

"How old are you?"

"I'm fourteen, and my brother's sixteen; please let us go."

"Why don't you have jobs?"

"Every place we apply says we're too young, but we know cattle, and we can work hard."

"Do you want jobs?"

"Yes, sir."

"Okay, take these cattle back to where you found them, then come to my place. Ask for Tommy Sanchez. I own the spread next to his."

The older boy looked like he was in shock. "You're the famous gunman."

"Well, I don't shoot as many people as I used to, but that would be me."

"Are you going to give us jobs?"

"Yes, and I'm going to feed you as soon as you get these cattle back where they belong."

"Come on, Billy, let's move these cows back. We're going to get jobs."

The boys showed up at four in the afternoon. After they ate what two men would usually have for dinner, they were given bunks and told to report to Tomas in the morning. In between mouthfuls, they kept staring at the guns Tommy set on the table next to them.

CHAPTER 19

*F*our people were having lunch on the patio in the rear when the sheriff and five deputies rode down the entryway. Naomi saw them and made her way to the bunkhouse. She alerted Tomas, who came with ten armed Vaqueros. The six men rode to the front and tied their horses to the hitching post. They ignored Tomas and the Vaqueros.

The sheriff walked up to the front door and knocked. Tommy answered while Sarah, Silas, and Juan waited in the kitchen. "What can I do for you, Sheriff?"

"I have a warrant for the arrest of Silas Smith for the robbery of the Oxnard Train." He handed the warrant to Tommy, who took the warrant.

"You mean he was one of the six robbers?"

"He was the seventh man, the one who joined the group after the robbery and probably masterminded the job," the sheriff responded.

"Why don't we have Juan read this? He works out of the County prosecutor's Office periodically. He'll know if this is valid?"

Tommy called Juan, and his adopted son came to greet the two. He and the sheriff shook hands. "What's up?"

"Why don't you read this document and tell me if it's enforceable?" Tommy asked.

Juan read the short document twice and then looked up at the sheriff. Who is Judge Larkin?"

"He's new."

"Tommy, this warrant is valid and enforceable," Juan responded.

"Sheriff, you and I went to the scene where I found Silas. We didn't find any evidence implicating Silas. Did you find something after I left, or is this just a fishing expedition?" Tommy asked.

"This is no fishing expedition, and I have solid evidence; it was enough for the judge to sign the warrant. This was a courtesy to you that I showed you the warrant. I've come to take Silas with me. Are you going to interfere?"

"No. Silas is in the kitchen. I'll call him."

When Silas and Sarah joined the three men, he asked what was happening. The sheriff handed him the warrant and told him he was under arrest." If you give me your word that you won't resist, I won't put the cuffs on you." Silas gave his word.

"Silas, I'll represent you unless you prefer someone else. As soon as I talk with Tommy, I'll come to Santa Barbara. I'll meet you tomorrow morning at the jail. Don't worry. This may all be just a big misunderstanding."

The three went back into the kitchen after the sheriff left. "I remember you saying that you didn't find anything at the scene where Silas was shot. What could they have that a judge would sign off on?" Juan asked Tommy.

"I made a thorough check of the area. There was nothing."

"Then where else could he have found something?"

I checked his pockets for identification, but I didn't thoroughly check all his clothing. The only other place would be the hospital. When you're in Santa Barbara, why don't you talk with the nurses and doctors who treated Silas?"

"By the way, what are the polls showing?" Sarah asked.

Rodgers has a slim lead over Williams, but Jacob Thunder has a solid third position. He could win with some help", Juan responded.

"Why don't we contribute ten thousand dollars to his campaign? I don't think Silas can afford to have Rodger's win. That man has something against him. I know Rodgers was friendly with Marjorie some time ago. Maybe that's it. It would be more comfortable for Silas and ourselves if someone else was the sheriff", Sarah said.

Tommy smiled. "I'll take care of it."

All the fire had gone out of Frances since she was brought back after almost reaching Santa Barbara. She could've continued by foot, but she'd have to give up her child. She couldn't do that. She wondered if there would ever be another chance to escape. A feeling of acceptance had taken over this fiercely independent woman. Lenny's outward attitude had changed for the better. He no longer lost his temper at the drop of a hat, and she no longer was beaten or forced to do sexual acts that disgusted her. They had sex whether she wanted to, but it usually occurred when they were in bed.

She tried to stay away from Lenny as much as she could. Rising early so that she could avoid him was her norm. He spent most of his days with their increasing herd. It fell upon her and the Indians to take care of the three planted acres. Much of the produce was given to them. Three acres of lettuce, tomatoes, and corn was more than they needed. They could take the crop to the market in Santa Barbara, but Lenny wouldn't let that happen. She had a few dollars Hiram left with her, but that wouldn't last forever. Lenny didn't seem to have any money, so what would they do in the future? She wondered if Lenny was hiding out from the authorities.

She'd just finished feeding the chickens when Lenny came into the barn. She tried to exit through the rear door when she saw him. He grabbed her arm and forced her against the barn wall. Initially, she wanted to ignore him, but he started unbuttoning her blouse with his right hand, and she pushed him away. He laced his fingers in her hair, and she couldn't move. With her blouse unbuttoned in the front, he slipped the straps of her slip off her shoulders and began to rub her left breast. She tried to pull away, but he was too strong, and the hold on her hair made it impossible.

Lenny had a smile on his face as he continued to rub her bare breast. Frances was embarrassed because she was becoming aroused and started to flush. Lenny saw the color in her cheeks, and he leaned forward and kissed her. Usually, she'd turn her face, and his attempt would fail, but today she allowed the kiss on her lips.

When he forced his tongue into her mouth, a feeling of passion arose within her body, and she returned the kiss. Lenny was encouraged and continued undressing her. When she was completely nude, he whispered in her ear, "put your arms around my neck."

She complied, and he lifted her off the ground. He placed both hands under her buttocks and pushed her against the wall. When Frances wrapped her legs around Lenny, he entered her and continued to thrust. There was no doubt that Frances was uncomfortable, and when she moaned, Lenny became more intense, and the couple climaxed together.

Frances still held on to Lenny's neck as he slowly slipped to the barn floor with her on top of him. "Frances, that was fantastic. I hope you act this way every time we have sex."

She didn't know what to say. The man she was on top of had abused her so much that she hated his every touch. How could she act this way with him? She was flushed with passion, something she'd never experienced with her husband, Hiram. "God forgives me; I'm ashamed of myself." She hung her head.

Yet, Frances didn't release her hold on Lenny. When he suggested they enter the cabin, she allowed him to put his arm around her shoulders and hold onto her breast as they walked to the house. When they went inside, he sat down on a straight-back chair and pulled her to him. She sat on his knee and continued to respond to his kisses while he caressed her breasts. When he put his fingers inside her vagina, she spread her legs even further apart and enjoyed the sensation; when she climaxed, she held onto his hand. She knew this was the transition to a husband-and-wife relationship. No longer could she ignore him. No longer could she think of ways to kill him. No longer could she seek avenues of escape. This solo action was a commitment on her part, and she knew it.

They retired as husband and wife, and instead of sleeping with her back to Lenny, she lay in his arms with his hands on her breasts. When she awoke, he wasn't in bed with her. She panicked and rushed into the kitchen. Lenny sat in the rocker, holding his son while humming a lullaby. Two months later, Frances knew she was pregnant again, and this time, she shared the news with Lenny. "I hope we have four kids, and they're all boys." He laughed.

CHAPTER 20

*I*t was a warm, sunny day when Frances gave birth to a seven- pound boy who she and Lenny named James, after her father. She relented and allowed the first boy to be named after Lenny and thereby reducing some of the friction between them. The Indian woman assisted in the birth; Lenny sat outside smoking a cigar. Every once in a while, he came into the room where the birthing was taking place to be sure everything was okay.

Frances was up and around in two days and started making Lenny's breakfast again. She wanted to talk to him, so she joined him at the table. "Lenny, we have to start looking to the future if you're going to be part of this family."

"What are you talking about? Of course, I'm going to be part of my family."

"Then what do you suggest we do for money? These babies need clothes and playthings. There isn't any money to buy things for them unless you have some. You don't have a job, and what produce we grow, we give away to the Indians."

Lenny was reluctant to tell her about the money he buried; that was his getaway money. Santa Barbara was too close to the robbery site for him to start passing some of that money around. He didn't think the Pinkertons had given up on the seventh man yet, and he wasn't about to find out. And the easiest way to make that happen would be to spend the loot in this area. "We can sell some

produce and cattle. Later, we can add another three to five acres and plant more crops. The Indians can help."
"But my question is the same. What are we going to do for money?"

"I'll get some. Give me a list of the supplies we need, and I'll fill up the wagon with our extra produce and take two cows. We can spare two out of thirty head of cattle. Let me see what the market is like; then, we can discuss what we should do after I get back. "You aren't going to try to leave again, are you?"

"No. I'll be here when you return."

Juan made his way to the hospital by noon the next day and spoke with the doctor who operated on Silas. He couldn't answer Juan's questions about the sheriff's investigation. He recommended that Juan talk to the nurse who oversaw his treatment. She was at lunch, but he found her at the nurse's station after she returned. "I'm Juan Sanchez, the attorney for Mr. Silas Smith, who you treated at this hospital this past year. Mr. Smith has been arrested for Train Robbery and is in the Santa Barbara jail. Did Mr. Smith leave anything here when he was released from the hospital; did you turn anything over to the sheriff?"

"I did, but I don't know how much I can tell you. I met with Sheriff Rodgers last week, and he told me to keep everything we discussed between us. I had him sign for the items and give the receipt to the hospital administrator. I want to help, but I don't want to get in trouble. I was doing my civic duty. Other than that, you'll have to talk to the sheriff."

Juan was being stonewalled, and he was angry. "Do you realize my family is a member of this hospital's board, and we contribute annually to its budget?"

The nurse started to cry. "I don't know what to do. I don't want to lose my job, but the sheriff was adamant about me not telling anyone what I found. "

Juan was no dummy. He knew the sheriff was playing hardball and wouldn't give him the time of day. He didn't want to badger the nurse and didn't want her to lose her job. Instead, he walked over to the county prosecutor's office and asked to speak to Jim Briger, whom he knew well. "I know why you're here, Juan." The prosecutor got up and shook Juan's hand as he entered his office.

They sat down, and Briger offered Juan coffee, which he accepted. "You weren't here for the arraignment this morning, so, out of courtesy, I postponed it until tomorrow. I know you want to talk to your client beforehand."

Briger opened up a desk drawer and removed some papers from a file. "When Smith was treated at the hospital after Mr. Sanchez brought him there, a nurse undressed him to prepare for surgery. Inside both boots was some money, well actually, currency. On the surface, that doesn't seem unusual. You go hunting, and you put some money in your boot."

When the sheriff visited the hospital after he returned from the trip with your father, he asked the nurse if Smith had left anything behind from his hospital stay. At first, Nurse Hoover said she didn't remember finding anything, but she'd look in a storage room where they kept things that patients left behind. She returned with an envelope. It contained the money found in Smith's boots.

The nurse said she would give it to the hospital administrator to send to Smith. The sheriff asked her if he could give it to Smith. She saw nothing wrong with that since the sheriff signed for the money.

The sheriff is a cagey old fox who sensed for some time that Smith was involved in the Oxnard Train Robbery. He checked the currency the nurse gave him against the list of bills the express messenger had. They matched."

Juan was stunned. "How can this be?"

"Well, you have a man who says he can't remember who he is, found within a few miles where a known member of the Oxnard gang is found dead. Your stepfather tracked the horse someone was riding from where the man was found dead to Silas' campsite. Subsequently, we learn that he left behind some of the train currency in the hospital that treated him. It all adds up to me. I won't tell you I have an open and shut case, but I have one a jury will believe."

"How much money was left at the hospital?"

"Five dollars."

"You can't be serious. Five dollars out of eight thousand doesn't sound like a major clue."

"Maybe not to you, but there's a chance some of the remaining money may turn up."

"Where's the rest of the money if he stole it."

"The sheriff has a search warrant for your stepfather's ranch. I tried to talk him out of it, but he's hell-bent, and Judge Larkin signed it. Is there bad blood between Tommy and Rodgers?"

"If there wasn't before, there will be now. Who do you think hid the money, Smith or my stepfather?"

"I'm positive that Tommy Sanchez is not involved in anything other than being a good Samaritan, but I can't say what the sheriff thinks. If I were your stepfather, I'd watch my back."

I'm going over to see Silas. I appreciate this information, Jim. I'll see you at the preliminary hearing tomorrow. Why don't you do the sheriff a favor and have him skip the search of Tommy's ranch."

The sheriff was being his usual disagreeable self. He made Juan wait an hour before he let him in to see Silas. Other than the loss of sleep, Smith had no complaints. He wanted out of jail as soon as possible, though. "We have to wait for the preliminary hearing tomorrow morning. That's when the judge will set bail. I have a series of drafts, up to one hundred thousand dollars, drawn on the Commercial Bank in town. Tommy is not going to let you down. Don't worry about my fee. My stepfather will pay for that. Our main concern is to clear your name."

"That sheriff seems to be taking this personally."

"He may be. He's upset with Tommy. He might be taking it out on you to get even with him. And then there's Marjorie Hawkins. The sheriff escorted her around town for six months before you showed up."

"She told me."

"Silas, tell me about the money you had on your person when Tommy found you."

"This is the first I've heard about it. I don't know anything about the robbery. Perhaps whoever shot me put the money on me to take the pressure off himself."

"That's how we'll play it. Leave everything to me. I'll try to get you released tomorrow. Let's meet at the courthouse tomorrow at 9."

Linda De L'Ortega had been seeing Juan for two years and was anxious for him to make his intentions known. Her father was worried that she'd become pregnant and that there would be a family scandal. Her mother was tired of answering her friend's questions about the relationship. The family had gotten over the embarrassment that Juan was half Sioux and had been in trouble with the law when he was young. However, he was now one of the preeminent attorneys in this area and more than capable of supporting a wife. Although the legend surrounding his stepfather and mother was significant, the L'Ortegas steered clear of any comment on Juan's parents.

Over the past year, Juan was a frequent dinner guest at the De L'Ortega house. Tonight was a celebration of her parent's wedding anniversary. There were only a dozen guests, mostly friends of the older couple, with one exception. They were hosting a distant cousin named Hernando Guitterez from Mexico City. Mr. Guitterez was the owner of a company that specialized in selling wine and its byproducts. Juan had met him once when Guitterez came to the valley to meet with Tommy Sanchez.

Linda's parents were anxious to learn about the trial like anyone else. Juan was going to represent the seventh train robber apprehended by the sheriff.

After many inquiries from everyone at the dinner table, Juan told them he couldn't comment on any evidence. He just said Silas Smith was innocent, and the seventh man was still free.

"Didn't they find some of the holdup money in his clothes?" Guitterez asked.

"Five dollars of the missing eight thousand was found in his boot. We believe it was put on him by the real seventh man who shot him in the back and left him for dead."

Guitterez appeared to be forcing the issue when he asked Juan, "Didn't your stepfather find your client? It would only seem natural that he would look in Smith's pockets to see if there was any identification."

"My stepfather was more interested in getting Mr. Smith to the hospital as soon as possible."

"But there are eight thousand dollars still missing. No matter how rich you are, that's sum would be very tempting", Guitterez countered.

"Sir, I don't care for your implication. My stepfather is an honorable man, and his reputation is beyond reproach. Besides, one-third of the stolen money was his. I expect an apology."

"Oh, I was making conversation. I apologize if I've caused you any embarrassment."

Juan was slightly flustered and wondered why the house guest was forcing the issue. "It isn't that I'm deliberately being evasive, but this conversation is more appropriate in a trial." Juan smiled at Guitterez.

After dinner, the guests departed, and the family and their house guest excused themselves, allowing Linda and Juan to have the parlor. "Before dinner, Papa asked me when we would let him make the announcement?"

"I know this is hard on you, but my caseload is such that I can't get away."

"That's the excuse that I've been using with my parents. It's getting old, and they're not buying it. They think you are dallying with me. Your caseload will never decrease because you're a victim of your success. I think you have to put your priorities in order. What do you say, my love?" She turned toward him with a smile and a hand on his arm.

"There was a silence that seemed like an eternity before Juan cleared his throat and got down on one knee.

Linda De L'Ortega, I love you very much; will you marry me?"

"See, that wasn't so hard. I accept, conditioned on you setting a date.

"I believe the Smith trial will be completed in six months. Any time two weeks after that date will work for me. What about you?"

"I will talk with my mother and father and see what date is convenient for them. I would love to be married on your parent's ranch. Do you think they'll agree to that?"

"Tommy may be a little obstinate, but my mother will say yes."

"They have you sleeping in the guest house tonight. They want to keep you far away from me until you propose. I'll wait an hour and join you there. What do you say?"

"Wow."

Hernando Guitterez was listening to their conversation. If he were to win the hand of the beautiful and rich Ms. De L'Ortega, he'd have to keep the pressure on Juan Sanchez and his family.

Linda was careful to wait until her parent's bedroom light went out before she ventured outside, down a walk, and through their botanical garden. She knocked lightly on the guest house door. Juan opened the door, and Linda quickly entered and told him to turn out the lights.

They'd been intimate for a year, and it was a wonder Linda wasn't with family by now. They celebrated their unofficial engagement, and Linda returned to her room around four in the morning with a smile. She didn't see Guitterez hiding in the garden as she left her lover.

Guitterez was angry. He had to come up with a plan that would discredit Juan Sanchez and allow him to take Juan's place. He wondered where he was most vulnerable. Perhaps his early years would shed some information that Hernando could use, and then there was his mother, an Indian squaw. Maybe the De L'Ortegas hadn't thought about who their daughter's in-laws would be. He smiled as he let himself into his room and thought all was not lost yet.

The following day, Juan and Silas met for an hour before the hearing and went before Judge Larkin, who'd signed Silas' arrest warrant. The sheriff and county prosecutor were present. Mr. Briger presented a straightforward case and asked that Silas be held without bail until trial. The judge only asked, "Where is the rest of the money?"

Briger responded quickly. "We haven't found it yet, judge."

When it was Juan's turn, he said he was shocked that the court would deny bail over a robbery. "Remember, judge, only five dollars was found on my client. He could have found that in the street. Silas Smith isn't my client's real name; it's one my parents gave him because he had amnesia. Someone shot him in the back, and he was left for dead for almost a day. It's also possible the person who shot him planted the money on Silas to confuse law enforcement. The only evidence against my client is five dollars out of a thirty-thousand-dollar robbery. They claim it was found in his boots at the hospital where he was operated on. The nurse didn't even remember the money existed until the sheriff visited her. I also note that the chain of custody over the money has been broken. Anyone could have access to it. I ask for bail of ten thousand dollars, your Honor."

"What's this about chain of custody?" the judge asked.

"It was held in an envelope in a storage room at the hospital for over a year. The room wasn't locked. Anyone could have access to its contents", Juan replied before Briger could speak.

"Trial is set for three months from today, and bail will be ten thousand dollars. Do you have the money with you, councilor?"

"Yes, your Honor. I have a draft for that exact amount."

"Court is adjourned, and as soon as bail is posted, the defendant is released."

CHAPTER 21

The ride over the pass was time-consuming, and he wished he hadn't pushed this issue. He knew he had made a wrong decision to initiate a search of Tommy Sanchez's property for the stolen money. Still, he made an even bigger one when he decided to perform the investigation himself.

Being sheriff was his whole life. His wife was dead, and his two boys moved away to Alabama and weren't inclined to visit. He didn't know what he'd do if he lost the election. One thing is for sure; he'd have to move away. Santa Barbara had become more expensive, and the meager pension the county would give him wouldn't pay for his cigars.

He and six deputies left early so they'd have time to return the same day. The hospitality Sanchez' showed in the past wouldn't be forthcoming this time. That didn't bother him so much; the election was on his mind. He thought he'd be a shoo-in for retaining the position he'd held for twenty years. He should've known that the voters were fickle and could be easily swayed. The Indian, Jacob Thunder, was gaining ground daily. If something didn't happen soon, he'd overtake the sheriff.

The rumor was that Sarah Sanchez had donated ten thousand dollars to the Thunder campaign. If Thunder needed more, she'd probably donate more. They arrived around noon and were greeted by Tommy, Sarah, and Juan. Silas had been sent to the south end of the ranch to check the gates. Off to his left was Tomas, the new foreman, and eight armed Vaqueros. The word had gotten out that he was coming.

Tommy and Sarah didn't say anything. It was Juan who asked what the purpose of the visit was, and when Rodgers told him, Juan asked for the search warrant.

After reading the document, Juan said, "We'll comply with all aspects of this warrant. However, one of our Vaqueros will accompany each of your men during the search."

Rodgers was angry. "I won't allow that."

Juan was smiling. "Show me someplace in the warrant where it says we can't. No, this is a way to be sure there are no surprises. We'll make everything available; we're just going along to be sure there aren't any. If that's not acceptable, then you can leave. I'll be present when this warrant is applied for again."

The sheriff's face was red. "Are you suggesting I would plant evidence?"

"It wasn't me that gave his word to Tommy Sanchez that he would get off Silas Smith's back if they didn't find evidence to convict when they visited those two campsites."

Rodgers knew he couldn't arrest Juan for his comments, even though he was embarrassed in front of his deputies, and that he wouldn't find anything significant over this large ranch. He just wanted to tell Tommy Sanchez that he wasn't above the law as long as Jack Rodgers was on the job. Although he had six deputies, he wasn't against Tommy Sanchez, so he agreed. He and his deputies, followed by seven Vaqueros, searched the ranch. They started with Silas Smith's room, the barn, and the bunkhouse. As much as he wanted to, he wasn't going into the Sanchez house.

Four hours later, the sheriff concluded the search while Tommy and his family sat in the kitchen and monitored what was happening. The only thing of significance that occurred during the investigation was a picture of Silas and Marjorie falling from a table next to his bed, and the glass in the frame was broken.

Sarah went out on the front porch and watched as Rodgers and his deputies departed the ranch. When she came back into the kitchen, she asked. "He didn't even say goodbye. Do you think that's the last we'll see of the sheriff?"

"This was just a petty trick to get in your faces. He'll realize it backfired on him and won't try anything like this again unless he has you stone cold, and then watch out", Juan said.

Tomas reported to Tommy in the kitchen and verified what had happened. "Put ten Vaqueros on alert tonight in case we have some unannounced visitors. I also want one of the Vaqueros who wasn't part of the search to track the sheriff and his deputies back as far as the pass. Have the Vaquero stay far enough behind so they don't know he's following."

Rodgers was no fool. He knew that Sanchez would be on alert if they came back tonight. And it wouldn't surprise the sheriff that someone was watching to be sure he and the deputies were headed home. The trial would start in less than ninety days, and the election in one hundred twenty. A conviction of Smith would increase his chance of reelection. He had to find something else that directly implicated Smith.

Although Marjorie Hawkins was anxious to go forward with the wedding, Silas wouldn't hear of it. "My name has been smeared; it must be cleared before I can look people in the eye. If it's okay with Tommy, I'll work at his ranch until I'm acquitted. Then we'll marry."

He returned home with most of the supplies Frances said they needed, but Lenny knew they couldn't exist this way. The cows were sold for twenty-five dollars each, and the produce for pennies. "Our herd isn't big enough, and the surplus produce is too small. You're right; we have to do something. It'll be lean for us until we build the herd bigger and plant more crops", Lenny told her at dinner that night.

"You could escape with the money you hid and escape from under this."

"What money?"

"I don't know what money, but I know you're hiding out from something and probably hid the money you stole."

"You don't know nothing."

"I know you, Lenny. You want to leave, yet you want to stay. Despite everything, you like our children, and you even like me."

There was no doubt in Lenny's mind that she was correct. He'd always taken the easy way out. This might be the right time to leave. The problem was he had a family he wanted to be part of for the first time in his life, and he was scared. "I want to stay with you and our children, but I don't know what to do?"

"I do. I have some money that Hiram left me at a bank in Santa Barbara. James needs nursing for a few more months before I can go and get it. We'll be okay until then."

"You had money all this time, and you didn't say anything. You could have left me. Why didn't you?"

"I couldn't figure out how to escape other than that one time. Now I don't want to." She flushed when she said that.

CHAPTER 22

*T*he election for Santa Barbara County Sheriff was heating up. The two leading candidates for the position, Jack Rodgers, the incumbent, and Jacob Thunder, his opposition, were everywhere, actively raising money. The sheriff has come to Santa Ynez for a speech this Saturday at 2 o'clock; Thunder would arrive the following week. Tables and chairs for the speaker were set up on the front porch of the thirty-room Central Hotel. Before the debate, attendees mingled in the large courtyard surrounding the hotel. There was a spirited turnout to hear the twenty-year veteran, and after his presentation, he fielded questions from the crowd.

Most of the questions were essential for his position, but near the end of the questioning, one of the voters asked the sheriff if he had ever thought that Tommy Sanchez was behind the jailbreak of the Sioux Brave, who was convicted of murder. Instead of fielding the question as a typical politician would, he said that the only involvement of Sanchez and his wife that he could prove was that they employed the killer's two brothers at their ranch in Santa Ynez for six months before the jailbreak. The two brothers had broken their brother out of jail and left the area on horses belonging to Tommy Sanchez.

Sarah Sanchez was one of those sitting on the hotel porch, listening to the sheriff. She couldn't believe what Rodgers implied. It was tantamount to an accusation. She knew better but couldn't control herself and stood up. "What you're implying is a downright lie.

My husband has given much of his free time to helping this community.

You've called upon him several times yourself when you couldn't control the crime in this area. Most recently, it was he, my son, and one of our employees who captured the Jenson gang who were robbing supply wagons and rustling cattle. You ought to be ashamed of yourself."

The sheriff could only say, "I'll stand behind my comments."

Sarah knew she'd gone too far, but she was angry. "I plan to contribute more funds to Jacob Thunder's campaign. Anyone who hasn't met Mr. Thunder yet should come back next week and hear him speak." It was as though a loud murmur had blown through the crowd. The sheriff didn't respond.

The political rally wasn't the main reason Sarah and Naomi were in Santa Ynez. In her own right, Sarah was an accomplished Native Artist. She took up charcoal sketching when she was a captive of the Sioux and gradually progressed to painting with oils. Before she met Tommy, she had several exhibitions in San Francisco where she sold her paintings.

She was treated like a slave by the tribe who captured her. She slept outdoors at night, as close to the embers as she could. She needed to keep the fire going to survive. She initially used charcoal to send messages to some trappers who traded with the tribe. When she was forced to marry Crazy Horse, the Indian Hero of the battle of the Little Big Horn, she developed her artistic skills even further. There was a time when selling her paintings to white visitors at the reservation was the War Chief's and her only income.

Her forte was oil sketching, mainly of Native Americans and their villages. Since she and her husband were early investors in the hotel, she used the lobby to display her works for weekend exhibits twice a year. It had been a productive morning and early afternoon; she sold four paintings. She hoped that tomorrow would be just as successful. The paintings that hadn't sold would be on display in the hotel lobby for the rest of the day and evening.

Tomas had some supplies to pick up, but most of the time, he sat waiting on Naomi and Sarah in the lobby. Around three o'clock, he drove them back to the ranch. Her husband was waiting to hear how the sales went. As Tomas helped her down from the carriage, Tommy gave her a glass of Chardonnay they had bottled last year and kissed her. "I don't know which I prefer more, the kiss or the wine. The kiss will last longer." Sarah smiled.

"Tell me about your day?" He asked.

First, she told him about the sales, and he rewarded her with another kiss and refilled her glass. When she told him about the sheriff's remarks, Tommy was angry. When she told him what her response was, he couldn't help but grin. "Good for you. From everything I've been told, he will lose the election. The only thing that could save him would be a Silas conviction."

Two Vaqueros were breaking a couple of green horses around noon the next day when Naomi handed

Tommy a wire from Sarah. She'd left with Tomas for the Central Hotel early that morning. "Paintings vandalized; come to the hotel."

A Vaquero saddled up his horse, put a Remington in the sheath, and off Tommy went to the hotel. Sarah was with the Hotel Manager when her husband arrived. All her paintings on display had been slashed with a knife; nothing was salvageable.

"Tommy glared at the manager. "Don't you have someone on duty all night?

"Yes, sir, but the night clerk had to attend to an incident in the kitchen at about eleven o'clock. He left the front desk unoccupied for about half an hour. When he returned, he saw the damage and sent one of the clean-up crew to get me. I tried to determine if anyone saw anything. I even went to Joe's saloon. I'm sorry, Mr. Sanchez. Those were beautiful paintings; it's a shame.

Tommy took his time before he spoke. "You seem like a competent individual. How many people did you recognize at Joe's?"

"Oh, I don't know if I want to get involved, Mr. Sanchez?"

"You're involved already. I want the names of the people you saw."

He tried to look away, but he kept returning to the medium-sized man in the black hat whose steel gray eyes penetrated his soul. I know several by sight, but I don't know their names."

"Give me the names of the ones you do."

"I remember these three; Harry Vance, Leroy Strait, and Jonny Gomez."

"Now give me the descriptions of the ones whose names you don't know."

"There was a tall guy with a tattoo on his right hand and a short man with a red checkered shirt. They are the only others I remember seeing there."

"Sarah, you wait here; I won't be long, but I'm going to find out who did this."

"Are you taking your guns?"

"Yes."

Tommy went to his horse tied to the railing and took out the revolver he always carried in his saddle bag. Tomas had come out the front door of the hotel by then. He handed the Remington to Tomas. "Go in the back door of Joe's saloon, don't let anyone out, and watch my back. We're going to find out who did this."

He waited a few minutes for Tomas to get in place, then strolled across the street. Anyone in that saloon that morning had to know trouble was on the way. The most lethal man in this county was coming over. Most in the bar the previous night knew why he was coming.

Tommy stopped outside the saloon and looked over the cafe doors to see who was inside.

He made his way through the doors and spied the bartender, who was about to pour whiskey for a patron but stopped with the bottle still in his hand when Tommy spoke. He saw Tomas and about ten other patrons; five were at the bar to his left. The others were sitting at a round table directly in front of him. Silence fell over the twenty by a thirty-foot room with a pot-bellied stove near the corner and six tables with chairs in the center.

"Is Harry Vance, Leroy Strait, or Jonny Gomez here?"

Again, there was silence, but two of the guys at the bar looked at one of the men sitting next to them. Tommy asked him what his name was.

"I'm Jonny Gomez, but I didn't see anything."

"We'll see. I want you to put your gun on the bar and sit right where you are until I say it's okay." Gomez did as he was told.

"What about Strait and Vance?"

"They're not here," the bartender said.

"If you're lying, I'll visit you at night when you're at home."

Vance lit out of here when he saw you walk across the street", the bartender said.

"Where does he live?"

"He has a room in the back of the livery stable on Sagunto Street."

"What about Strait?"

"He hasn't been in here today."

Tommy took his time and carefully walked around the room, looking at   everyone. A short guy with a red checkered shirt was alone at one of the tables.

"Are you packing?" Tommy asked while staring at the man.

"No, sir. I don't carry."

"Come over here."

"Why, I don't know anything."

"Well, find out. What's your name?" "Jon Smith."

"Well, Mr. Smith, I want you and Gomez to walk to the back door and step into the alley."

"Isn't anyone going to help us?" Gomez asked.

When there was no answer to his plea, he hung his head and started toward the back door. While Smith and Gomez were walking to the back door, Tommy turned and faced the other patrons. "If you hear some shooting, I wouldn't come out to see what's happening. You might get in the line of fire."

There was a feed warehouse behind the saloon with multiple bales of hay stacked against the wall of that building. Tommy asked Tomas to bring his equipment from the wagon Sarah used that morning. Tomas returned a few minutes later with a bow and about twelve arrows in a quiver. "I want you two to lean up against those bales behind you. "I'm going to ask you both the same question. Who slashed my wife's paintings? When I get the right answer, you can go."

He adjusted the string and bent the bow several times to determine its flexibility. The two men leaning against the bales all this time watched him intently. Tommy put an arrow on the bow and let it slip; it flew down the alley.

The two saw this and stated firmly that they didn't know anything. Tommy fired the next arrow at Gomez, which came within inches of his head. The third arrow flew at Smith and nicked his long hair. When Tommy fired the next arrow, which grazed Gomez's cheek, he yelled out, "It was Larry Vance, Joe Frazier, and Bill Tullis that slashed the paintings. They paid the night clerk to look the other way."

"Where do they live?"

Gomez gave Tomas their address. All four walked back to the hotel and met with the hotel manager. Gomez repeated what he told Tommy. The night clerk's shift was over, and he'd gone home. The manager had his secretary write up Gomez and Smith's statements; both men signed them.

The following day, Tomas took a copy of their statements, along with the addresses of the three implicated in the vandalism, plus that of the night clerk, and took it to the sheriff in Santa Barbara. He wasn't very friendly, but he took the information and said he'd arrest them.

This wasn't the first time the Sanchez family had been subject to vandalism and discrimination. His two children and Naiwa's two children had been victims of intense hatred toward minorities. Tommy had fought against it and, at least for a while, put a stop to it. He worried that his children would have to go through that experience again.

CHAPTER 23

*T*ommy drove the buckboard home with Sarah and Naomi. Tomas had taken his employer's horse to Santa Barbara to deliver the statements to the sheriff. When Tommy told Sarah who did the vandalism, she was surprised. "Larry Vance's wife was ill last year, and I brought her soup and groceries so she, the little ones, and her husband wouldn't go hungry. Larry had gotten hurt and lost his job."

Sarah wasn't finished. "We seem to have experienced this situation years ago. I remember when the children were repeatedly harassed in school, and we had to work hard to end it. Let's hope it doesn't flare up again. We've been lucky. Our two children look white but Naiwa's look like Sioux. I don't think I could bear it if they again became the target of discrimination. The last time was unbearable." A tear formed in Sarah's eye.

When they pulled up in front of their house, an old friend was sitting on the porch, enjoying a glass of their red wine. "You're a sight for sore eyes." Sarah was smiling as she greeted their friend.

"James Jefferson of the Pinkerton Agency at your service, my lady." He reached up, helped her down from the carriage, and then shook Tommy's hand.

"Can you stay for a few days?" Sarah asked.

Jefferson was a friend of Tommy Sanchez, but he was a friend of Sarah's first. He'd helped her soon after her husband, Crazy Horse died. Juan couldn't adjust to being a half-breed, living on an Army Post.

The young soldiers were constantly ridiculing him. When he retaliated, the provost marshal would put him in jail for one or two nights.

He left the post, joined a renegade gang, and became a nuisance to the area. The team didn't kill anyone or commit any major robberies, but they'd steal food, whiskey, and an occasional horse. Jefferson caught Juan once and turned him over to his mother, but he ran away and rejoined the gang.

When Tommy and Sarah decided to marry, she told him about her son and how she wanted to see if he could be reformed. Tommy and Jefferson tracked the boy and his gang to a bar in New Mexico. Some of the team decided to test Tommy Sanchez, and he shot their guns out of their hands. Juan was impressed enough to talk to Tommy. After several months with his mother, Juan decided to see if he could change.

From then on, Juan became responsible, went back to school, and studied   for the bar. Tommy adopted him and gave Juan his name.

"Where is the boy? I want to say hello to him."

"He's no longer a boy. He's a grown man and a prominent attorney here in Santa Ynez. He hasn't been around lately because he's got a client arrested for the Oxnard Train Robbery. That, and a fiancé in Santa Barbara, keep him busy", Sarah said.

"That's why I'm here. I want to know everything about Silas Smith, the money they found on him, and why they think he's the seventh man?"

"Why not talk to the man, see what he has to say? I'll get him. You can have a guest room in the house. Supper will be in an hour." Tommy walked out to the barn to find Silas.

"Raoul, Naiwa, and the children joined the family for dinner. Usually, it was just Naomi, Silas, and their two children, and they'd eat in the breakfast nook. Tonight, they sat at the big table, which seated twelve. Silas was quiet most of the dinner; his appetite wasn't much. The pending trial was like an albatross around his neck.

When the children went to bed, and Naiwa's family left, Sarah and Naomi cleaned up the dishes.

The three men went to Tommy's office and had cigars and brandy. That seemed to loosen Silas' tongue.

Jefferson sat in the chair with the ottoman. He leaned back and put his feet up. "I want you to know that I'm a friend to Tommy, Sarah, and Juan. I won't do or say anything tonight that would make them uncomfortable. I'm here about the money. The Pinkertons have tasked me to find the remaining money and trace it from its origin through all the arrests to the present time. So that you know, I don't believe you're the seventh man and will testify to that at your trial. I've talked to the sheriff, but I'm not moved by anything he said."

Silas was stunned, and it was as though a balloon had burst, and all the air had dissipated. "Why do you say that?"

"Let's say the seventh man is still alive, and it's not you. Let's set him aside for now. Three of the bandits were captured by Tommy; one died in the shootout. The two who survived were hung for their part in ambushing Sheriff Gray. We accounted for their shares. Another was killed, and his body was found. That leaves two of the original six alive, and both serve thirty years in jail. I don't understand why they didn't charge you with the murder of Richards if you're the seventh man.

Tommy smiled. "Good point, Jim."

"I met with the Hitchen Brothers in Missouri and discussed their part in the robbery. They told me the brains behind the holdup were neither Butch nor the Sundance Kid but a drifter named Lenny Harris. I asked them for a description of Harris, and they both said he was about five foot ten, one hundred sixty pounds, and nearly thirty years old."

Silas shifted in his seat. "Did you tell the sheriff this?"

"Yes. He said it wasn't true. He said the Hitchen Brothers just told me that to throw us off the trail."

"Pinkertons have access to a lot of information, and we can talk to law enforcement personnel, so we decided to check up on Harris. He was a known drifter in the Oxnard and Venture area.

His specialty was to waylay a traveler, rob him, and then get drunk and blow his money. He liked to play poker on Saturday nights at a saloon in Ventura, but he wasn't fortunate. The description Hitchens gave us was the same one the bartender at that saloon in Ventura gave me."

"How he found out about the special train carrying all that money is a mystery. Hitchens said that Harris was a friend of Sundance. He introduced Harris to Butch. It was Cassidy who funded the robbery and provided the men. Harris paid Butch and Sundance $2,500 off the top, and the gang split the rest seven ways. This is consistent with what Snake Eyes said before they hung him. Each of the four we apprehended said it was an even split; each got slightly less than four thousand, making the total from the train robbery about $30,000."

"Why can't we get the brothers down here to testify for me?"

"That's not going to happen. The prosecutor will say that the Hitchen Brothers would try to escape or that they'd expect you to give them a big chunk of money for their testimony. Tommy and I are the best witnesses you will get.

"What has happened to Jack Rodgers? He used to be a straight shooter, but what I'm hearing is that he's now a man that's manipulating the evidence." Jefferson continued.

"What's your plan for the next few days?" Tommy asked Jefferson.

"I plan to head down to Ventura, see if I can get a picture of Harris from some of my acquaintances, and then dig up as much background on him as possible. If I can get that picture, I intend to take a police artist to interview the Hitchen Brothers. I want them to describe Harris to the artist. The next step is to compare the artist's rendition to the photo, but my real job is to find the remainder of the money."

Two weeks had passed since Tomas delivered the names of the vandals of his wife's paintings to the sheriff, but nothing had been done. Tommy decided to help law enforcement. He had a letter drawn up for the four who Jonny Gomez had identified. The letters were delivered by one of his Vaqueros.

The letter named the three as the ones who destroyed Sarah's paintings and the night clerk who accepted money to look the other way. It stated that they had five days to turn themselves over to the sheriff and confess.

Five nights later, after none of the four had turned themselves in, a flaming arrow hit the front door of the Vance residence. The flame took some time to burn out, leaving a metal arrow and a burnt circle in the door. The next night the same thing happened at the Frazier home; the next night, Tullis received his flaming message, and the following night the clerk was visited. The four men met the following day to decide what to do. "He wants us to turn ourselves in. I'm not going to do it. Why don't we turn the tables and do it to his house," Tullis?

"Wait a minute. That may be just what he wants; then he can shoot us for trespassing", Frazier responded.

"I say we do nothing. I'm not afraid of an arrow. What else can he do?" Vance, the ring leader of the group, responded.

"How did we get ourselves into this mess?" Frazier asked.

"We were drinking, and it seemed funny at the time," Vance responded.

Two days later, Vance and Frazier exited Joe's saloon at eleven o'clock at night. They were walking across the main square when a flaming arrow landed at their feet. Frazier ran up the alley behind the hotel while Vance ran down the street toward the Chumash Village. An arrow flew over his head, and another landed at his feet. As he continued to run past the village, he stumbled. A flaming arrow landed at his feet. "Okay, I'll turn myself into the sheriff tomorrow."

Out of a connecting alley, a black rider on a black stallion with a flaming lance raced toward Frazier, who looked back and stumbled, landing on his stomach. The rider stopped next to Frazier and threw the flaming lance between Frazier's legs.

Frazier thought he had escaped and doubled back to where his horse was hitched. The fallen man screamed for help, and when none was forthcoming, he yelled at the rider that he would turn himself in tomorrow.

Later, someone knocked on the Tullis's door; the family was asleep. When the father opened the door, the smoke from the flaming arrow at his door made him cough, and tears came to his eyes. He slammed the door shut and looked out the window. There was a flaming dummy hanging from the tree in his front yard. He vowed that he would turn himself in tomorrow.

The night clerk had been fired; the money he received from the other three had been spent. He decided to leave Santa Ynez and look for work in Lompoc. Around midnight, he was five miles from his destination and decided to stop along the road. He'd brought a bedroll and found a spot under a Sycamore tree where he could spend the night. Around two in the morning, he was visited by a rider dressed in black, riding a black stallion, and carrying a flaming lance. He rose quickly and ran through a field next to the Sycamore tree, but he stumbled over a gopher hole and fell on his face.

The rider took the burning lance and threw it right beside him, and he screamed out that he'd confess to the sheriff.

At two o'clock the next day, the three men confessed to Sheriff Rodgers that they vandalized Sarah Sanchez's paintings, valued at seven thousand dollars, and the night clerk said he'd been paid by the three to find something to do while they were at it. The sheriff wanted to know why they were confessing, so he asked them, "Did anyone intimidate you into confessing?"

The four looked at each other and answered in unison, "No."

The sheriff wasn't finished. "Did Tommy Sanchez or any of his employees threaten you?"

"We never saw Sanchez or any of his employees. It was a rider on a black horse who threw the burning lance at us and told us to confess."

"I'm going to notify the county prosecutor. He'll inform you when your trial is. Until then, you're released. I'd stay away from anything related to Tommy Sanchez."

CHAPTER 24

*N*o sooner had James Jefferson left for Ventura to check on Lenny Harris than a close relative came to call. Sarah hadn't seen her brother in nearly five years. Their relationship growing up was strong, but after being captured by the Sioux who killed their parents, a wedge developed between them.

Her brother, James Hansen, had been rescued early from his captivity. But Sarah was initially mistreated by her captors, then adopted by an Indian Couple, and subsequently forced into a marriage with one of the Indian Chiefs. By the time she could've been rescued, she was a widow who constantly faced a life of starvation with two children to support. He was not forthcoming when she reached out to her brother for help. He was ashamed of her. When his conscience finally got the best of him, he transferred part of her inheritance from their parent's estate. However, this recognition was offset by keeping Sarah at arm's length because of her marriage to an Indian. To say that he was embarrassed that she was related to him was an understatement. James had become a snob.

Years later, when her brother suffered from a bad marriage and loss of his assets, Sarah and Tommy Sanchez came to his rescue. James was forced to run up substantial debts, seeking relief in the courts after his wife and her brother had conspired to steal his assets. Sarah paid off his debts, and Tommy forced his in- laws to transfer his assets back to him. Since that time, James has been absent from her life. He'd only made a feeble attempt at maintaining contact, and he never reached out to his niece and nephew. They were like strangers to him.

When Sarah saw the man get out of a wagon and walk up to their front porch, she didn't know who it was. It wasn't until he called her name that she realized it was her brother. James' face was bloated, his eyes were bloodshot, and he was at least forty pounds overweight. She didn't hesitate but threw her arms around his neck and kissed him on the cheek. She asked Tomas to get his baggage and then escorted him into her home and to the kitchen, where Tommy was sitting, having a cup of coffee.

Tommy got up and shook James' hand. He immediately noted the bloated face and sensed that James had been drinking. When Sarah offered him some coffee, he asked if they had anything more substantial. Since they had an active vineyard at Rancho Del Prado, they were more than willing to share their wines with family members and guests. The reunion lasted until midnight. Sarah   suggested they all go to bed and meet tomorrow for breakfast. "The children will be very excited to meet their uncle," Sarah said as she led James to the guest room.

Over the next few days, it became apparent that her brother had a severe drinking problem and probably needed some counseling. Sarah tried to approach the subject with James delicately, but he got angry and said he didn't have a problem. Tommy decided to try his hand at helping James and invited him, Juan, and Silas to go fishing at their pond in the southern part of their ranch.

They planned to stay overnight, so Naomi fixed enough food for the four; Tomas provided the fishing gear and bait. Tommy brought along a half dozen bottles of his wine. They arrived around three in the afternoon, and Silas set up the fishing gear for everyone. James took to fishing. By six that evening, they set aside their rods. The four savored the food Naomi provided and especially the wine Tommy brought along.

James was even more flushed within an hour; he became very talkative. The conversation was heavy as Tommy tried to probe into what was bothering his brother-in-law. After initially denying anything was wrong, he started to open up, though it took some time. Finally, James divulged that his ex-wife was pregnant, and she claimed that James raped her and was the father of her child. She'd hired a high-priced law firm and has filed suit, seeking five hundred thousand dollars and another five thousand a month in child support.

"Have you had relations with your ex-wife?" Tommy asked.

James was quick to respond, "No."

"Had you socialized or visited her before her accusations?"

"She sent me a note saying she was ill and would very much like to see me."

"I assume you visited her at her home."

"Yes. She wasn't ill at all but in excellent health. She said she missed me and wanted to get back together."

"When was the child born?"

"About nine months after my visit."

"How convenient."

"She's been hounding me ever since that visit. She shows up at restaurants I frequent and starts an argument. She shows up at my home and my office without any advance notice. At the office, she'll sit in the waiting room if I won't see her and start shouting hateful things. I'm at my wit's end. I thought if I came to see you, she wouldn't follow me, and I would be rid of her."

"Have you hired an attorney?" Juan asked.

"Yes. He suggested we settle."

"Have you offered her anything?"

"No, I just took the train out here. I know it's cowardly to bring this to your doorstep, but I was scared and hoped you could figure out what to do."

"What about her brother?" Tommy asked.

"I haven't seen him, but this is just the thing he would do. They hate you, Sarah, and of course, me. I don't think he'll ever forgive you for turning the tables on him in front of everyone."

"Do you think any of the family followed you here?"

"I don't know. They may have. I'm so sorry for bringing this to your home. I'll leave tomorrow, go back and face it."

"James. Why don't we see what they do and take it from there? What do you think, Juan?"

"I've not met these people, but Tommy tells me they're equally vulnerable to a lawsuit. Maybe when they find out Tommy's involved, they'll leave you alone", Juan said.

"Why don't we turn in now, get up early and catch some fish? Everyone is going to laugh at us if we don't come back with dinner for the family", Tommy   smiled.

CHAPTER 25

*J*uan rented a home and an office in Santa Barbara so he could be near the courthouse, keep up with anything new in his case, and be closer to Linda. Her father was going to announce the upcoming nuptials, and he needed to spend more time with her and her family.

It was a complete surprise when the California Supreme Court ruled that Ventura County had jurisdiction over the Trial of Silas Smith and that Jim Bridger was no longer the prosecutor. Juan didn't know that the counties disagreed on who had jurisdiction.

Rather than travel back and forth to Santa Ynez to meet with his client, Juan wired Tommy with the news. He asked that Silas meet him in Santa Barbara at his office the day after tomorrow.

Today, Juan took the train to Ventura to meet with the new prosecutor, Frank Hilliard. They'd never met, but Hilliard had a reputation of being a tenacious attorney but a straight shooter. Hilliard was gracious and agreed to meet with Juan on short notice.

"I've heard good things about you, Mr. Sanchez. Is it true that the famous gunman is your father?"

"He's my stepfather, but closer to an older brother than a parent."

"I had a long discussion with Jim Briger over dinner last week, and he's turned his entire file over to me.

He was convinced of Smith's guilt, and everything seems to point in that direction."

Juan smiled. "I didn't come here to plead my case. I wanted to meet you and ask if you've uncovered anything new."

"No, but if something crops up, I'll inform you immediately. I have a strong case but won't do anything underhanded to win." The two men shook hands, and Juan took the train back to Santa Barbara.

When he returned from Ventura, he had a message from Linda at his office. Her father wanted to make the announcement a week from Friday at home. If it were alright with Juan, they'd invite all their friends and his family to be present when her father announced their engagement.

He took a carriage to their home and told her in person that the arrangements were okay with him. They had lunch on her patio. Her brother and sister joined them. "How is the trial going?" Linda asked.

"They moved the trial to Ventura County."

"Is that a problem?"

"It's a logistics problem. My office is here. I either have to get a temporary office there or operate out of here and commute daily by train. And then there's you; I may not have as much time for you as I'd like until the trial is over."

"Don't worry, Juan. There's plenty for me to do to prepare for the wedding. It will be the biggest thing that's happened in Santa Ynez. I promise you'll like everything."

Silas was waiting for Juan at his office the following day. The two were cordial and reminisced about the number of fish they caught at Tommy's ranch last week. The sheriff seems to have made this case very personal. I know he'd been squiring your intended around, but I didn't realize he was angry about that.

The money issue is what puzzles me. I know you don't recall anything about the attack, but I wonder if you'd consider being hypnotized to see if you might remember anything about your assailant. I know a doctor who specializes in that treatment and has had some success.

"I don't know, Juan. I don't want some quack making me do silly things. I'm willing to try anything as long as you're present and won't let me be embarrassed. I keep thinking I'm an educated man; I must have some family or assets somewhere. Maybe it's my ego talking. What do you think?"

"Tommy and I have discussed that subject many times. You have polish, fine manners and can converse on many subjects. You sound like a New Englander. I wonder if we shouldn't make some inquiries back in that area, say Boston. We could contact the banks and see if anyone knows you. I'll have my secretary contact the top five banks in Boston to see if we can get some response."

"I'm concerned about the cost of the trial. I work for Tommy Sanchez, and he's footing the bill for everything. I'm embarrassed."

"Don't be. I was in trouble with the law when my stepfather came to my rescue. Like you, I thought I was tough, but Tommy showed me what tough is, mixed with compassion. The way he treats my mother is amazing. She had a lot of baggage when she met him, but all he sees is the inner person. I wouldn't be here with you today if it weren't for my mother's husband. I'm a good attorney; I will do everything I can to represent you and have you set free."

A week from Friday came sooner than he thought, and it was time to announce the engagement to his beautiful Linda. There must have been one hundred guests at the formal union announcement between Linda and himself. Most of the people were new to him, but his mother was there, still a radiant beauty at nearly fifty years of age. Tommy looked distinguished, standing next to her in his new tuxedo. He was, by far, the most well-known celebrity in the gathering. Everyone would go home and say they sat next to the legendary gunman-turned-businessman. Juan smiled as people shyly approached Tommy. They wanted to shake his hand, but some were reluctant, and they didn't want to   stay and talk to the legend.

When it was time to make the announcement, the parents and the young couple stood side by side. Linda's proud father introduced Linda and Juan and established their wedding date. The guests were friendly, and there must have been a hundred toasts to the engaged couple. There was one individual who gave Juan the creeps,

Hernando Guitterez. Juan wondered what his agenda was. He seemed like a person who hovered around, waiting to pounce.

Tommy also noticed it, and he wondered what Hernando was doing here. He looked more like a jilted lover than a friend of the family. After the announcement, there was dancing to a local band. Tommy intercepted Hernando by grabbing his arm as the house guest made his way toward Linda.

"I wonder if you and I could get some fresh air and chat. I've not seen you for a couple of years." Hernando was more interested in dancing with Linda, but Tommy's firm grip on his arm persuaded him to go along.

When they reached the garden, Tommy found chairs they could sit in. He offered Hernando a cigar, but the wine merchant already had one, and the two men lit up. "I sent a consignment of our wine to you, and although I received a check for the correct amount, I wanted to know how our wine was received."

"I'm sorry I didn't let you know, but the Grenache you sent was the more popular, though the other varietals were warmly received. I assume this wasn't the reason you escorted me out here."

"I have a wonderful relationship with my adopted son, Juan, and I'm very protective of him. From all outward appearances, I see a young couple who seem to be in love. I don't want anyone to interfere with that relationship unless one of them wants out of it. I don't know your relationship with the De L'Ortegas, but you seem too interested in what Linda is doing. I advise you to let the young couple figure out what they want from each other without any undue influence on your part."

"Okay, you've said your piece. Am I free to leave now?"

"Why yes. I don't want to unduly delay any plans you may have if they don't interfere with mine. Do we understand each other?" Hernando didn't respond as he made his way back inside.

Linda and Juan were dancing together when Tommy entered the large hall. He found Sarah, and she insisted they dance. This wasn't Tommy's forte, but he accommodated his wife and did his best. He and Sarah were one of the last to leave. He hadn't seen Guitterez since their talk in the garden.

CHAPTER 26

*N*ow that her second child was six months old, Frances believed she could leave both boys with Lenny for a few days and travel to Santa Barbara. Money was short, and they needed some staples; Lenny worked hard on the ranch but didn't contribute any money. It was all on her to make this work. She needed to go to Santa Barbara to get the cash Hiram had set aside for her. She desperately needed clothes for the two boys.

Lenny was totally against her going, and an argument broke out at the breakfast table. He was shouting, and the children were scared, and they cried. But Frances held her position, and as defiantly as she could, she said, "I'm going by myself, and you're staying home with the children."

"When he didn't respond, she came over to him, put her arm around his shoulders, and said, "I'm not going to leave you. You're my man until we die."

"What if they get a fever or a cold? What will I do?"

"I'll have the Indian woman stay with you while I'm gone. It should only be four days."

The following day after breakfast, she hitched up the wagon and left; this was an adventure for her. Besides the train ride to the west coast, she always did something with others. But today, she was a lone woman in the wilderness enjoying her freedom. She thought about the last two years with Lenny and wondered how she survived.

She wasn't being unrealistic when she felt that he was dependent on her now. She constantly had to encourage and compliment him on keeping up his self-esteem.

She slept the first night under the wagon with a rifle clutched to her breasts. She got a quick chill down her spine when a coyote howled but fell asleep and rose at daybreak. It was near noon when she saw the outskirts of Santa Barbara, so she stopped along the trail, took some water from the bucket she carried in the wagon, cleaned her face, and combed her hair. The next step was to change her dress so she'd be presentable in case the bank refused to give her the funds.

Hiram had deposited five thousand dollars in an account made out to her. With interest accruing for three years, she had fifty-three hundred plus in the account. She asked the bank manager if she could have two hundred dollars and leave the balance for another time. It took her only fifteen minutes to complete the transaction after he verified her signature. She was so happy that she almost skipped out the front door, but that would have made the banker suspicious.

She found a general store near the bank and bought clothes for her two sons, a new dress for herself, and pants and a shirt for Lenny. She found some canned milk the boys could drink if she left them for any appreciable time. She wasn't sure about toys, but she bought a child's wagon for the oldest boy. She asked the clerk if she could pick up her purchases the following day since she planned to stay that night. The clerk parked her wagon in the alley behind the store and threw a tarp over it in case it rained. She took the dress with her, found a reasonably priced boarding house, and rented a room for the night.

What a treat to have indoor plumbing. She soaked in the tub for at least an hour before dinner. She didn't want to leave the soothing, warm water. Seven other adults were sitting around the boarding house table when she entered. The conversation was light, and most guests went to their rooms early.

She stopped in the parlor before retiring and picked up the Santa Barbara Register lying on the coffee table in front of the couch. She sat down and thumbed through the weekly.

On the second page was a narrative about the upcoming trial of the seventh man in the Oxnard Train Robbery. Halfway down the page was a grainy picture of the accused. It was Hiram or someone who looked like her late husband. Could it be that he was alive and had participated in that robbery?

She continued reading the entire article and found that Silas Smith, as he's called, was found by a man named Sanchez in a remote valley southeast of Santa Barbara. The victim had been shot in the back and was near death. Sanchez brought him to the hospital in town, and the doctors saved his life. The problem was that the kept man couldn't remember who he was, so Sanchez gave him the name of Silas Smith and hired him to work on his ranch in Santa Ynez.

She noted the date of the robbery, December 22, 1899, and knew that Hiram couldn't have been involved with the theft. He didn't go on his hunting trip until late January 1900. She knew at that moment that Lenny had shot Hiram, left him for dead, and deliberately came to the ranch to take over Hiram's life. If he were here right now, she'd kill him for sure.

One of the things she wanted to do in Santa Barbara while she was here was to go to the library and see if Hiram's body had been found or if perhaps some of his hunting equipment had been recovered. She didn't sleep that night while tossing and turning in bed. The same question was always coming up to her. Is he still alive? If he is, what is she going to do? She married him but had two children with another man at his ranch.

The eight people who gathered around the breakfast table at the boarding house were actively discussing the trial as she took her seat. It was the biggest thing that happened in Ventura over the past year. "I heard that he still hasn't told the authorities where the money is." One young woman said.

Another of the patrons chimed, "he's guilty and should be put in jail."

Frances had been quiet during the give-and-take between the breakfast crowd, but she asked the man next to her, "Wasn't he found shot and lying in the bushes?"

He looked at her as though she was dumb. "Yes."

Frances had to be sure it was Hiram who was on trial. She knew now that he couldn't be the seventh man.

That was their first Christmas together. If it's him on trial, then they have the wrong man. Rather than pick up her purchases, she decided to go to the courthouse to see if it was Hiram who was on trial. She didn't know what that would accomplish, but she was determined to go anyway.

Lenny would be angry when she didn't come home immediately, but he'd get over it. It would do him good. She'd turn him into the sheriff if it weren't for the children.

She took the nine AM train to Ventura and arrived in court after it started. The judge called a brief recess of fifteen minutes at eleven while the two attorneys met with the judge in chambers. Many in the court went outside, including Hiram, with a beautiful woman on his arm. Behind the couple was a medium-sized man dressed entirely in black, escorting a beautiful blond woman. They followed Hiram and his lady outside.

There was a gate separating the spectators and the court officials. When he returned, Hiram entered the gated area and shook hands with a tall slim man who looked like a Native American. Hiram's two friends sat in the front row outside the gated area. The court was called to order, and jury selection began. After each side made preliminary statements, the judge called a recess for lunch. Before he left the court, Hiram had a short discussion with the tall Native American, who appeared to be his attorney. When they were finished, Hiram spoke to the attractive woman, and they walked down the aisle toward Frances.

She had to know if it was him. It had been three years since he left on his hunting trip. She stepped into the aisle and blocked his way as he and the woman approached. He looked right at her but didn't acknowledge her. It was him, but he didn't remember her. Of course, he could be faking it, but she didn't think that was true. He didn't know her. Maybe he lost his memory.

It was the man, dressed in black, who noticed her. He stopped in front of her with the blond woman beside him, preventing her from leaving. "Do you know Silas Smith?"

"Who?" was all that Frances could say.

"You know who I mean. The man you purposely approached." "Tommy, you're scaring her."

Sarah looked into Frances's eyes and asked if she knew Silas Smith or the man calling himself Silas Smith.

"I don't know what you're talking about."

Sarah was pleasant but firm. "I think you do. You know who he is, and that's why you're here. Please, we'd like to know, we're his friends. He's on trial and needs all the help we can give him."

At that exact time, Silas and Marjorie Hawkins came back into the courtroom to talk to Tommy and Sarah. Frances used that moment to walk past Hiram and out into the clear dry summer air. She walked with a couple of other spectators and quickly disappeared into one of the stores. She did have time to ask another woman walking out at the same time who the man in black was with the blond woman. "Why, he's Tommy Sanchez, a former Sioux Brave. He's the one who found the guy who maste4rminded the Oxnard Train Robbery. The woman is the former wife of Crazy Horse, who massacred the Seventh Army at the Battle of the Little Big Horn. They make quite a couple. Both have blood on their hands."

Tommy wasn't the only person who noticed the recognition on Frances' face when she confronted Silas. James Jefferson was in the back of the courthouse when the meeting occurred. He followed the mysterious woman outside, and when she entered the general store, he walked to the corner to see both the front door and the alleyway behind the row of stores containing the general store.

He watched as she came out of the alley and made her way to the train station two blocks away. He followed discretely and watched as she bought a ticket and boarded the train. It was a thirty-minute ride, and when the train stopped at the station, the woman exited and walked to the Santa Barbara Bank and Trust. Jefferson followed at a discrete distance. He watched as she approached the bank manager. "I think I bought too much yesterday and have very little left out of the two hundred. I want three hundred dollars before I go home."

"No problem. I'll take care of it, Mrs. Bookers. I just remembered that I had to ask you about Mr. Bookers. Is he well?"

"Yes, he's home with the children." That was the only thing Frances could think of to say."

Sign this withdrawal slip for the three hundred, and you can be on your way." Frances quickly signed the title, thanked the manager, picked up her money, and walked out the front door. Jefferson was near enough to the two as the transaction was completed, but he had his back turned so she wouldn't think he was listening.

When he was sure she had left, he walked over to the manager, showed him his credentials, and introduced himself. "My company has been hired to find a missing person. Jane Walters was last seen two years ago in Los Angeles, California. She left behind a husband and two children. Her husband and father have been searching for her since. That young woman who was just here talking to you remarkably resembles Mrs. Walters."

"I'm sorry, Mr. Jefferson, but her name is Frances Booker. Her husband Hiram and she own a ranch about twenty miles southeast of Santa Barbara."

"I'm sorry too. My client had been hoping that we would find her by now. I appreciate your help. By the way, while I'm in this beautiful city, I'd like to find a house I can use as a vacation retreat. Can you recommend a realtor who could help me?"

"Why yes. Norman Harkins has been in the city for over twenty years, and come to think of it; he's the one who found Booker's property. Here's his address. Have a nice day."

Jefferson took the train back to court to watch the proceedings. The prosecution was presenting its arguments this week. Juan would have a chance next week to put on his case. Jefferson was a good part of that strategy. It was three o'clock when the court adjourned. Jefferson asked Tommy and Sarah to come have a drink with him after they returned to Santa Barbara, but Sarah begged off.

"I'd like to return to Arlington and take a warm bath. Tommy can fill me in when he comes back." She left with Silas and Marjorie.

On the way to the real estate office, Jefferson filled Tommy in on what he found out. "You know, the saddle we recovered where I found Silas had the initials H.B inside. It could be Hiram Bookers. Then my question is, why didn't she identify herself? She had to know that Silas was Bookers and probably didn't commit the robbery. Why didn't she come forward? Something had to be holding her back." Tommy said.

They arrived at Harkins office, told him what they wanted, and he took a map out of the file and showed them where the Bookers ranch was. "That's within ten miles from where I found Silas," Tommy whispered to Jefferson.

"Do you remember what Bookers looked like?" Jefferson asked Harkins.

"Somewhat, he was about fifty years of age, standing five foot ten inches tall and weighing one hundred eighty pounds. He wore a nautical hat all the time. He and I visited the ranch before he bought it. I also met Mrs. Bookers after they were married at the Arlington Hotel. She was a mail-order bride from the Boston area." Harkins said.

"Can you describe her?" Tommy asked.

Heath thought for a moment and described the woman who came to court today.

Tommy put it together quickly. "Let's go back to the hotel, change and go to The Booker's place. We can get two good horses at the livery."

"Do you think we should take Silas with us? Perhaps seeing his spread could make him remember some things. She has to be the wife he married in Santa Barbara." Jefferson responded.

"We'll be gone for at least three days. Juan needs him in court. If she's the   wife, why didn't she come forward? We need to talk to her and find out the entire story. Maybe she shot Silas." Tommy said.

They went to the hotel, changed, and told Sarah what they'd found out. "You mean she could be his wife?"

Tommy responded. "I believe she is."

CHAPTER 27

They didn't want to get to the ranch ahead of her, so they took their time and slept overnight using their bedrolls. "I'm not used to mother earth. I've gotten soft and like the boarding house or hotels." Jefferson said and then turned over and went to sleep.

At about three that afternoon, they saw the cabin and the livestock. A wagon was tied up out front. They took their time ensuring no one else was on the property. A man came out of the barn with hay and threw it to the cattle. Tommy nudged Jefferson, and they waited to see what the man would do next. He went back into the barn. "We'll leave my horse here. You ride to the cabin as soon as I make sure the man in the barn isn't armed. Give me a few minutes to come up behind the barn. Bring the horses down as soon as you see us, and we'll visit with the woman." Tommy said.

Lenny was pitching hay to the barn horse when Tommy walked up behind him. "I have a gun trained on you and won't hesitate to use it if you make any move. Stay still while I pat you down. We're going into the house and talk to Mrs. Bookers and see what this is all about."

When Lenny turned around to face Tommy, he seemed defeated. "I knew you come someday. I stayed too long here."

"You're Lenny Harris, aren't you?" Lenny didn't respond.

Jefferson waited a few minutes until Tommy got behind the barn. When he saw both men exit the barn, he made his way to the cabin. All three arrived at the same time. Rather than knock, Jefferson and Lenny, followed by Tommy, entered the house. The woman had her back to them as they entered. "I'll bet you can't guess who I saw in Ventura yesterday?" she said.

When she didn't get an answer, she turned, and the shock on her face registered on all three. "Who did you see in Ventura?" Tommy asked.

Frances didn't respond. She looked at Lenny and then at the two men and started crying. Tommy still had a gun trained on Lenny. "Let's sit down at the table. There's a lot the two of you have to tell us. This is James Jefferson, a Pinkerton Detective on the hunt for the final robber of the Oxnard Train. I'm Tommy Sanchez, the man who found Silas Smith with a gunshot wound in his back, or should I say, Hiram Bookers, your husband."

Frances put her head down on her arms and cried out loud. If the color wasn't lost on Lenny's face when he heard Tommy mention a Pinkerton Detective, it did when he listened to the name Tommy Sanchez. Although he never met him, even Butch Cassidy spoke in awe of the legend. Jefferson turned to Lenny. "I guess you're Lenny Harris, the seventh man in the train robbery."

The Indian woman with two small boys, one in her arms, walked into the kitchen and continued into the room attached to the cabin. The door behind them opened a crack, and Tommy sprung around with his gun pointed at it. Frances screamed. "Please don't hurt my sons."

Tommy lowered his gun but kept Harris in sight. Jefferson, who knew some Indian dialects, followed the Indian woman and the children into the room. They could hear him discussing something with them, and then he returned. "The woman knows that she and the children are not to come out until we finish."

"Can I go to them," Frances pleaded?

Tommy quickly responded, "Not until we know the full story of who this man is and who shot Silas Smith."

At that moment, Harris started to get up from the table, but with only a flick of his gun, Tommy hit Harris on the side of the head, and he fell to the floor with blood pouring from a gash. Frances rushed to Lenny, but Jefferson grabbed her arm and made her sit down. "Put these handcuffs on him, Tommy, and I'll get a wet rag to stop the bleeding."

It was only a superficial cut, and after Tommy put the handcuffs on Harris, he helped him up and sat him back in his chair. Jefferson cleaned the wound, pressed hard on the spot, and soon the blood stopped flowing.

"Okay, who wants to start with the truth?" Jefferson was looking at Frances when he spoke.

Through sobs and pleading to talk to her children, Frances told of her marriage to Bookers and how he went on a hunting trip with his horse and mule and never came home. She went out looking for him and found Lenny with a broken ankle and separated shoulder. She nursed him back to health, and he abused her physically and sexually for six months. After six months, she learned that she was pregnant and had reached the point where she accepted that Hiram was dead and that Lenny wasn't going to leave. After the second child, she took the fact that Lenny was, for all practical purposes, her husband.

They had enough food but needed money, and since Lenny didn't have any or wouldn't use his, she remembered the trust fund Hiram set up for her. She went to Santa Barbara to pick up clothes for the children and some staples for the family. While there, she learned about the trial and, "you know the rest. Can I go to my children?"

"Conditioned that there are no firearms in that room. Jim, check it out while I talk to Harris."

Harris responded immediately. "I'm not going to say anything, and you can't make me."

"I don't think you're as well off as you think. We've already established that you are the seventh man. Snake Eyes gave us a description and a name before he was hung.

The bartender in Ventura, where you used to drink and play poker, gave us your description. I'm pretty sure we have you. The question is, what are we going to do with you? The most logical thing is to take you back, get the witnesses who can identify you, and free Silas.

More than likely, they'll hang you. Now if the money were to turn up, they might settle for life in imprisonment. Either way, Bookers will be back here to claim his property, wife, and probably your kids. Of course, he may not want the wife since she took up with you. He'll probably throw her off the property. In that case, the kids will go to the orphanage."

The color again drained from Lenny's face. "You can't do that to small boys. They didn't have anything to do with this. They're innocent victims."

Frances was calm as she returned to the kitchen, fixed some coffee, and joined the other three at the table. "I heard everything you said, and it looks grim for Lenny, me, and the kids. Can you suggest another alternative?"

"First, tell me everything you know about Hiram Bookers."

Frances took a sip of coffee and sat back in her chair." I met Hiram through an ad he placed in the Boston Globe Newspaper looking for a mail-order bride. I responded, and after a few months, he invited me to come to California to meet him and see where he lived."

"He was forty-five when we met, and we married after two days at Arlington. That was three years ago. He'd come from a sailing family and had sailed his entire adult life. When his father died, he became the sole owner of an eight-ship merchant fleet. I believe he wanted something else, so he sold his company. I think he was a boxer for some time. He tells of his fight with Jack Dempsey and his subsequent friendship. He got tired of his life back east, and when a significant storm shut down the east coast, he came out here and bought this property. I suspect there may have been a failed romance that may have contributed to his move to California. He has no living relatives other than me.

Tommy understood how Silas had taken to fishing readily: "Before we traveled to this place, he set up a trust fund for me for five thousand dollars, which I drew upon recently. I believe Hiram has over three hundred thousand dollars in that bank, but it's not in my name, and I can't access it."

Tommy was more confident than he led Lenny to believe. The main problem for Silas was Sheriff Jack Rodgers, who didn't care about finding the real seventh man. He wanted Silas to swing for the crime. The reasons were obvious. Marjorie Hawkins had dumped the sheriff and now was taking up with Silas. Tommy and the sheriff had been hunting buddies, but now there was vindictiveness on the part of the sheriff to punish Tommy for aiding in the escape of a convicted murderer. He was using Silas to get even. The third reason was the election. Rodgers needed a conviction now, not later, to secure a victory.

Tommy felt for the kids. He didn't want any kids to go to an orphanage, but he didn't know how far Jefferson could go to make everything right.

"Where's the money?" Tommy asked.

After a few moments of silence, Frances looked at Lenny and demanded, "tell him."

"I buried it in a can out in the field by those two twin trees."

"Do you think they'll acquit Silas if the money's returned?" Tommy asked Jefferson.

"No, I don't think so. They'll say Silas had the money returned to get off."

Tommy thought for a minute before speaking. "Are the bills still being tracked by the banks?"

Jefferson smiled. "What are you thinking about?"

"What if the missing bills were suddenly in circulation?"

"They'd arrest the individual, check out his story and see where he was on the robbery dates. I don't think Silas would get off if that individual had an alibi. Silas has to have an alibi for the dates of the robbery, and he has to explain why the bills were found in his boot."

Lenny started to speak, and Tommy told him to shut up. Jefferson was starting to think about how to get Silas acquitted. "The only way Silas will get off is if Frances testifies that Silas is her husband Hiram Bookers, and Lenny tells the court that he was the seventh man and that it was he who shot Silas."

Lenny wouldn't be quiet. "Forget it, you may get me to court, but I'm not going to testify, even if Frances does."

Frances didn't understand what they were saying. "I can prove that I'm Hiram's wife, and we can find someone who will tell the court that Silas is Bookers. Isn't that enough to get him off?"

"They want Silas to be the seventh man, and they don't care if he's Bookers. Lenny put some stolen loot in his boot after he shot him."

Frances glared at Lenny. "You are a bastard, aren't you?"

Lenny wouldn't be quiet. "No one can prove that I shot Bookers or whatever his name is."

Jefferson had been quiet, but he turned to Tommy. "But I know how your mind works. You have something else in mind. Don't you?" Jefferson was smiling.

Tommy looked at Jefferson. "I could be wrong, but I don't think just Frances telling the court that Silas is her husband and he was with her during the robbery will get him acquitted. I think money is the key. Having someone spending the money would take a lot of the heat off Silas. What if we were able to get the funds in circulation and the one or ones circulating the money have no connection to Silas or us."

Jim Jefferson was listening intently." How would you accomplish that?".

"That's where Lenny's old trade comes into play and whether he's willing to try to get us out of this situation. Let's say that Lenny exchanges the money for other currencies. Maybe there's a poker game, and the big winner is drunk when he leaves the game. At the right moment, Lenny exchanges the money with the man so that he doesn't know about the exchange, and he'll later spend it in many locations."

Jefferson followed Tommy's lead. "The poker winnings have to be at least eight thousand dollars. The exchange should take place after the man falls asleep. When he wakes, he checks his money, and it's all there. He goes to breakfast or lunch and, spending some, goes to the general store to buy something for loved ones or himself. When the bills are turned in to the bank, they raise the alarm, and eventually, the Pinkertons can trace it to the victim. He, in turn, says he won it in a poker game and only remembered one other individual who was in the game that night."

Tommy couldn't help but smile because Jefferson was visualizing the same plan as him. "All five in the game will point to the others, but the beauty of the plan is it will remove Silas from the equation. He didn't have the money, and he didn't spend it. They've searched his room and our ranch, so they can't say he was the one who introduced the money into the game."

Lenny listened to the give-and-take between Jefferson and Sanchez. "If I do this, what do I get out of it?"

"Maybe your life. I don't know anything about amnesia, but the doctors I consulted with think that if Silas hasn't recovered his memory in three years, he may never." Tommy responded.

"What about this place? Will my children and I be able to live here?" Frances asked.

Tommy responded. "I think that will be up to Silas. I don't have all the answers. Silas may not take back his real name. Our main goal today is to see if we can devise a plan to clear Silas and perhaps not adversely affect anyone here."

"What's to prevent Lenny from skipping out with the money?" Frances asked.

"I'll be in the background the entire time. If Lenny tries to flee after he has the money, I'll kill him." Lenny shifted in the chair when he heard Tommy say that.

Frances wasn't finished. "If you can free Silas, what about Lenny?"

"That's up to Lenny. He can run as far as he can or come back here. Tommy was serious. That's between you two."

Frances had made a fresh pot of coffee and got up to get the pot. As she rose, Tommy's attention was diverted to one of the walls in the two-room cabin. He wondered why he didn't see it before, but there was a painting of Crazy Horse on the wall. He walked over to see if he could determine who the artist was. Neatly in the lower right-hand portion of the picture was the name Sarah Hansen.

"Frances, where did you get this painting?"

"It was here when Hiram brought me here. I love the colors. They're so rich. Are you familiar with the painting?"

"It was painted by my wife and hung in the lobby of the Central Hotel in Santa Ynez.

CHAPTER 28

They talked through the night before they had an agreement on the plan. The first thing that had to be done was for Lenny to retrieve the money. Tommy made sure Lenny watched as he checked his guns before he holstered them. The two walked to where Lenny said he buried the capital, with Tommy staying a discrete distance back. Ha dug around the tree until he found the money.

Tommy demanded it when he recovered the can, and Lenny handed it over. "Keep in front of me on the way back. You better know that I think you're a killer and a scoundrel, and I won't hesitate to shoot you if you screw this plan up."

Frances had breakfast ready when the two returned. Frances asked if she could talk to Tommy in private when they were finished. They went outside and walked to the barn. "I know I asked this before, but If this succeeds, what's going to happen to Lenny? She asked.

"Do you care?"

"Yes. As bad as he was, he's a part of my life and the kids. I think he's changed and should have another chance, especially if he can make things right."

"I won't promise anything. I think he'll try to get away from me any chance he has and his instincts are to protect himself? My priority is to my friend Silas or if you want Bookers. I don't care about Lenny other than he must perform the task that's needed"

"I don't say he's completely vindicated himself, but he's changed enough to get some consideration."

"Are you going to be okay here by yourself while we try to put this plan in place?"

"I have some money, enough food, and the Indian woman will stay with me. If necessary, I can get one of the Indian men to come over and do some work or take me to Santa Barbara. There's almost five thousand in my name in the Bank of Santa Barbara. Thank God, I'm not pregnant at this time."

Before the three men left, Jefferson had a private talk with Lenny. I know you've heard of Tommy Sanchez, but you don't see that he's the best tracker alive. He'll find you and kill you. You may try to get away, but you do it at your peril. Do you understand?" Lenny nodded.

Frances knew that she might never see Lenny again. Before the three men left, she had a private meeting with Lenny. "I think what happens next is up to you. They've given you a chance to reform. You can either run or come back and face up to your responsibility. Whether you accept the gift they're offering will be determined by either the old Lenny or the new Lenny. With the money Hiram left me, I can make a living here; the kids and I won't starve. Of course, there's no way to know whether another Lenny could come by and do to me what you did. So be on your way and think about what I've said."

The three rode toward Santa Barbara, veered around the city, and headed toward Ventura. Jefferson went his way about two miles out of town, and Tommy and Lenny headed toward the Ventura Hotel in the downtown district. They checked in separately and had rooms on different floors. Tommy carried the money.

They didn't eat any of their meals together but met secretly in the alley behind the hotel at night to determine what they'd do the next day. Harris indicated there'd be a game tonight at a roadhouse about one mile north of Ventura on Oxnard Road. The weekend of the games was small, and the opportunity wasn't there. Tom y left early to scout the game and determine if there would be a winner big enough to put their plan in motion.

On Monday, Tommy got an idea, went to the cattle yards, and talked to the auctioneer to see if any significant purchases or sales were contemplated shortly. The manager of the stockyards said there was a herd expected soon, but they didn't know when. There were none that day, so Tommy went to the stockyards each day until Friday. Then, he saw a herd of about four hundred head of cattle being brought into the stockyards. He didn't learn the exact same amount, but at an average price of twenty-five dollars a head, he knew that somewhere around ten thousand dollars would change hands. They completed the count about seven that evening, and the principals went into the Railroad Hotel Bar to sign the bill of sale, pay the trail herder in cash and have a few drinks to celebrate the deal. Tommy tried to be inconspicuous and, at the same time, attempted to hear what the cattlemen said.

He learned that the ramrod and the cowboys would return to their camp about a mile out of town that evening. They had another two hundred heads to bring in and planned to be at the yards at nine the following day. It was then that the cowboys would be paid off. If they could make a money switch tonight, the cowboys would more than cloud the issue by spending everything they were paid, starting tomorrow.

The buyer and seller went into the dining room, and Tommy went back to his hotel and found Lenny in his room. "I think we have an opportunity tonight if you can pick the seller's hotel room lock and make the switch without waking him. From what I can see, he will have lots to celebrate and has already started."

"What happens if I'm able to make the switch? I mean, what happens to the money I switched?

"I know what you're getting at. I don't want to turn you in unless I have to. That would muddy the waters and make it a bigger scandal than it is now. The chances are that Silas won't recover his memory and will remain as Silas Smith. It looks to me that you have some options. You can skip with the money, or you can take the money and go back to that woman who bore your children. I think she has feelings for you. You can't be a complete scoundrel; there must be something of worth inside you, but I don't know. If you screw this up, I'll come down hard on you. Believe me, when I say this, I can find you if I want.

Stay out of sight until this is over. I suggest you eat in your room. I'm going to dinner at the hotel where the cattlemen are partying and monitor what's happening. I'll come back and fill you in, and then we can determine when to make our move."

Tommy was going to make sure Lenny didn't try to make a break for it. He'd look in on the cattlemen, but his main focus tonight was on Lenny. At midnight the cattlemen said good night and went to their rooms. Tommy had checked which room the seller was in when the man checked in. He returned to Lenny's room and woke him up, and the two went out into the alley.

"Let's wait an hour before we go in the back way of the hotel and up the stairs to the second floor. I saw him put the money in a saddlebag. That should be the first place you look. I'll be your lookout while you're making the tradeoff. Don't worry; I'll get us out of here. I don't want to get caught either," Tommy said.

Tommy stayed down the hall next to a window overlooking the street. He also had a clear view of the steps from the lobby to the second floor. Lenny took off his boots and handed them to Tommy, who gave him the money, and Lenny made his way to the seller's door. He took out a couple of small metal pieces from his pocket and, in thirty seconds, turned the handle and entered the room. There was limited visibility from the streetlight outside the hotel, but Lenny could see the cattleman's profile on the bed with his clothes and boots on; he was snoring.

The saddle bags were on the floor next to the nightstand on the other side of the bed. Lenny got on his knees, crawled toward the saddlebags, and took out all the cash. It was difficult in the limited light, but he counted eight thousand dollars and set that amount on the floor near his leg. He took the robbery money from his pocket, mixed it with the remaining bills, and put it back in the saddlebag. Lenny picked up the eight thousand on the floor, made his way to the door, closed it, and relocked it.

Just then, the cattleman turned over and looked in Lenny's direction, but he didn't wake up.

He joined Tommy at the end of the hall, and they went down the back steps, and Lenny put on his boots. "I think we should leave town right now. We're paid up through tonight, so the hotel is taken care of. Let's go to the livery, pick up our horses and get out of here.

We accomplished what we set out to do. I don't know if I'll ever see you again, but you know your options. Jefferson will monitor the train money from this point forward. You can keep the money you switched."

Tommy headed to Santa Barbara and arrived at daybreak. He was tired, so he dropped his rented horse at the livery, took his saddlebags, and went to his room. Sarah had stayed the week, taking the train back and forth to Ventura each day to attend the trial. Lenny made a gesture to shake hands with Sanchez but was ignored. Tommy was quiet as he took off his clothes and crawled into bed next to his wife. He reached out to touch her, and she was completely nude. He caressed   her body, and she moaned. "I don't know if you're my husband, but I like what you're doing to me."

"Ha, ha, funny lady." She spread her legs, and he entered her while kissing her passionately.

"You ought to be gone more often, whoever you are." Tommy squeezed her hard, and she giggled.

After they climaxed, he held her in his arms and drifted asleep. She didn't have the heart to wake him for breakfast or to tell him she was going shopping; she came back around noon, and he was awake. He looked up as she entered the room. "How is the trial going?"

"They're just about ready to hear yours and Jefferson's testimony and then turn it over to the jury for deliberations. I know he's innocent, and Juan's doing a great job, but that money found in his boot is brought up by the prosecutor constantly. We need a miracle now. How did you make out?'

"We got lucky, but now the gods of the winds have to take over." He told her about the cattle sale and what he and Lenny did.

"That sounds great. It's up to the banks and Jim Jefferson to make it work. Those cowboys will spend everything they got after a long cattle drive. How about some lunch, Sioux Man?"

Lenny didn't waste any time getting out of town. He went the opposite way from Tommy. He planned to go to San Diego and get lost in the big city. The city was far from the Ventura Courthouse and close enough to Mexico if he had to get out of the country.

It took him a week to reach the outskirts of San Diego. Although he had a couple of drinks each night, he didn't participate in any poker games at the saloons where he stopped. He was carrying too much money to act like he used to. He didn't want to take any chances, so he took another week to reach the border and cross into Mexico. "He'd bought a gun in San Diego but was nervous every time he stopped at a cantina or hotel. He had transitioned from a predator to prey, and that bothered him. He rented a little house on the beach over the border, and one of the girls from a nearby cantina would come If he wanted her. He enjoyed his freedom, but after a week, he knew something was missing.

He didn't want to go back to the states and face prosecution for what he did, but he missed Frances and the two boys. The more he sat in the sun doing nothing, the more he missed the farm with plenty to do. What was wrong with him? He was free of all that, and good riddance. Who wants to work his ass off for a few crumbs? If that guy is acquitted, he'll throw her off the place. If Lenny is with her, Bookers will send the Indians for the sheriff, who'll throw him in jail and probably hang him for Richard's murder and the attempt on Booker's life. He drank another beer and then thought of Frances and the two boys. If they arrest him, the kids will end up in an orphanage; he didn't want that. But what was he going to do?

CHAPTER 29

His timing was near perfect. As soon as Tommy returned from the Booker place, Juan was ready to present the defense's case, and Tommy would be the first witness called by his adopted son.

Silas, Marjorie, Tommy, and Sarah stayed in Santa Barbara at the Arlington. Juan arranged to have Tommy prepped for his testimony on Saturday after he returned. He would be the first witness Juan would call on Monday Morning. "Tommy, I want to concentrate on your trip with the sheriff to see if you can remember any evidence, you or the sheriff found that would implicate Silas."

"What about the money found on Silas?"

"It is what it is, and although the prosecutor is going to hammer that point home, I'll concentrate on the fact that anyone could have planted it on Silas, especially since he was shot and left for dead."

Linda joined Juan and the other two couples for dinner on Sunday night, and it was the first time she'd been allowed to hear some of the strategies that Juan was to employ. "I hope you don't mind if I come to the courthouse and listen to my future father-in-law's testimony?"

"I'll be a little nervous knowing you're watching me, but come. I want you to be part of our life."

Court opened at nine on Monday morning, and the defense called Thomas Sanchez to the stand.

Juan walked Tommy through his discovery of the unconscious Silas and the time the defendant worked for him at Rancho Del Prado. The testimony took the better part of the morning, and the Judge recessed early for lunch, recognizing   that the afternoon might become contentious.

Linda had accompanied Sarah and the others by train, and the three couples went to lunch. Everyone was reserved and ate very little They knew that Tommy's testimony and the subsequent cross-examination by the prosecutor would go a long way to determining Silas' guilt.

Since Tommy was already under oath, Juan continued with his questions. I understand that Sheriff Rodgers approached you to visit the scenes of the two shootings, the murder of the bandit Richards and the shooting of the defendant, Silas Smith. What was the purpose of this trip?"

"The sheriff visited me at my home and suggested that he suspected Silas Smith of being the seventh member that robbed the Oxnard Train. He wanted to know if I could track the horses at the Richards' murder scene and see if they could have been ridden to where I found Silas Smith."

"Were you reluctant to perform this task?"

"Yes. I felt a year had passed, and it would be difficult to track anything after a year."

"If you had those concerns, why did you accompany the sheriff?"

"Sheriff Rodgers said that if we couldn't find evidence of Silas' guilt, he'd get off the man's back and drop his investigation."

"Objection. There is no way the sheriff would've agreed to that stipulation."

"Mr. Sanchez is what the prosecutor is saying, true."

"No. I would not have gone on the trip if he didn't make that promise."

"Is it true that the sheriff has called upon you on at least ten occasions to track escaped prisoners?"

"Yes."

"What was the percentage of escapees you tracked and apprehend?"

"One hundred percent."

"Is it also true that you were the senior deputy sheriff for the Santa Ynez Valley and were appointed by Sheriff Rodgers on at least two occasions?"

"Yes."

"Would you please summarize what you found at the two shooting sites you visited with Sheriff Rodgers?"

"There were two horses at the Richards crime scene. Those two horses traveled to the Silas shooting scene. One horse was ridden, the other tethered to the other horse. When the two horses from Richard's site arrived at Silas' site, there were now three horses, a mule, and a skinned deer.

"What was your conclusion?"

"The man who killed Richards came to the Silas camp and left the camp with the same two horses, except the one that had been tethered now carried something on its back, probably the skinned deer. The horse and mule at the Silas Camp had been run off to the south. We also found a broken Sharps Rifle, bedding, other gear, probably belonged to the man who'd been shot in the back. Obviously, Silas, his horse, and mule were not at Richard's Camp, so he didn't shoot Richards and therefore couldn't be the seventh bandit that robbed the Oxnard Train."

The prosecutor jumped to his feet. "Objection, the witness should not be making conclusions."

The judge responded immediately. "Sustained."

"Please continue, Mr. Sanchez," Juan said.

"The person who shot Richards came to the Silas Camp and left a seriously wounded man, a broken rifle, bedding and run off his mule and horse before he rode off."

"Thank you, Mr. Sanchez; I have no further questions now. Your witness Mr. Prosecutor.

"I'd like to remind you, Mr. Sanchez, that you're still under oath. Thank you for your continued community service and helping the sheriff get to the bottom of this mystery.

I have very few questions for you. Did you search Mr. Smith's pockets for identification?"

"Yes, I did."

"Did you look in his boots?"

"I did not. My main concern was to treat the wound, keep him warm and get him to the hospital as soon as possible."

"I want to compliment you, Mr. Sanchez, for being a good Samaritan. Is it possible that Mr. Smith may have owned the horse you attribute to Richards?"

"Anything is possible but not probable."

"Isn't it also possible that Smith rode to Richard's site, killed him, and then came back to his camp?"

"Again, it's possible but doubtful. I spent nearly a week tracking the horse hoofs leading from Richard's site to the Silas Camp. I didn't find any evidence that the horses were traveling in the opposite direction." If what you say is true, who shot Mr. Smith and rode off with the horses?"

"In this court, I ask the questions, Mr. Sanchez. I have no further questions of this witness, your honor."

The three couples again had dinner and talked about Tommy's testimony. "Tommy, you were fabulous. I hope the jury was paying attention." Sarah said.

"Have you heard from Jefferson?" Tommy asked.

"He wired the prosecutor that he'd be in court at nine tomorrow morning. He was trying to get a picture of Lenny Harris."

The defense kept putting on their case and called James Jefferson to the stand. His initial testimony covered his credentials and how long the Pinkerton Agency had employed him.

"What are your current duties with the Pinkertons?" Juan asked.

"I've been tasked with finding the remaining money from the Oxnard Train Robbery. As a secondary task, I've been asked to account for all the money taken from the train."

"Have you been successful?"

"Moderately. All the cash, gold, and notes have been accounted for except eight thousand dollars."

"Where do you think the remaining assets are?"

"I believe, as does my company, that the seventh man has the money."

"Do you know who the seventh man is?"

"We believe that he's a man named Lenny Harris. Two bank robbers, namely Joe and Harvey Hitchins, have called him the seventh man.

I have two affidavits for their statements, which I had given to Sheriff Rodgers and the prosecutor... Two of the bandits who were hung, namely Snake Eyes Jack Porter and Larry Jeffries, gave a detailed description of the seventh man. Harris, who grew up in Missouri and came to Oxnard about ten years ago, fits that description. Until the Oxnard Train Robbery, he was a petty thief who frequented saloons when there was a poker game. He made his living rolling drunks and waylaying winners from the poker games.

At least two saloons he frequented here in the Ventura locale where the owner remembered him and gave his description, which matched the one

Jeffries and Porter offered. The Pinkertons believe Lenny Harris is the seventh man, not Silas Smith."

"As you said, you presented this information to the local authorities."

"I showed the affidavits and briefed Sheriff Rodgers on what I'd found out. He is unwilling to investigate that scenario."

"Why do you think that is?"

"Objection." The prosecutor jumped from his seat.

"Objection sustained." The judge ruled, but Juan was able to get that point across to the jury.

Both sides made their closing statements, and the judge turned the case over to the jury. The jury foreman had taken an initial poll of the jurors and found nine would vote guilty and three not guilty. He was calm and had spent thirty years in the classroom handling teenagers and young adults. Two male jurors were very vocal and called the three who were holding out gutless and wasting everyone's time.

After two days of constant bickering and arguing, the jury foreman told the judge they were deadlocked on a verdict. The judge sent him back to have the jury continue to deliberate and come back with a verdict.

The three couples had dinner together each night and discussed what could be swaying the jury.

Tommy didn't at any time indicate to the others, especially Juan, what was in play in Ventura. They hadn't heard from Jefferson since his testimony; Tommy assumed he would be on top of the money trail.

A conscientious clerk at the Mechanics Bank in Ventura first spotted the Train Robbery Money. After that, three other banks notified the Pinkerton Office in Los Angeles they received some of the stolen money from the Oxnard Train Robbery. From that point on, things speeded up significantly.

In one week, over six thousand Oxnard Train Robbery Currency had circulated in Ventura. Special agent James Jefferson rode the train to Ventura and took charge of the stolen bills. After taking control of the money,

Jefferson interviewed the four bank managers and learned about the cash transaction that funded a trail herd purchase.

The purchaser of the cattle was still in town, and the Pinkerton man met with him for two hours and then notified the Ventura County Prosecutor about the four affidavits he had in his possession. "How convenient for the money to show up at this point," was the first thing he said to Jefferson.

Juan and the judge were notified, and his honor asked that the opposing attorneys meet with him at ten the following day in his chambers; the jury was still deliberating.

The county prosecutor filled in both parties on everything that Jefferson told him, plus the affidavits signed by the bank managers and the purchaser of the cattle. The seller was a Mexican National and had since left Ventura. "The jury has to be notified of this development," Juan said immediately.

The prosecutor could see that this new piece of information could significantly impact the jury, and he was going to fight hard not to have it introduced. "I think finding this money is irrelevant to the case. It does not in any way explain the money found in Smith's possession and would only cloud the issue,"

Juan knew this was his big chance. "You honor, if this information were available before the jury sat down to deliberate, it would be admissible in court.

Therefore, I believe the only fair thing to do is call the jury back and have Mr. Jefferson testify to the existence of the money."

The three talked for another hour, but the decision was based on whether the new information would've been allowed at the time if known; the answer was yes. The judge sent a message to the jury that further information had been found and the court would reconvene at one that afternoon.

Jefferson took the stand, and after explaining what was found, he was grilled by the prosecutor." Isn't it true that you're a close personal friend of the Sanchez Family who employs Silas Smith?"

"Yes, I've known the defense attorney since he was a teenager. But I didn't manufacture the currency, I didn't issue the money, and I didn't spend the money. I have affidavits from the parties involved about how the transaction took place and who had the funds."

"Didn't your friendship with the Sanchez family make you pursue this issue on your off time?"

"I didn't decide to pursue this matter on my own, nor did I suggest to my company that I be put in charge of this inquiry. My company was trying to satisfy the concerns of its clients and assigned me the task of recovering the currency over six months ago, which I did to the best of my ability."

When it was Juan's turn to cross-examine Jefferson, he went directly to the most crucial point. "Isn't it true that it was the Bank of Ventura who released these funds to the purchaser of the cattle?"

"That would seem to be the most logical explanation. They gave the money to the purchaser, who paid for the cattle. The trail herder paid his cowboys, and they went on a spending spree."

The county prosecutor had one last question. "If the money was in the bank, how come their employees didn't find it."

"Jefferson responded. "I don't know. As you can see in the affidavits, I asked that question, and the response from all four banks, especially the Bank of Ventura, was that they didn't know."

The prosecutor wasn't finished. "I believe those funds were switched with other funds after they left the bank."

Juan jumped to his feet. "Objection. That's pure speculation on the part of the prosecutor."

"Sustained." The judge said.

"Since there are no further questions for this witness, the jury will retire to deliberate." The judge adjourned the court and left the bench.

Three hours later, the jury returned with a verdict of not guilty. The Sanchez Family, including Linda, who was so proud of Juan, Silas, and Marjorie, took the train back to Santa Barbara and had lunch at the Arlington. Everyone congratulated Juan on his victory, especially Silas, who was now free of suspicion and could marry Marjorie. Tommy thought it would be wise if Jefferson said goodbye at the courthouse and returned immediately to Los Angeles. The celebratory lunch carried into afternoon cocktails and a late dinner. The group planned to return to Santa Ynez the next day. Linda and Sarah had a lot of planning to make the ranch suitable for the big wedding, which was to be held shortly.

They took the stage home, stopping off at the Kinevans and then going to their Ranch. Silas dropped Tommy, Sarah, Juan, and Linda at the Ranch and took Marjorie home. They didn't expect to see him for a few days.

"I know you have something you haven't told me. It was significant that you and Jim went off for a few days. I didn't ask. I knew you'd tell me in good time." Sarah asked.

They sat in the kitchen nook after the children and Naomi went to bed, and Juan and Linda went to the guest room in the barn.

He told her the entire story, including the exchange of money. "My god Tommy, you took a chance with that scoundrel. You could've gone to jail. Please don't do that again. I don't think I could bear being away from you."

"I promise."

"Are you going to tell Silas? He's planning on marrying Marjorie, yet he's still married to that other woman. What's she like?"

"Down to earth. She got caught in a situation not of her choosing and made the best of it. She had two children that she had to look out for."

"Sounds a lot like me."

There were still some issues that needed to be resolved. They talked it over late into the night, and when Sarah was satisfied, they went to bed.

Jacob Thunder was elected sheriff, with Jack Rodgers a close second. In this county, the winner assumed office immediately, which was good news for Silas. Rodgers used the time between the verdict and the election to refute the money transfer everyone agreed to. He vowed to get to the bottom of the transfer but came up short. He contended that someone switched the train money at the last minute. He just couldn't come up with a reasonable explanation as to how it happened. To some of his close acquaintances, he said since Sanchez found Smith, it was likely that he also found the money and picked the perfect time to release it. In public, he refuted that suggestion. He remembered the editor who used the newspaper to give Tommy such a bad time. That guy lost an ear lobe one night when he was sound asleep. With his political career over, Jack moved to San Diego to be near his daughter.

Jacob Thunder took over the sheriff's office and pledged that all minorities would be treated fairly. He came to the ranch one afternoon and asked Tommy about the investigation Rodgers had been conducting after the trial. "It seems like sour grapes to me. He was a good sheriff once. I guess he didn't want to give up the office." Tommy responded.

"As far as my office is concerned, the Silas Smith issue is closed forever." Thunder shook Tommy's hand and left.

Jacob thanked Sarah for her two contributions. "Your help was greatly appreciated. I will try to be the sheriff you expect. One of the first things I did when I took over the office was look at those issues that had not been resolved. It seems there was vandalism of your paintings in the hotel lobby in Santa Ynez. The previous sheriff failed to take action even though all four perpetrators signed a confession. I have arrested the four and put them in jail, waiting for a hearing before a judge. I'm sorry that your valuable work was destroyed. It's now up to the judge to determine their penalty."

CHAPTER 30

*T*he wedding was one month off, and the three women who would decide the logistics of the wedding were Linda De L'Ortega, her mother, Diane, and Sarah Sanchez. Linda had her heart set on the wedding at the Sanchez ranch, while her mother Diane was opposed. Sarah wasn't taking sides, but the decision had to be made soon.

She invited Diane and her daughter to the ranch for a week to make the final decisions and put things in motion. When Tommy saw the women sitting in the nook in their kitchen, he excused himself, got on his horse, and rode into Santa Ynez to meet with Juan. He would be as far away from any decision on the wedding as he could. He decided to sneak back to the ranch with Juan, pick up their fishing gear, and stay out of the way.

"I know the decision where the wedding is to take place belongs to you and Diane. But if we don't decide in the next few hours, we'll be in a catch-up mode the rest of the way." Sarah said to Linda.

Diane wasn't going to be left out. "The logistics are impossible. You can't house a hundred guests on the ranch; you can't transport one hundred guests not only from Santa Barbara to here but to the lake site where you want the wedding. Facilities are nonexistent. If we forget something, it's hours back and forth to bring it to the wedding site."

"I guess other than that, you're not opposed," Linda said to her mother as   Diane reached over and grabbed her daughter's hand.

"I agree that Santa Barbara makes more sense. There're plenty of hotels, yet most guests would go home after the party. In addition, the facilities are adequate. Another way of approaching this decision is to see what we could do at the ranch to satisfy Linda's desire." Sarah said.

Linda's face lit up. "Thank you, Sarah. Why don't you summarize what you could do at the ranch."

"I believe we can put up tents to accommodate 125 guests at the lake site. Getting enough bedding might be a reach, but it's possible. The Vaqueros should build twenty outhouses and put them discretely out of the way. The Vaqueros have cooked for a hundred guests before and could move the cooking equipment out to the lake. Breakfast the next morning for those who stayed over could be steak and eggs. We can borrow rigs and wagons from neighboring ranches to bring the guest from here to the lake. It would be up to the guests to get here. We can make this an extraordinary event, but I think one hundred guests is the limit that we could accommodate."

"If we need to cut down on some of the guests, that's okay, but I want the wedding on the knoll overlooking the lake on the south part of the ranch. It might be uncomfortable for some older guests, but if we tell them, it's an adventure of a lifetime, they'll buy into it." Linda responded and looked at her mother.

"Sarah, you're a wonder. I'm not going to raise any more objections. If this is what my daughter wants, I'll support it and tell my husband this is how it will be. This is going to be a tremendous burden on you and your husband. Why don't we divide up some tasks I could do, such as bedding and providing all the food? One thing that is not negotiable is my husband, and I will pay for everything."

Naomi provided lunch and beverages for the three women as they wrote down who would perform which task.

Tommy and Juan made their way to the lake on the south side of the ranch, and after they unloaded their fishing equipment, Juan shared with Tommy the civil lawsuit that was filed in Santa Barbara County against James Hansen.

"Who is the plaintiff?"

"James' ex-wife."

"What's the claim?"

"She claims that James is the father of her son. She's asking the court for five hundred thousand dollars and five thousand a month in child support."

"This is an out-of-state plaintiff versus an out-of-state defendant. Is there any merit to her suit?"

"Well, you never can be sure, but my best guess is that she's whistling in the wind and that the case won't go anyplace. I think she's desperate and is looking for a settlement."

"I haven't seen James since we went fishing. His frame of mind wasn't too good then. What would you advise him to do?"

"I would advise him to ignore it. We must be alert that the brother may come to California and cause trouble. He's the wild card in this suit."

"I understand you had a conversation with Hernando Guitterez?"

"How did you know?"

"He told me you threatened him if he didn't leave Linda and me alone. He also said he was going back to Mexico. As he was leaving, he asked me if you would shoot him?"

"I looked at him and said yes.'"

Tommy laughed. "I just said I was protective of you and Linda and would be upset if you weren't allowed to pursue your lives as you wished."

"I'll just bet you did." Juan laughed.

CHAPTER 31

*T*he gods the Sioux prayed to must have been listening today. The sky was clear, and the temperature was in the high seventies; there was no wind. This was Juan's wedding day. He was nervous and wasn't sure he could adjust to married life. He had a successful practice and could dictate his schedule without asking someone else if it was okay. But then he looked at Tommy Sanchez. There never was anyone more independent than he, yet he could work with his wife on significant issues.

Almost one hundred guests from Santa Barbara made their way to Rancho Del Prado this morning. Those that needed a ride to the wedding site near the lake were driven by one of the Vaqueros. Their names were listed on the tents, and with few exceptions, no one complained that they were spending the night in a tent. The majority looked upon the experience as an adventure.

"The bride and groom arrived in separate carriages. Tommy and Sarah rode with Juan while Linda's bridesmaid and parents came with her. It was a little out of the ordinary, but Sarah and Tommy were the joint best man for Juan. They were his parents, best friends, and the ones he loved the most. The minister tried to talk Juan out of it, but he was adamant.

The Vaqueros did the cooking, the singing, and the cleanup afterward. Tommy and Sarah toasted the couple, who left early in the afternoon to start their honeymoon. Sarah made reservations for Tommy and the family, except Naomi, at the Central Hotel in Santa Ynez for three days, and the young married couple used their home for that time and then took the train to San Francisco.

During their three-day honeymoon at the ranch, Linda and Juan went horseback riding, picnicking by the lake, and dinners on the patio. They seldom saw Naomi, but their meals were always there for them.

After the family returned to the ranch, they spent two days tearing down the canvas tents used by the wedding guests. Linda's parents came up for a day to help, but the vaqueros had everything in hand, and the restoration went smoothly. Linda's parents spent the night in the guest room in the house and didn't want to leave. After a couple of bottles of the Sanchez wine, everyone relaxed and saw Sarah and Tommy as themselves. "Where do you think they're going to live?" Diane De L'Ortega asked.

"Juan has a good practice in the valley but a much more lucrative one in Santa Barbara. I believe that where they're going to live most of the time, Juan and Linda have asked if they could build a home in the western part of the ranch that they could use on weekends or vacations. We've agreed to their request. It'll take at least six months to complete." Sarah said.

"What about us?" Diane asked.

Sarah put her hand on Diane's arm. "You are always welcome. We have a nice guest room in the house and plenty of wine. My question is, why don't you stay a couple of days and relax? We have work to do, but our people will cater to your every need, and the ranch is open for you to enjoy."

CHAPTER 32

It took him a month to decide, but Lenny saddled up and left Mexico. He read in the San Diego paper that Bookers had been acquitted. He felt good that he helped the jury reach that verdict even though he'd never get credit for it. He took the most direct route he could to the Bookers Ranch. That's where he wanted to be, and he hoped she felt the same way. He'd do everything he could to make up for how he treated her in the past. He'd never been in love before and therefore couldn't confirm that's what he was feeling. All he knew was that he cared for Frances and the children and wanted to be with them.

Frances was busy in the barn, so she didn't hear him when he rode up. He came up behind her and put his arms around her. When she got over the surprise, she cried.

"Frances, I'm back for good if you want me. If you don't, I understand." Without speaking, she grabbed his hand, and the two entered the cabin.

Tommy waited weeks after the trial before he sends a note with Tomas asking Silas to come and have lunch with him at the Ranch the day after tomorrow. Silas had left the Ranch and now was living with Marjorie. Their wedding was scheduled for two months. He responded immediately and accepted the invitation. Their greeting was warm, and Tommy escorted his friend into the kitchen. Naomi had prepared a chicken and cole slaw lunch for the two, and Tommy opened a bottle of wine.

They discussed his pending marriage to Marjorie, but gradually Tommy shifted the conversation to Silas' finances.

"I saved a good bit of my salary from you, and Marjorie has some funds. I think I can expand the herd of cattle, plant some hay for sale and make it comfortable for the two of us. I won't be rich, but we'll be okay. Then there's the cost of the trial and Juan's fee. I don't have the money now, but I promise to repay your kindness and generosity."

"I'm not worried. I know a man of character when I meet him. This isn't what this lunch is about. By the way, where are you and Marjorie banking?"

"Marjorie had an account in Santa Maria. It's a little easier to get there since there's a train service. I plan to use her account. I've already put the funds I have into that account.

"Although I don't know everything about your former life, I've recently learned some things I'd like to share with you, and then sometime later, I want to divulge more. Please bear with me; I have only your interest at heart.

Your real name is Hiram Bookers, and you're from Boston, Massachusetts. You were the owner of a fleet of ships, having inherited them from your father. Before coming to California, you sold your merchant fleet. The proceeds from the sale were deposited into the Santa Barbara Bank and Trust three years ago."

"Hold on here. You say you know my name and where I'm from. How do you know this?"

"We found someone who knew you."

"Who?"

"Can we set that part aside for a moment? I want to discuss your money in the Santa Barbara Bank and Trust. The person who gave us this information wasn't sure, but they thought there were near three hundred thousand dollars in the account. I talked to the bank manager, and he remembers Hiram Bookers, who you are, and that you have an account with his bank. Since you're still Silas Smith, and I believe you'll remain, Silas Smith, I suggest you move the funds to an account in Santa Maria. I think that'll protect your future."

"My god. You're saying I'm rich, and I felt guilty that I would live off Marjorie. When did you find out this information?"

"About a week before the jury went to deliberate."

"Shouldn't you have told Juan or the court about my name?"

"I can see why you're confused, but the main issue was the money found on you, and that wasn't going to go away unless we found the remainder of the stolen money. But let's stick with your bank account and work on that being transferred so you can use it."

"Do you think I can go there, and they'll give me the money?"

"Yes, if I'm with you or a man named Harkins, who sold you some real estate. I don't believe you have a middle name," he remembers you, and then there's your signature card on file.

"You say I own property?"

"Yes, you have a thousand-acre ranch about fifteen to twenty miles southeast of Santa Barbara."

"Have you been there?"

"Jim Jefferson and I went there. It was the four days we were gone near the end of your trial."

"Are there any improvements or stock on the property?"

"There's a cabin, barn, and utility buildings. Three acres have been planted, and there's a mule, a horse, and sixty head of cattle."

"Who's managing the property while I'm gone?"

"Your wife."

"Oh, my god. What am I going to tell Marjorie?"

"I suggest you don't tell her anything at this time. My advice is to take care of the money first, and then you and I will go to your Ranch and meet with your wife."

"Are you sure she's, my wife?"

"I am. I confirmed a marriage certificate and that you were wed at the Arlington Hotel in Santa Barbara. Here's a copy. You may not want to take it with you for fear Marjorie will find it."

Silas read the certificate and handed it back to Tommy. He just stared at the ceiling for about a minute. They sat for another two hours and talked about various things before Silas left for Marjorie's place. He was confused but agreed that moving the money was the first thing to do. He decided he wouldn't discuss this situation with Marjorie but would wait until he learned more from his wife.

A week later, Tommy and Silas rode to Santa Barbara and met with the real estate agent Harkins, who sold him the property southeast of Santa Barbara. He confirmed that Silas was Hiram Bookers. Silas and Sanchez went to the Santa Barbara Bank and Trust with that information and met with the bank manager. The manager recognized Bookers immediately and asked him how he could help. Hiram explained that he was moving to Santa Ynez and that the Central City Bank in Santa Maria would be more convenient for conducting his business.

"Are you going to sell your acreage?"

"No. I have someone who wants to lease it. Since it has improvements and three acres planted, it's a good deal for a young couple."

"Is it someone I know?" The manager asked.

"No. It's someone Mr. Sanchez referred to me."

The manager didn't want to lose such a large account. He suggested they could do anything the other bank could. Still, when Hiram insisted, the manager was helpful and arranged for a cashier's check to be made out to Hiram Bookers and Silas Smith, who Hiram said was his business partner.

Silas wrestled with the situation for another three weeks after transferring his funds to the Santa Maria bank. He didn't share with Marjorie that he was rich and had a separate account at her bank. One day he showed up at the Sanchez Ranch and talked to Tommy. "I'm ready to face my wife and see what else I have to learn about my former life. I've not told Marjorie anything about the money. It took me some time, but Juan finally gave me a bill for his fee and told me how much he paid out during the trial. I have a cashier's check for you. The money is a small gesture of what I owe you and Sarah. I didn't know until recently that she was with you when I was found."

They left early in the morning, made good time, and camped out the first night. It had rained most of the day intermittently, and when they stopped, they spent considerable time taking care of the horses, getting dry kindling, and having a cold dinner. They were tired, slept early, and tried to stay dry. They rose at dawn; luckily, most of the rain had passed in the night, and after coffee, they were on their way. They reached the camping spot Tommy had selected at three in the afternoon. They set up for the night, had an early dinner, and enjoyed a bottle of wine Tommy brought along.

When they were relaxed and enjoying the wine, Tommy asked Silas if this location had any significance. "I don't think I've been here before. Is it someplace I should know about?"

"I wasn't sure. There are some things you need to know about your previous life that I'm privy to, and you need to be aware of to determine how you want to proceed in your life/."

"You make it sound sinister," Silas sounded concerned.

"Some of it is. To start with, this is the location where Sarah and I found you lying in the bushes with a bullet in your back. I guess you were on a hunting trip, and Lenny Harris joined you in this camp. After learning that you were a former sea captain named Hiram Bookers, owned a spread within ten miles from here, and had a mail-order bride, he shot you and left you for dead.".

Silas sat up straight. He was stunned and probably didn't hear everything Tommy told him. "What are you saying? You say I was shot by someone named Lenny Harris. Is this the same man Jefferson said was the seventh man in the Oxnard Train Robbery?"

"Yes."

"Where is Harris now?"

"Bear with me for a little longer. I've known about Harris for over two months. I could have turned Harris in, but our main concern at the time was getting you acquitted of the robbery. Sheriff Rodgers was tenacious and wouldn't let up even after the jury freed you. Harris was important to free you. He produced the stolen money, snuck into a hotel room at two AM, and exchanged the funds with the cattle seller so that the funds could be circulated and found by the Pinkertons."

"How do you know all this?"

"It was my idea, and I went with Harris to be sure he went through with the plan to exchange the money."

"Christ, you stuck your neck out for me. Where did Harris get the Train money?"

"He was the mastermind behind the robbery you were accused of. He was the seventh man who shot and killed Charley Joe Richards just before he shot you. He'd buried the eight thousand dollars on your property."

"You mean he volunteered to dig up the money so he could help me' I'm the guy he shot."

It was dark, and Silas couldn't see the smile on Tommy's face as he responded. "Well, he had to be encouraged. The bottom line is, he did it."

"Did you turn him in or let him go?"

"I gave him a couple of options after the exchange. I don't know where he is now. It depends on what's inside the man."

"You took some liberties with my life on the line."

"Not really. I had your best interest at heart, and after we found Harris, we had the card that could free you. Harris only left my sight once he exchanged the train money with the money paid to the cattle seller. The only question was how we would orchestrate it. That took considerable luck. If I turned Harris in, he never would've confessed to anything. If I need to find Harris, my skills are such that I could accomplish that."

"What am I going to do? I promised Marjorie that we would be married in two months. What am I going to tell her?"

"You need to assimilate all of this very slowly. We should go to your place and meet Frances, your wife, and find out how she feels."

"You say I was a sea captain. Where am I from?

"I told you before that you're from Boston, have no living relatives, and owned a merchant fleet you sold five years ago before coming out here. You had significant funds in the Bank of Santa Barbara under your name with a separate account for your wife, Frances, in the same bank. Your wife withdrew some funds from the account set up for her, and the banker recognized her as Mrs. Bookers. That's how we traced her."

"This may be too much for me. I need help getting my hands around a new identity since I've been Silas Smith for at least three years. How am I ever going to explain this to Marjorie?"

"Again, let's not get ahead of ourselves. There are still some things that I still need to share with you. I suggest we go to your ranch tomorrow and meet with your wife. I'll let her tell you."

"You make it sound as though she knew all the time what was going on with me."

"Somewhat. She came to Santa Barbara during your trial, took the train to Ventura, and saw you in court. That's how we found her and devised a plan to free you. Before that, she thought you were dead."

"Why didn't she come other times?"

"You'll have to ask her."

Silas barely slept that night. There were too many unanswered questions. Tommy seemed reluctant to answer them. He wondered why.

They were up early and barely spoke. Tommy knew that Silas was trying to filter all the information he'd been furnished, and he needed to do it better. If he was confused now, Tommy knew that when he saw his wife and her children, he would panic. And then there was Lenny Harris. Tommy wondered whether he'd run off or if he was back at the ranch. How would that go if he met Silas?

The ride to Silas' place was smooth but quiet. Tommy didn't want to create unnecessary problems, so he remained silent. The final points that Tommy wanted to share with Silas would come when he met the wife he didn't know and the children that were hers. They saw smoke coming from the cabin's chimney as they went over the rise. As they got closer, they saw a man working behind a plow in the field. "Silas, wait here. I want to talk to that man before we meet with your wife."

Lenny didn't see Tommy's approach. He just finished one row and turned around. When he looked up, he saw the man in black about twenty feet away and froze. He wondered if the man was here to kill him. He dropped the reins and walked toward Tommy. "What do you want?" He asked.

"I've brought Bookers with me. He's here to meet his wife, who he doesn't know. He knows about you but won't recognize you. Let's skip the introductions until he understands what's happening."

"What are you going to do about me?"

"Nothing. However, I am still wondering what Silas is going to do. That's the big question. Do you have any guns around that I should know about?"

"They're hiding in the barn. We didn't want the children to find them. By the way, she's pregnant again."

"Can you stay outside until they resolve a couple of issues?"

"I can wait if that's what you want."

"Lenny, remember. I don't want to see any guns in your hands. Could you leave them in the barn? The best thing you can do now is to stay out of sight. Let   Bookers get adjusted before he finds out you're here. Again, there will be no gun play."

"Can you be sure Bookers will see it that way?"

CHAPTER 33

*T*hey knocked on the door, and Frances opened it. The first thing she did was step back. She hadn't planned on seeing her husband come to the door. "Frances, can we come in and talk?" Tommy asked.

She didn't respond but backed up and pointed to the table with four chairs in the kitchen. Hiram stared at the petite woman, but there was no recognition there. It was as though he'd drawn a blank. She, in turn, had her head down. He looked around the room as though to find something he recognized.

Tommy waited a few minutes to let the moment sink in. "I know this is hard on both of you, so I'll start with Hiram or Silas, whatever name you're comfortable with, and then Frances can fill in the rest."

The two of you were married at the Arlington Hotel in Santa Barbara over three years ago, and the marriage license is recorded in that county registrar's office. Frances was a mail-order bride from Boston, where you came from. As part of your married life, you went hunting every six months to add some deer to your diet. The last time you went hunting, you didn't come back. Frances went looking for you and found your assailant instead. He had a broken ankle and a separated shoulder. She brought him back here and nursed him back to health.

This man assaulted her sexually and physically and thwarted any attempt she made to escape. After she found out she was pregnant, the abuse stopped. She attempted to run three to six months after her first child was born. An Indian woman and her brother helped, but your assailant caught up to her and the Indian and brought them home.

Frances then reconciled to the fact that you were dead and she'd have to make the best of her situation; she accepted this man as her natural mate. A second child was born before she remembered the money you set aside for her at the Santa Barbara Bank and Trust. Her family needed clothes and some food for the children.

When she arrived in Santa Barbara, she came across the local newspaper covering your trial, and that's when she saw your picture. You probably don't remember the confrontation at the courthouse because you were busy with Marjorie, but Jim Jefferson and I did. He followed her back to Santa Barbara and the bank, where she made another withdrawal."

Frances, who had her head bowed, looked up at Tommy, and he nodded for her to continue. "When I saw you, and you didn't recognize me immediately, I thought you were someone else. As I listened to the court testimony, I realized that Lenny Harris had shot you and left you for dead. He intended to come to the ranch and take your place. I went home to confront him, but before I could, Mr. Sanchez and Mr. Jefferson came to the farm, subdued Lenny, and I told them my story. Eventually, Lenny told them much of his."

For the first time, Hiram spoke. "You might have told the judge who you were."

Tommy answered quickly. "I'm not defending Frances, but she didn't know you had amnesia. Initially, she thought you were someone else. She got scared when she guessed what might have happened and rode back home."

"Why didn't you run away again from this monster?" Hiram asked.

"Where would I go? I have two small children to look out for; this is my home. Initially, I tried to stab him, but he was too strong and took the knife away and beat me." Just then, the oldest, Lenny, who was two years old, came out of the added room and walked to his mother. Frances picked him up, put the child on her lap, and hugged him.

"Is that your child?"

"Yes, Lenny is the father of both my children."

"Where's Lenny now?"

Frances responded. "He's outside. I think he was harrowing the lettuce field   you planted."

"Did I plant the crop outside?"

"Yes, and you and the Indian built the cabin, the shed, and the barn. From the ten head of cattle, you stocked the place with, Lenny has built it into a herd of sixty. He rents a bull from a farmer about three miles away at least once a year. We butcher one cow annually for meat" Frances didn't look up when she responded. Her head was touching her son's.

Silas got up from the chair. "I'm going outside to talk to Lenny."

Tommy was reluctant to have the two meets without him being present. "Okay, but I'm going outside at the same time. There are some guns in the barn, and I'll be there while you talk with Lenny."

As Tommy made his way to the barn, Silas walked toward Lenny, who gave the cattle water. Lenny turned to the noise when he heard someone walking toward him. Silas stopped in front of him and asked him why he shot him.

"To be honest, I was looking for a hideout, and what you described would be perfect. A posse was on my trail, and I needed breathing room."

Silas hit him as hard as he could, and Lenny fell. When he rose, Silas hit him twice more with the same result. When Lenny was hit and fell the third time, Silas rubbed his hands together and walked back into the house. Frances was watching the confrontation through the window. She handed her son to the Indian woman and rushed through the door, past Hiram, and knelt beside Lenny. After a few minutes, with her help, he rose, walked with her into the house, and sat at the table with the other two men.

Frances grabbed a towel, put it in a bucket of water on top of the kitchen counter, wrung it out, and then wiped Lenny's face, which was covered with blood. His lip was cut, his nose broken, and at least one tooth had been knocked out. No one said anything as they watched the scene play out in front of them. It was as though the curtain was coming down on a dramatic play.

Lenny was still groggy, so the two men helped put him to bed and covered him up. Frances, who had been preparing dinner when the two arrived, set three plates on the kitchen table without asking. The Indian woman, after feeding the two children, put them to bed. She slept on the floor next to their cribs.

"It looks like you have some decisions about all of this. You see how it is between Lenny and me, and then there are the children, and oh yes, you own the ranch. What do you want to do?"

Rather than answer, Silas looked around the room at the nautical furnishings. "Are the furnishings yours or mine?" he asked Frances.

"Everything is yours."

"The painting of the Indian seems out of place here. Did you buy it somewhere?

"No, it was here when you brought me here."

At that moment, Tommy spoke up. "Silas, I want you to go over to the painting and read who the artist is."

Silas did as he was asked and then turned to face Tommy. "How can this be?"

"You must have come to our valley sometime in the past and purchased it. It was hanging in the Central

Hotel in Santa Ynez, and as you can see, It's Sarah's painting of her first husband, Crazy Horse."

"It's magnificent. May I take it with me?" he asked Frances.

"They ate in silence. After dinner, Frances gave them blankets, and Tommy and Silas made their way to the barn, pitched enough hay for two beds, and lay down for the night.

Tommy was up at daybreak, but there was no sign of Silas. He walked into the cabin and saw Frances preparing breakfast. Lenny was still in bed, and she prepared a bowl of mush she would spoon-feed to him. "How's he doing?" Tommy asked.

"He had a bad night. I know he deserved it, but that was a vicious beating he took. It's not like him not to fight back. He's probably more man than you or Hiram thinks he is."

Around ten that morning, Hiram showed up, and Frances gave him a cup of coffee. "I walked the property, and I've been in all the buildings. I can't find one thing that I remember. It's as though I'm seeing it for the first time. It's beautiful, and I can see where a man could be happy here, but not me."

"How much money do you need annually to keep this place working?"

"Right now, we need about three hundred a year from outside sources to break even. It's mostly for children. In five years, we'll be self-sufficient and have a good life. In ten years, we can put aside money for our children's education."

"If I put enough money in your account, will you forget I exist?"

"What are you driving at?"

"I'd like to go on living as Silas Smith and forget about my life before that. I won't give you the ranch, but I'll put another five thousand dollars in your account so you and your children and whoever can have a productive life living here. I don't want to see you again unless it's a dire emergency, such as life- threatening. I believe that Thomas Sanchez can act as our interface if needed. I don't know you, but from what I've seen this past twenty-four hours, you're a strong woman and would make anyone a wonderful wife.

From what I've heard from you and my friend here, you did everything you could to survive. I admire you for it, but I don't know you" You and I have someone we care about. Let's go our own way."

There was no hug between the two as they said goodbye, just a handshake. Frances wrapped the painting in an old sheet, and though it was cumbersome, Silas wouldn't part with it. Tommy looked in on Lenny, who was still asleep, as he and Silas left the ranch and rode home.

On the way back, both men talked freely. "Although I might have done things differently, especially about Lenny, I can't fault you in any way. You had my interest at heart, and I'll always be grateful for everything you did. You saved my life."

"What about Marjorie?"

"You asked me to wait before I made a decision. What Marjorie doesn't know won't hurt her. I don't want to go through the scandal of a divorce and the breakup of Frances' family. I detest Lenny, but she made her bed, and that's fine. I'm a little nervous about any of this coming out. What do you think?"

"I think if you told Marjorie, she'd worry about someone breaking the news and then worry about what other people would think. You have enough money to relocate if the story gets out. I say marry the woman and forget about this. Frances and Lenny don't want anyone to know about this because Lenny would probably go to jail and be hung. I wouldn't be surprised if they didn't become the Bookers."

ABOUT THE AUTHOR

James S. (Jim) Kelly is a retired United States Air Force Colonel with over 100 combat missions during the Vietnam Conflict. Prior to his retirement, Jim was the program Director for a communication program in the country of Iran, working directly with the Shah.

Jim and his wife Patricia own and operate High Meadow's Horse Ranch in Solvang California. Nearly eighty percent of his novels use the beautiful Santa Ynez Valley as a backdrop for his plots.

He and his wife are heavily involved in a charity supporting our troops in forward operating locations. in hostile territory.

To contact Jim, send an e-mail to asyougo90@gmail.com